THE OCEANS

BETWEEN STARS

Book Two of the
CHRONICLE OF THE DARK STAR

KEVIN EMERSON

WALDEN POND PRESS
An Imprint of HarperCollinsPublishers

Walden Pond Press is an imprint of HarperCollins Publishers.
Walden Pond Press and the skipping stone logo are trademarks
and registered trademarks of Walden Media, LLC.

The Oceans between Stars

ISBN 978-0-06-230674-6

Typography by Carla Weise
18 19 20 21 22   CG/LSCH   10 9 8 7 6 5 4 3 2 1
❖
First Edition

FOR ANNIE, COPILOT, ALWAYS

PRELUDE

2ND PLANET OF THE 28TH PLANETARY SYSTEM 8TH SECTOR—SPIRAL GALAXY 93— GALACTIC SUPERCLUSTER 714

Just over fifteen light-years from the solar system you call home, inside a small triangular dwelling whose surface shimmered like a road in midday sun, a light began to blink. The light was on a phone, or something like a phone. Picture the newest, sleekest phone you can—probably that one your friend just got; you know, the friend who always gets the newest things—only now imagine it bent into a ring and hovering just above the skin of your wrist, except that skin is the lavender color of a predawn sky, and covered in millions of tiny bristles, which are in this case grayish-black but can be other colors, too. Also, you must imagine that the phone has a sort of fluttering warmth on its underside that is synced to your pulse, while its outer surface displays no numbers or symbols but only intermittent blooms of light in wavelengths that your

3

human eyes would not even be able to perceive. . . .

Let's just call it a phone.

The wrist with the phone rested on a table, and the blinking caught the attention of its wearer. She paused from eating her cereal and watching a comedy show on a small screen. The phone sang to her in infrared light. Her eyes, which were shaped like human eyes but were sky blue where yours are white, and had black irises and gold pupils, saw the different temperatures of the light the same way that you would see colors.

Most of the features of this being, known as a Telphon, were similar to a human's. Her two eyes were in the same position as yours; she had one nose in the middle of her face, and two arms and two legs in the same spots as you; she walked upright and had the same number of vocal cords and ears and allergies and dreams. If you basically picture a young human girl only with the different eyes and skin and also a tight white braid of silky hair spiraling around the crown of her head—technically she had a tail too, just a small one, but let's remember that you once had one, too—that will be fine for the moment.

The girl's phone was delivering an urgent message. The message was not good.

The girl, whose full name was Xela-4 but who went by Xela, was about ten Earth years old. In Telphon years she was twenty-seven, but years are just revolutions around a star, and Xela's star was quite a bit smaller than yours.

She looked up and saw other blinking lights around the room. Her mother, sitting across the table, and her father, standing in the kitchen, were getting messages on their phones, too.

Mom and Dad shared a look. "Turn on the TV," said Dad.

Mom whistled and the television rippled to life. Xela whistled off her pad. The television and the pad, the table Xela was sitting at, as well as the cereal and spoon and even the milk, were all somewhat similar to what you would have seen on Earth, as most things on Telos were. Give a planet four or five billion years to get organized, and you will often get something Earthlike. You will also often get something very different, depending on a great many variables, but in this case, Telos and Earth shared enough similarities that their life-forms had much in common. (It's worth noting that what you will get after eight or even ten billion years can be quite different, but what was happening this autumn morning on Telos was only the latest proof that making it that long in this universe is extremely rare.)

The television showed a live scene from the far side of the planet. Tiny sparks of light in the crimson evening sky. Millions of them, raining down from space.

"Are those shooting stars?" asked Xela. She did not call them shooting stars, exactly. This is just an approximate translation. Even the minor differences between Telphons and humans are enough to create a language that to you would sound sort of like the chirping and clucking of large birds.

Mom, whose name was Marnia-2, peered at the screen. "Maybe xanodites?"

Calo-6, Xela's dad, frowned at his phone. "The lab says the initial readings indicate metal . . . and electronic signals."

The view on the TV zoomed back, revealing the copper-colored ocean off the coast of Ocelia, one of Telos's major cities. Xela stared, transfixed by the rain of golden lights nearing the planet's surface; she thought it was lovely. Later, she would remember thinking that, and she would feel so stupid.

"Did one of our orbiters explode?" Mom wondered.

"They're trying to find out," said Dad. "They—"

At that moment, the first of the falling embers hit the water, and there was a flash of brilliant white light. More of the objects landed and the light grew bigger, and bigger.

"Oh no," said Mom.

The blast spread, ballooning into the sky and racing across the water toward the city. Churning and convulsing, a wall of fire. It hit the first glittering buildings along the shore, and Xela thought it must be a trick of the light because the buildings seemed to vaporize—

The scene cut out. A newscaster appeared, frantic. "We've lost all contact with Ocelia," she said. "Reports from the surrounding districts describe a wall of fire advancing in all directions. I'm told now that we've just received this satellite imagery—"

The scene switched to a view of the far side of Telos from space. Half the planet was still lit in the rusty light of their red dwarf star, the other half in shadow. The brilliant firestorm bloomed in the dark, spreading like a spill, a perfect circle growing and growing, enveloping more and more of the planet's surface.

"We have to go," said Dad softly, reading from his phone. "We have to go right now."

"What is it, Dad?" Xela kept staring at the expanding light.

The newscaster reappeared. She was looking off camera, her face pale. "We what?" Now back to the camera. "Ladies and gentlemen, we—"

The broadcast went dark.

"What's going on?" Xela asked.

Mom's hand closed around Xela's arm. "Come on, Xela, now!"

Her cereal bowl smashed to the floor as Mom dragged her toward the door. Xela felt her heart galloping in her chest. "But I don't have my jacket, or my backpack, I—"

"There's no time!" said Dad, holding the front door open for them. He checked his phone. "They're saying eighteen minutes."

"Until what?" asked Xela.

Dad didn't answer. He bolted past them as they stumbled down the steps and led the way across the ruby-colored lawn.

"But you didn't lock the door!"

"Mica, pick up!" Mom shouted uselessly at her phone. "He's probably not even awake yet."

"Call your mother!" said Dad.

"She never has her phone on."

Xela struggled to keep up, Mom's grip on her wrist burning. Mica-3 was her younger brother. He was with Nia and Niho, their grandparents. They'd taken Mica to the Telphon version of a soccer game the night before and it had run late so they'd taken him to their house to sleep over, and were going to take him to school this morning.

"Will they be okay?" Xela asked.

"Yes," Mom answered breathlessly. "Just keep moving, honey!"

Xela wanted to disagree. That firestorm on the

TV, the things Dad was saying: none of it sounded okay. She wanted to stop, to freeze right there in the middle of the street and scream *No!* She would turn and go back to her house and finish her cereal and her cartoon and go to school and hate math just like every other day.

But she did what she was told, just like she always did, and kept running, the pristine lavender morning sky a blur through her tears.

Later, those who survived the events of that morning on Telos named the cosmic phenomenon that destroyed their planet the *Tears of Ana*.

Their great sun goddess, weeping.

Passing her Judgment.

In those frantic early moments, though, newscasters simply called the fiery objects falling through the sky *xanodites*, as Xela's mom had. This was the Telphon word for asteroids and comets and meteors. The term came from Telphon history; many millions of years earlier, their sister planet, Xanos, had been struck and destroyed by a comet. Three enormous pieces of the planet had remained in orbit, forming a broken sphere, and much of the debris had coalesced to form Telos's lovely multicolored rings, which were only a distant shimmer by day, but then at sunset they glittered like jeweled necklaces and by night glowed

9

like strings of pearls. However, a few of the larger chunks of Xanos had crashed into Telos's surface, causing massive upheaval.

It is interesting to note that at the time, Telos had been well on its way to being colonized by a particularly crafty and very toxic species of fungus. The fungus had been firmly in control, and just beginning to have the most basic of sentient thoughts—something about the universe, and blueberries—when the xanodites rained down and drove the fungus to extinction. This had been a great development for the invertebrate worms that had managed to survive inside a few crevices of the xanodites and that would, over millions of years, evolve into the Telphons—yes, technically, the Telphons were aliens to their own planet—and a terrible development for the fungus. But such a thing is not uncommon in a universe like this one.

In other words: these things happen.

Of course, that's an easy thing for us to say about some fungus, but it didn't feel that way to Xela as she and her family raced out of their house that morning. All across the planet, people were doing the same: running for their lives.

There were six billion Telphons when the Tears of Ana arrived.

Only two hundred and thirty-eight survived.

Of these few survivors, some believed that the firestorm was indeed a message from their unhappy goddess, but those who were scientifically inclined understood within the first few hours of the tragedy that the Tears were not the work of a deity, nor were they a random cosmic event that had *just happened.* No, what certain survivors learned from their initial analysis was that the tears had been created, and had been aimed specifically at their planet.

Someone, somewhere, had done this on purpose.

As Xela sprinted across her yard, then up her street, she knew that they were all in grave danger, but she would have been shocked to know how bad her odds of survival that morning really were.

Here is what had to go right for you to be one of the two hundred and thirty-eight Telphons who survived the Tears of Ana:

First, you had to live on the opposite side of the world from where the Tears had landed. It ended up taking the firestorm only sixteen and a half minutes to engulf the planet. A full third of the population had been asleep; they literally never knew what hit them. Another third had only enough time to either turn on the television or start to consider what they should do before being vaporized. The final third was an ocean or two away and had enough time to get out of the house and head for shelter, only it turned out that almost no place was safe. At least most of these Telphons had time to say their good-byes.

Second, if you happened to be one of the lucky ones on the far side of the planet, you or a member of your family had to not only be employed by the military of your country—there's no reason to get into the political history or geography of Telos at this point, as every country and city and historical site and petty squabble was about to be obliterated—but you also had to be stationed at the one particular base where the International Advanced Cosmic Studies lab was located. That this base was located on the far side of the planet in the first place was an incredible stroke of luck.

The Telphons had a space program somewhat similar to humanity's. They'd sent a few astronauts up into the Xanos Rings, and built telescopes to study the stars and also to keep an eye out for objects that could destroy their planet. Unfortunately, this warning system was of little use when the Tears of Ana arrived. Each of the Tears measured barely a Telphon meter long. To the telescopes, they just looked like a harmless meteor shower, and like any other planet, especially one with such significant rings, Telos was being bombarded by thousands of small meteors each day, most of which burned up in the atmosphere.

Third, you or a member of your family had to not only be stationed at the IACS lab, you had to know about, and have clearance to enter, the top secret high-security subterranean laboratory *beneath* the base, where a small international team had spent many years studying a fascinating artifact: the first proof (before the Tears arrived, that is) that the Telphons were not alone in the universe.

But even more than that had to go right: within moments of the Tears' arrival, you had to begin running, heading directly for the elevators to that underground lab. You had to reach those elevators and use them before the power cut out, a mere nine minutes after the initial explosion that vaporized Ocelia.

Because even if you made it to the staircase that switched back and forth down to the lab, even if you somehow navigated the crush of people trying to use that staircase, and even if you made it all the way down to the one spot from which anyone could hope to get off Telos in time . . . even then, you would have only another few minutes before the hurtling wave of atomic fire washed over everything and everyone.

★

As Xela dashed across the paths of the base, a hot electric wind buffeted her back. She risked a glance over her shoulder. The rim of the sky had begun to glow white hot. Black thunderclouds reared their heads over the horizon, lightning shooting from their crowns in all directions.

"Farther!" Dad shouted over the searing wind.

They reached a triangular building. Just like almost every other structure on Telos, its exterior was tiled with infrared-absorbing panels that shimmered in the deep orange of the rising sun.

They burst through metal access doors into a cool hallway. Dad wrestled to get his security badge out of his pocket, only to find that the guards at the checkpoint had abandoned their post. They sprinted down a long hallway and threw themselves into one of the three elevators.

"I still can't reach Mica or my parents!" said Mom.

"Did you send them a message?" said Dad, stabbing the door-close button over and over. "We're about to lose service."

"I did, I—I told them to come here as fast as they could. . . ." At the far end of the hallway, the light from outside began to darken.

Another group crammed into the elevator and they were packed shoulder to shoulder. The doors began to hum closed. "Take the next one!" Dad called at the people rushing toward them. They shouted in protest, but the doors slid shut and the elevator whisked downward.

Mom kept refreshing her phone until a message appeared: *No signal.* She started to cry.

The elevator opened and they sprinted out into a massive cavern with glittering black walls and a high cathedral-like ceiling, a cavern that was believed to have formed when one of the giant chunks of Xanos struck Telos long ago. This turned out to be untrue. In fact, something else had made this cavern, something only a few on Telos knew about and even fewer understood, and when Xela saw it now for the first time, it made her gasp:

A huge, spherical orange crystal, as tall as a house, floating in the center of the cavern. The scientists of Telos had built a catwalk around its equator.

Xela and her family raced toward it. Xela saw people standing on the catwalk and placing their hands against the humming surface of the crystal. As each person did, they briefly glowed and then completely vanished.

She wanted to stop and blink and ask what exactly she had just seen, but Dad kept pulling her along, and in moments they were jostling their way toward the sphere, shoulder to shoulder with the other scientists and their families. They inched along the metal walkway that led to the circular catwalk, the huge crystal bathing them in orange light.

"Eight minutes," said Dad.

Suddenly, the power went out. The elevators stopped working, and all the lights went out except for the orange glow of the crystal. There were screams and shouts, and Xela followed Mom's gaze back over her shoulder to where people where stumbling and falling on the staircase that zigzagged down the side of the cavern, wild shadows lit only by the lights from their phones.

"I've got to go back for them!" Mom shouted, trying to turn around against the crowd.

"Marnia," said Dad. She looked at him, and now her tears flowed freely. Xela felt a great, hulking shadow slip beneath her thoughts, like the Telphon version of a whale, but with black eyes and horrible teeth. She refused to hear it. Refused to think it: her brother, her grandparents . . .

Dad kept pulling her toward the crystal. Pushing and nudging ahead. Telphons kept vanishing into it, two, now three at a time. Xela had no idea what was happening to them, but whatever it was must be preferable to staying here.

What her father and mother and the other members of the team knew after decades of study and thousands of experiments was that this seemingly simple crystal was actually an incredibly complicated device that did a great many things, but its single most important function was its ability to create a wormhole through space, which beings or objects could then transit. Before today, it had never allowed a Telphon to do this, despite their many efforts, but thankfully, in this desperate moment, the crystal seemed to have changed its mind.

Or rather, the being standing beside it had changed its mind. As they inched closer, Xela's heart skipped a beat at the sight of the strange figure on the catwalk, overseeing the Telphons' departure. (This was, in fact, the second alien to show up on Telos that day. Moments before, a being known as a chronologist had arrived elsewhere on the planet to log the Tears of Ana in her records, but she had kept her visit to herself.)

This delicate, ancient being standing beside the crystal had appeared once before. Xela's mom and dad had been there, though that encounter was strictly classified. The Telphons translated the being's name as Styrlax. A couple of centuries earlier, one of these same beings had also appeared to a small collection of earthlings, who had heard its name as Paha'Ne. Neither of these were quite the true name of the beings, but they didn't mind. When you'd traveled over a quarter of the known half of the universe, you learned to be easygoing about nomenclature.

Interestingly, even these Styrlax, easily one of the oldest and most advanced races in the universe, did not know about the chronologists. They knew about the blueberry, but not the pie, so to speak.

When the Styrlax had first appeared five years ago, he had kindly explained the business of the giant orange crystal to the Telphon scientists who had been studying it, and who were quite shocked to see an otherworldy being materialize out of it. He'd said, apologetically, that the Styrlax had intended to use the crystal as part of a plan to colonize the planet and turn the Telphons into mindless drones, only to learn that because of some slight oddities in the Telphons' chemical composition, the Styrlax mind-control technology would not in fact work on them.

"Sorry about that," the Styrlax had added. "It's just that our planet blew up, as they sometimes do. We've been homeless ever since, but unlike *some* beings, we believe that all life in the universe is precious, no matter how insignificant."

Before leaving, the Styrlax told the Telphons that, when the Telphons were ready, he would be happy to assist them in journeying out into space. "As an apology for nearly enslaving you all. Really, it's the least we could do."

At the time, the Telphons had no idea what the Styrlax was saying. He was, after all, speaking Styrlax. Xela's mother was part of the linguistics team that had worked on translating the language in the years since. Until today, they hadn't known for certain whether they'd gotten the translation right, as they had attempted to send numerous messages into the crystal but had received no replies. Then this morning when the first scientists raced down to the lab after the Tears had struck, and sent a desperate plea for help, they'd been relieved to see the Styrlax appear moments later.

"Place both palms on the surface," the Styrlax had said, and the Telphons had correctly translated. "And I'd suggest closing your eyes," he'd added.

Now Xela and her parents were almost to the crystal, only a few groups ahead of them. Arcs of energy erupted like solar flares from its surface, cycling around it like a miniature sun. The next few Telphons put their hands on it and disappeared in a wash of light.

"What about Mica?" Xela asked, but her voice was choked and barely more than a whisper. She couldn't quite see over the adults behind them, but the sounds of screaming and wailing had grown so loud behind them . . .

Mom kept checking over her shoulder, fire glimmering in her tear-filled eyes. She rubbed Xela's back and forced a smile. "They'll make it."

The group directly in front of them disappeared into the crystal.

"We have to go," said Dad. "It's now or never."

Mom nodded, tears falling faster. She put her arm around Xela and they stepped up to the crystal. Its humming vibrated her teeth.

They'll make it, Xela said to herself over and over.

"Tarra," Dad said to a scientist beside him, "any idea where they're sending us?"

Tarra-8 motioned to the Styrlax, who watched the crowd mildly, his translucent arms crossed. "He says they have a ship in orbit."

Dad glanced around. "Golan and the kids?"

Tarra checked her phone. It flashed *No Signal*. "He took them early to practice. I should have gone for them. . . ."

Dad put a hand on her shoulder. "They know to come here, right?"

Tarra shrugged. She motioned with her phone. "Golan has subnetwork access, but even that's down."

"That fire is spreading fast," said Dad.

"Not a fire," said Tarra. "A fusion-driven plasma storm."

The Styrlax spoke from nearby: a voice you might describe as a human computer imitating the sounds of an excited dog, crossed with a dinging microwave.

"*Please hurry*," Mom translated.

"Go," said Dad, pushing Xela.

She found herself face-to-face with the glittering electric crystal interface. But Mica! And wait, were

20

they really leaving the planet? How would they get back? They—

"Now, Xela!" Dad urged.

Later, and for years after, Xela would wonder how she did it, because placing her hands on that warm surface had meant never seeing her house or anything in her world again. No one had told her that, and yet she'd seen her parents' faces, seen that storm. It meant traveling to somewhere completely new when only moments before she'd been eating cereal and preparing for yet another day at school. Still needing to brush her hair and coil her tail, to remember to bring her friend Dia-7's charm bracelet with her to class, otherwise there would be *drama* at lunch, and what about that vocabulary quiz? Wait, what would happen to Dia? And her classmates?

As she placed her palms onto the warm, buzzing crystal, it hit her like a wave. None of those things would ever happen, and her brother, and her grand-parents—

Her body lit up. She experienced a light and stretching feeling like she was a pysal flower (similar to an Earth dandelion), like her very molecules were catching the wind and blowing free. And it felt like there was air between her fingernails and her skin, a wind behind her eyeballs, a gray hole in her thoughts . . .

The next thing Xela saw was the midnight-blue

floor of the Styrlax space cruiser. She sucked in a breath that seemed to reorganize her from toe to spine. The gray hole was still there, though, the sense of something missing, something lost. After a moment it faded, but not all the way.

It never would.

She stumbled to her feet and looked around at the small crowd of Telphons. Everyone was silent. Facing the same way. Light flickered on their faces. Xela pressed up on her tiptoes but once again couldn't see over the adults.

"Xela, don't," said Dad.

"I want to see."

Dad sighed and lifted her up by the armpits; when was the last time he'd picked her up? He strained to hold her against his side. It had been so long since she'd smelled his brand of gel. Everyone wore it to keep their bristles from drying out. Dad's smelled like hot sand and the Telphon version of chocolate. All of this brought fresh tears to her eyes. She felt younger, and older, so much older, all at once.

Xela saw, over the crowd, a giant liquid window. Below were the glittering rings and magenta curve of Telos. Her world. The copper hues of its oceans, the red and pink dabs of its landforms. She'd seen images of it from orbit but never really imagined how beautiful it was.

And yet, before her eyes, the energy storm swept over the planet rim, preceded by a foam of black clouds like breaking surf. It charged over land and water and crashed against itself in splashes of fire, and when it had covered the entire surface, their planet looked as if it had become a star. Then the storm died out, leaving a swirling gray breakwater, ashen, here and there blooming with flashes of leftover flame, like fireworks in a cloudy sky.

Everyone wept. Someone wailed. An older man nearby just repeated, "No, no, no. . . ."

Xela craned to see behind her. The crystal interface—a smaller sphere up here on the ship—hummed quietly. No one else was appearing in front of it.

"Mica?" she whispered.

Mom put a hand on her shoulder but didn't answer.

"We should have stayed!" Xela yelled. "We should have waited!"

Dad hugged her tighter. "Shh."

"No! Let me go!" She thrashed out of her father's grasp and fell to the ground. He grabbed her by the shoulders and hugged her again. "We'd be dead, too," he said, his voice choked. "You have to see that. We'd be gone."

Xela quieted. He was right. But now that she had lived, how long would she feel this terribly alone?

Eventually, the murmurs and tears and wails of

agony coalesced into one swirling wave, a single question, ringing throughout the crowd of survivors.

"What happened?"

"Ana wanted to punish us!" someone yelled. "She wept for our sins!"

"It was terrorism!"

"We were attacked!"

Dad moved away from the shouting. Xela trailed behind him. He and Mom and Tarra convened behind the orange crystal, in a command area where the Styrlax who had come for them stood with two others of his kind.

"Do you know what caused this?" Dad asked calmly.

Mom translated the question. The Styrlax chirped and blipped in reply.

"He says they aren't sure," said Mom, "but they can help us retrace the trajectory of the bombs and pinpoint their origin."

"Can they help us get there?" Dad asked.

The Styrlax made a sound like a breeze through wind chimes. He consulted with the others for what seemed like a long time, then replied.

"They will lend us a ship," Mom translated. "What we do with it is up to us. We can bring a small team. The rest can stay aboard here for as long as we need, but the Styrlax will not involve themselves further."

"Tell them we are grateful." Dad looked back at the survivors, then locked eyes with Tarra and another scientist who'd joined them, Barro-8. "I think we've ended up in command."

Barro motioned to Tarra. "You're the highest ranking among us."

Tarra grimaced but nodded. "Let's get everyone else organized."

Mom looked around. "There are so few of us. . . ."

"All the more reason not to waste time."

"Dad, what will we do?" asked Xela.

"We're going to figure out who did this, and why."

Xela sat alone by the window as the adults conversed in quiet tones. Below, the planet swirled in gray ash and darkness. She thought of Mica, of his auburn bristles and his feisty tail, the way he wouldn't leave her room each night even though it was bedtime, the way he jumped on her each morning . . .

Many hours, or maybe a day later—time had little meaning when you were in orbit, the sun slipping by every few hours—Mom came and sat beside her.

"Mica's gone," Xela sobbed.

Mom nuzzled her face against Xela's braid. "I know."

"We'll never see him or Nia or Niho again, ever. Or the rest of our family or any of my friends or our house or anything. I just want to die, too."

Mom hugged her tightly, tears falling. This was the kind of moment when, throughout Xela's life, Mom had said something like *It's going to be okay*, but not this time.

"We're going to go on a journey," she said instead. She rubbed her finger against the skin in the crook of her elbow.

Xela noticed that Mom had drawn three hollow black circles there. "What's that?"

"To remember your brother, and your grandparents."

"Can I have one, too?"

"It's permanent. And it hurts."

"I don't care; I want one. Where are we going?"

"To where the Tears came from. To find out who sent them, and why."

"And then what?"

Mom looked out the window. "We don't know yet."

"We need to kill them," said Xela, squeezing her own tail until it hurt. "We need to burn them up just like they did to us!"

"Calm down, honey," said Mom, rubbing her shoulders, and yet she didn't disagree. "Barro and Tarra are leaving soon. They will scout the system and report back. Then we'll go."

Xela nodded. "I'm waiting for you to tell me that you're going to leave me here where it's safe."

Mom shook her head and bit her lip, a pained look crossing her face. "We will stay together. Nowhere is safe anymore."

"I know."

"We may need to make some changes," said Mom. "To how we look and how we think. We may need to do things that, before today, we would never have imagined doing."

Xela gripped her tail tighter. "Good."

Mom left, and Xela gazed out the window. Below, the surface of Telos, in night's shadow, was as dark as the depths of space around them, a black hole where her entire life had once been.

She turned away from it and curled up on her side.

Many sleepless hours later, she boarded a Styrlax spaceship with Mom and Dad, Barro and Tarra, and ten other Telphons. The ship was powered by a smaller version of the orange crystal sphere, and they traveled many light-years nearly at once. And then again. And again.

One year later, after endless training and careful, quiet study, Xela had a new name and a new face. She had scars from the changes they had all made to blend in, changes that had left her in daily pain.

The strange planet she now found herself on looked stranger through her new eyes; even her voice no longer sounded like her own. She was an alien speaking an alien language, learning an alien history. But she appeared as one of them, except for the three circles she would draw inside her elbow, above the permanent, hidden tattoos beneath. Three circles that she would touch when she was alone, and say their names: Mica, Nia, Niho.

She would smile, and she would make alien friends, and pretend to laugh at their alien jokes, but inside, she would never forget:

They would be counted.

TIME LINE

2175: Humanity detects anomalous readings in the sun and discovers that it will explode in a supernova in less than fifty years. This behavior contradicts all previous scientific knowledge of yellow dwarf stars, and there is no way to stop it.

2179: The International Space Agency devises a plan: leave the solar system and journey to the planet designated Aaru-5, nearly fifteen light-years away. The journey will take one hundred and fifty years, with humans in stasis for most of the trip.

2185: Humanity begins moving to colonies on Mars. Starliner construction commences in orbit above the red planet. The ISA initiates Phases One and Two of the Aaru-5 colonization protocol.

2194: Eight years into its test voyage, the *Starliner Artemis*, the prototype of the ships that will make up the colonial fleet, is lost.

2198: The last humans leave Earth orbit. The planet is officially declared uninhabitable.

2200: The First Fleet departs on the ten-year journey to Delphi, the first waypoint en route to Aaru-5. Additional fleets depart yearly, then every few months as Red Line, the time when Mars will become too dangerous to inhabit, draws closer.

2209: Phase One is completed. Initial readings are deemed promising. The First Fleet reaches Delphi successfully and refuels to begin the journey to Danos, the second waypoint.

2211: Earth is consumed by the sun.

2213: The last colonists depart Mars on the *Starliner Scorpius*.

2216: The sun goes supernova, obliterating the solar system.

2223: The *Scorpius* begins its arrival procedures near Delphi. . . .

THE OCEANS BETWEEN STARS

1

EARTH YEAR: 2223

DISTANCE TO DELPHI: 557.3 BILLION KM

TIME TO ARRIVAL: 184 DAYS, 9 HOURS

From a far enough distance, the Milky Way galaxy appears to be hugging itself with arms made of soft clouds. Closer, those clouds can be seen for what they really are: trillions of stars, a spill of diamonds. It would seem that to fly through, you would need to carefully thread your way between their crowded edges, all the while being blinded by their gleaming. But when you get very close, those spiral arms, those rivers of gems, reveal their trick. The spaces between the stars get bigger and bigger, until you are alone in darkness, each star seemingly a lifetime away. You can be moving at nearly thirty thousand kilometers per second, a speed so fast it is like traveling from your house around the world and back in the time it takes to snap your fingers, and yet the stars never seem to get any closer. In a universe this vast, where the answer to *are we there yet* comes in decades, centuries, even millennia, you can almost feel like you aren't moving at all.

Better just to sleep.

And so humanity did, in billions of little pods on a hundred great ships, a jagged blinking ant line through the dark. And yet, again, so great were the distances that this was not a line you could see: the First Fleet, which had recently departed from Danos, the second waypoint, was a bit more than a full light-year ahead of the Final Fleet, which was just nearing Delphi, the first. More than twelve trillion kilometers separated the first starliner, the *Asimov*, and the last, the *Scorpius*, with the rest of the fleets scattered in between.

There were more ships behind the *Scorpius* as well: many private vessels, stragglers who had stayed to watch the sun go supernova seven years ago. They had pulled back to a safe distance and peered through high-powered scopes as the sun, now a smoldering red supergiant, all at once collapsed in on itself and exploded, sending a brilliant wave of energy in all directions. It vaporized Jupiter and Saturn (in the Rings of Gold casino, at the last table of lifers still playing cards, the dealer's final recorded hand was a perfect twenty-one), as well as Neptune and Uranus. It tossed Pluto and Charon like marbles out into the dark, to roam the night perhaps forever, or at least until they found another sun to enchant them. It bloomed into a feathery magenta-and-yellow cloud and eventually died away.

Humanity's home: erased forever.

Was it worth it? the stragglers had asked one another as they'd turned and shot away from the glimmering little neutron star that remained, a celestial tomb-stone to the solar system that was. *Definitely*, they'd all replied, and yet they were quiet as they prepared for stasis, their memories haunted by the ferocious blast, by the sight of those planets disintegrating, the irre-futable finality. . . .

Now all was quiet. Sleeping pods across the fleets, all the orphans inside dreaming their molasses-slow dreams, a light coating of ice on each small window. Here, a bot moving about, performing basic main-tenance. There, a human waking to take his watch on a starliner bridge, relieving another bleary-eyed colonial officer who trudged back to her pod, lonely footsteps echoing on the metal corridor floors. She'd seen enough of the infinite for a while, thank you very much.

On icy Delphi: the chugging of mining equipment

and trash incinerators, cleanup from the second-to-last fleet and the *Starliner Saga*. When its passengers had woken up and learned that their sun was truly gone, they'd had quite a party. To hear their raucous din, you might have thought theirs was a joyous celebration, but as with most funerals, if you studied their faces, you would have known otherwise.

On they went, the ships racing across the ocean of space, blips barely visible in the dark, the humans on their way to Aaru-5, the closest planet that might be able to support them still well over a hundred years away.

But see this:

On one small ship near the very back of the line, still a few months from Delphi, a girl who is not asleep. On a human ship, in human clothes, a girl . . .

But not a human at all.

She has left her pod, awakened by an alarm she set just before their last refueling stop ended. The other passengers are still asleep. This girl checks her link. She has little time, and much to do.

She floats through the ship in low light, little more than a shadow in her black thermal wear. She keeps one hand on the wall because balance has never been as easy since she had to lose her tail. As she floats, she slips her atmo pack over her shoulders and presses the plugs into her nostrils. Can't afford to have her cough kick in, though the air on the ship is far better than it ever was on Mars.

The skin on her hands, feet, and face is striped, some human color still, but the wider streaks reveal lavender with grayish-black dots. The putty-like skin covering is meant to be reapplied every few days, but she's been in stasis three years since their last stop, and even in the cold, still pod, the cream dries and flakes off. She has to wake up early to clean up the mess, to reapply.

But there are other things that must be done first.

She slips into the cockpit. The ship's panda-shaped bot sits in the pilot's chair in low power mode, his eyes glowing a mellow orange above his permanent, creepy grin. Carefully, she lowers herself behind him and places a metal cylinder against the back of his head. The cylinder is smooth and silver, as long as a pinkie finger, with a black suction cup at one end. She presses the cup tight against the metal, then pushes a red button. A white light starts to blink on the cylinder's opposite end. Normally the bot would awaken in the presence of a passenger, but this device will keep him asleep while she works.

The girl buckles herself into the copilot's chair and checks her link. She scrolls through the usual menus and then taps an icon that no normal human link has. A message awaits her. It is cold inside the ship, but before she activates the message, she slips off her gloves, pulls the link out of its port on her sleeve, and cups her hands around it.

The message is not displayed in the visual spectrum of light. Nor is it presented in her native language; the coverings that she wears on her eyes so that they appear human would make it impossible to read, anyway. Three years, or if you counted stasis nearly thirteen, of seeing the world as if it has lost its color, its depth, and by evening when the lubricant has worn off, the maddening irritation. Just one of many things she has never told even her closest friends. Nor has she complained. Her mother would just remind her of all the more important things they've lost.

The message arrives in pulses of heat, created by running the link's processors at full speed in quick bursts. She feels the heat as a code in her palms, long bursts and short, some hotter than others. Even that sensation is dulled, since her bristles were shaved off.

Slowly, she decodes the message, and it fills her with worry and frustration.

We know you are confused, but you must not forget our mission. We can forgive what happened at Saturn, but you must turn your link's locator back on so that we can intercept. It is what your mother and father would want.

The girl curses to herself. They don't know what they're doing. They thought they did, but they don't know what she now knows. She tried to convince Barro back at Saturn, while Liam ran off with the data key, but he wouldn't listen, wouldn't take her seriously. They never did.

She will show them this time.

Think of your brother. Of all those who must be counted. Think of your people. Our very survival depends on you.

Yes, she thinks, *it does,* and she grits her teeth and deletes the message.

She does not turn on her link locator. She has a plan of her own. But as she replaces her link, she shivers. It is a plan that means she is almost always alone.

The girl puts on her gloves. She taps the ship's navigation and brings up a holoscreen. A map of the journey to Delphi, with key statistics. Speed: thirty-five thousand kilometers per second. Time to arrival: one hundred and forty-two days, eight and a half hours. They are a day behind schedule because at their last refueling stop, three years ago, they discovered that they had drifted ever so slightly off course. This meant it would take them an extra day to catch the *Scorpius* at Delphi. The starliner will be moored there for five days, and they've been scheduled to get there on the second day; now it will be the third, and that's fine. They have enough fuel to make it without any more stops.

But she needs them to need one more stop. Just to be sure.

The girl pairs her link with the console and activates another icon that no human link would have: a viral program that slaves the ship's navigation and allows her to make changes to their course without the ship's computer, or its bot, knowing. Her father built it while her mother was decoding human speech— changing code and changing vocal cords, communication surgery. In a way, it's what she's doing now.

Except Dad would be furious, she thinks. Both of them would be. Maybe she will be able to convince them, when the time comes. But she still has no plan for that.

She loads their course plot on the holoscreen. Hours of study under her stern mother's eye, learning these systems, on top of all the human customs, the history. Many hours here in the dark too, before their last wake-up, figuring out just how much to alter their course.

She is betraying them now, betraying them all— *don't think about that.*

She makes the change: barely a hundredth of a

degree. That should do it.

The girl confirms the new settings, and the ship shudders as its lateral thrusters fire. A short pulse, just a momentary vibration, then silence again. So much silence out here.

She watches the ship's trajectory change just so, then taps off the holoscreen, exits the program, and disconnects her link. She removes the cylinder on the bot's neck and glides out of the cockpit.

Back in her compartment, she gets her backpack and heads to the bathroom. She looks in the mirror, her face half her own, half an imposter's. But since that last day on Mars, she wonders: Which is which? It feels like neither. It feels like both.

How will she make him understand?

She rubs the old putty off, the flakes floating in the air around her. When she's finished, she gets the ship's vacuum, switches it to zero gravity mode, and sucks up the mess. Then she unscrews a metal container, dips her finger into the cool, thick putty, and lifts it toward her face. Pauses again.

Why bother?

Why keep hiding who she is, when it is no longer certain who she should be hiding from?

But no, one thing at a time. There may still be a way to not lose everyone she cares about.

And so a half hour later she reemerges from the

bathroom, the mask reapplied and nearly set. She enters the compartment where her parents sleep. Carefully, she opens their pods, one at a time, with a hiss of frosted fog. The pods can't be open for long, less than a minute, or the temperature and fluid parameters of stasis will become imbalanced, forcing an emergency wake-up. This would jeopardize their health, as their wounds from the explosion on Mars are no better than they were ten years ago, merely paused. But also, then she might have to explain herself.

She moves swiftly. There's not time to remove their old masks, so she quickly vaccuums what's flaked off, dabs on fresh putty, and smoothes it as best she can. Before sealing them up again, she kisses each of their foreheads.

Finally, she returns to her room. Before she gets back into her pod, she pauses, a nervous flutter in her chest. She opens a drawer along the wall and pulls out a link. She turns it on, and as it powers up, her heart begins to beat faster. This makes the artificial pump just below her single ventricle speed up, and there is a strange sort of sucking in her lungs and she has to fight back a cough. Before, it was easy to blame it on the Martian dust. That had probably been part of the cause, but what excuse will she make now that it is only guilt and fear?

The home screen appears and she taps the video file there. When it starts to play, she fast-forwards until a boy's face appears, cheery, then she jumps ahead to his last appearance.

"See you soon, guys," Shawn says.

And this makes her heart race even more, and the pump labors to keep up, and, as tears spring from her eyes, the girl taps pause and doubles over, coughing until her insides ache. She looks back at the file, at her friend's face. "I'm so sorry," she whispers. "Goodbye." She shuts off the link and closes her eyes. Holds her breath. Too many tears might stain the putty before it has completely set. The lies, the lies, the lies.

The girl exhales and puts the link away. Returning to her pod, she pauses to gaze into the one beside hers, through the frosted flex-glass at the still face of a boy, her friend. Not an enemy, she has decided. *But if he knew* . . . And he'll need to. Soon. Is there any way he will understand?

She lets her forehead fall against the glass. "I'm doing my best." When his eyes are closed, she thinks that he almost looks like Mica. *They look nothing like us*, her mother had said when once, back on Mars, she'd given voice to this observation. It is true that there are so many differences. And yet, something about Liam's face . . .

She raises herself, takes a moment to check her

reflection in the top of the pod and to smooth the tear lines. The putty barely budges. It is so uncomfortable. Like having a wet towel draped over your skin, day after day.

Stop complaining, her mother would say. *Be strong. We can't afford not to be.*

You're right, Mother.

The girl floats back to her pod, buckles herself in, and activates the stasis sequence. As the flex-glass top lowers, she breathes deep, but her hearts will not slow their off-kilter beat, and tears threaten her trembling eyes once more, until the cold and gas coax her under.

Her thoughts begin to slow. She thinks of Shawn, and the others.

I'm sorry.

The world dims. Liam, Mica . . .

I'm sorry.

A moment later, orange lights blink on around the inside perimeter of the pod: *stasis reengaged*.

The ship, now still again, continues through the dark, ever so slightly off course from where it was headed. One one-hundredth of a degree, such a little thing . . . but perhaps just enough to determine the fate of this universe.

2

"Liam, do you see it?"

"Not yet." Liam peered out the canopy of the skim drone. A river of icy boulders floated all around him, looming shadows against the distant stars, their metal-and-frost surfaces gleaming now and then as they tumbled through the drone's exterior lights. The rocks were actually fragments of a pulverized comet that had once been the size of a small moon. They slipped along through the dark of space at eighty kilometers per second. Not that Liam could tell; he was moving right along with them, and the stars were all so far away in every direction that there was nothing to indicate that they were moving at all.

Nothing above, below, anywhere.

"How close am I?"

"It should be visible out your starboard side," said JEFF over the link.

A proximity alert began to flash on the navigation screen.

"Liam, look out!" said Phoebe.

"Got it." Liam hit the joystick control and fired the starboard thrusters. The skim drone jumped sideways just as a boulder twice its size spun down from above. His maneuver wasn't precise, though—it was hard to operate the controls while wearing this space-grade suit with its thick gloves—and the boulder clipped the back corner of the craft, sending a shudder through it.

"That was close," said Phoebe.

"They're all close." Liam's fingers tingled. His head and back still ached from reanimation, though at least his stomach had calmed down. He breathed deep and tried to relax, but it wasn't easy when he was navigating these boulders. Half of them were bigger than his ship, and they kept ricocheting off one another in sprays of dust. The biggest danger was getting caught between two of them. The skim drone's fragile exterior was little match for what amounted to multiton billiard balls.

Liam spied a midsized rock ahead. He tapped it on

the sensors. "What about that one?"

"Acknowledged, analyzing," said JEFF. "I'm afraid while the mass and composition are right, it contains too little water to suit our needs."

"And you're sure we can't just grab a couple of these smaller ones?" Phoebe wondered. Liam saw her in the rear camera, wearing a space suit and floating, upside down, it seemed, on a tether beneath their Cosmic Cruiser, the boxy spaceship that was only meant for travel around the old solar system, but which they'd now managed to fly for nearly a light-year with the help of a special engine they'd salvaged just before leaving Saturn. An engine that was now low on fuel. Again.

"We only have time for one, right, JEFF?" said Liam. The engine was powered by nuclear fusion, and water was its fuel source. There was plenty of it frozen inside these comet fragments, but they also needed to choose one that wasn't too difficult to mine: if the pockets of ice were too small, or if the composition of the surrounding rock was wrong, it could take many more hours to extract the water.

"Correct. Attempting to mine more than one fragment, even if they are small, will add variability, and thus further the risk of missing our rendezvous window with the *Scorpius*."

Liam held his breath against a flare of adrenaline

in his belly. "We don't have much more rendezvous time to lose."

"Unless you get crushed trying to find the perfect rock," said Phoebe.

"Well, yeah." The skim drone's sensors blared and a smaller rock clanged against the underside of the craft.

"See what I mean?"

"The fragment we pinpointed is the best option," said JEFF. "But you are the acting captain, Liam, so just say the word, and I will reply: *aye aye!*"

Phoebe sighed.

"Was that not funny?" JEFF asked.

Liam swallowed, a metallic taste in his mouth. He'd broken out in a clammy sweat, his heart rate increasing. "No, it was fine, JEFF. I'm just not in the mood."

It was true that Liam was the acting captain. While his parents were technically the owners of the Cosmic Cruiser, they were still in stasis due to the injuries they'd sustained on Mars, which required the advanced medical attention they could get only on the *Scorpius* or at Delphi. But he certainly didn't feel like a captain. These worries, spinny feelings that tied him in knots, had been getting worse after each stasis period. JEFF said some of it was due to disorientation from stasis, and some due to the prolonged time in low gravity, no matter how much the pods attempted to compensate for it.

But Liam knew it was more than that. It was also the time, and the distance. There was nothing, ever, anywhere, out here in the darkness. And if they didn't refuel fast enough, if they didn't make it to Delphi in time to catch the *Scorpius* . . .

Liam's hand left the controls and drifted to his other wrist. On the outside of his puffy white suit was the strange silver watch that he'd found in the hidden observatory on Mars, on the wrist of a dead alien being. The watch's face was split into two hemispheres, each with an odd symbol. There was also a dial around the outside. Turning the dial allowed the wearer to move through time—not to time *travel*, exactly, because Liam couldn't stay where he went. He could only observe.

It had been helpful on Mars, and at Saturn, allowing Liam to see potentially disastrous events in his future and find alternative solutions, but it had also been dangerous: when he used it, he entered a sort of timestream, and inside, Liam had encountered a metal-suited man who was part of the Drove, the beings responsible for blowing up the sun. That man had killed the alien in the observatory, and he'd wanted to take the watch from Liam. He'd also offered to bring Liam to something called the Dark Star. Liam had encountered the Drove again when he'd used the watch at Saturn, this time in strange, liquid black ships, and so, though he'd wanted to many times, he hadn't traveled into the future since. Also, using the watch made him feel very strange, not just the splitting headaches and nausea, but also like he was coming apart, unsticking first in his thoughts and then in his very molecules.

"Liam?" Phoebe asked. "Do you see it yet?"

Liam glanced at Phoebe in the camera. She and the cruiser had drifted—or maybe he had, who knew?—such that she now seemed to be floating on her side, with the cruiser pointing up and down. "No," he said. "Just a sec."

He returned his hand to the console, and as he did, for just a moment, he felt a hollowness inside that he yearned to fill. There was something else about the watch, an urge that the time trips stirred inside him—to keep going. To see what was out there even further into the future. Where did Liam and his friends end up? How did he die? But even beyond that—what happened to this galaxy? How did the universe end? It had seemed, during those moments in the timestream, like he could have found those answers if he'd just reached far enough . . . even though at the same time, he'd experienced a chilling fear, like if he traveled that far he might not be able to return. Still, if it hadn't been for the danger of the Drove, he felt like he would have attempted it, and this was something he didn't want to admit to Phoebe or JEFF.

Liam tried to put the urge out of his mind. They needed to hurry. After all, they weren't even supposed to be here right now. They should still have been asleep, due to wake up in just over three months at Delphi, where the *Starliner Scorpius* and his older sister, Mina, and best friend, Shawn, would be waiting. At their last refueling stop, they'd made what should have been their final course correction, but instead of coming out of stasis within sight of Delphi, they had been awakened by JEFF here, in the middle of nowhere, and he'd informed them that they'd drifted off course for the second time on the journey. The first time had cost them a day on their arrival time, and now this extra stop was costing them another. The *Scorpius* would be moored at Delphi for five days, during which time the crew would refuel and attend to any repairs, and the passengers would take a break from stasis for exercise, socialization, and wellness checkups. The cruiser was now due to arrive on day four. Any more delays, and they might miss the starliner altogether.

It was funny to even be referring to days anymore, since it was pretty much just night all the time out here, but Liam and Phoebe and the rest of humanity still lived by an Earth-standard twenty-four-hour clock. Up until recently, Liam had measured his life in Martian days, which were forty minutes longer than Earth's, but like so many things about Mars, that clock had been discarded the moment they'd departed, in favor of what was considered humanity's true chronological cycle. Liam had kept the Mars calendar on his link, though. It would have been the red planet's version of September, right now, when the sun, large as it had been, would angle lower in the sky, and the dust storms of the long summer would finally calm. But thinking about that only made Liam homesick. Worse, actually, because home no longer even existed. Erased from the universe, almost as if his memories were just dreams.

He tapped the thrusters to speed up and promptly nicked another boulder, but he didn't slow down. Would a ship carrying one hundred million humans wait around for two teens and their parents? It hadn't last time. Of course, back at Saturn, the *Scorpius* had been in danger. Even though Liam and Phoebe had the final Phase Two data—results from their parents' very last terraforming trials, which would make colonizing Aaru-5 possible—and even though they had their parents on board—the scientists who knew best how to interpret that data—that still might not be enough reason to keep a wary starliner from running toward Danos as soon as it could, trying to stay ahead of whatever threat was surely still lurking behind them.

Liam could relate: each time they stopped to refuel, he found himself eyeing the dark around them. Who was after them? Barro had been the name of the one they'd met. Were they pirates? But they hadn't just been trying to commandeer their ship. They'd also, he assumed, been the ones who blew up Saturn Station. Did that make them terrorists? But they'd also wanted the Phase Two data. Mercenaries? Working for whom?

Liam remembered what Barro had said: *It cannot change what the humans have done. It cannot undo Phase One.* There were three phases to humanity's plan to colonize Aaru-5. Liam knew a lot about Phase Two, the terraforming science that his parents has spent his entire life working on, and Phase Three was what they were doing right now: traveling to Aaru. But Phase One . . . he barely knew anything about it. How had they described it in school? *Gathering advanced data about Aaru and preparing the planet.* He'd asked JEFF about Phase One, but JEFF didn't have any more information because, as Liam already knew, the project was classified. The only people around who knew more about it—his parents—literally couldn't talk about it at the moment. And besides, he'd already asked them back on Mars, and they hadn't had much to say.

But whatever Phase One was, there was something else about what Barro had said that troubled Liam even more: *the humans*. He'd said that like he wasn't a human himself. Could that be possible?

Even though they'd been traveling for nearly ten years, they'd been awake for only five days of it, and so it seemed like barely a week had passed since the events on Mars. Liam had woken up that last morning worried about leaving his apartment and the only way of life he'd ever known, only to find out that there were not one, or two, but now possibly even three different races of aliens in the universe, most if not all of whom seemed determined to wipe out humanity. And as far as Liam knew, he and Phoebe were the only humans who had any idea about any of it. Once they finally caught up with the *Scorpius*, he could show colonial command the watch in order to explain about the dead alien. He also had a small orange crystal in his pocket, about the size of a golf ball, that contained data about the supernovas that the Drove had caused. And everyone had already seen what Barro and his people had done at Saturn.

And yet telling colonial, even catching up, all assumed that the *Scorpius* was still okay. Liam had no idea what else might have happened in the years since they'd left Saturn. Had the *Scorpius* been attacked again? What about any of the other starliners?

The Cosmic Cruiser's long-range communications had been damaged on Mars, so the only way that Liam and Phoebe could communicate with the *Scorpius* was by using the tiny pendant hanging around Liam's neck: a radio beacon. Mina wore its twin. They sent each other messages using an ancient twentieth-century language called tap code. That was how Liam had let Mina and the *Scorpius* know that they'd salvaged a faster engine and would be able to catch them. But there had been no communication since. Mina would still be in stasis on the starliner, not due to wake up until arrival at Delphi. Yet Liam had pressed the green glass top of the pendant each time he'd woken up anyway, hoping it might blink back.

She was probably fine. Shawn, all of them. Fast asleep. The *Scorpius* and the other starliners had defenses: military escorts, shields, robotic fighter drones, even an arsenal of nuclear warheads. But how could he be sure? Other than these brief refueling stops, Liam had been in stasis, too. Long stretches of nothing. If something had gone wrong on the *Scorpius* and Mina had woken up and tried to contact him, he wouldn't even have gotten the message. The beacon would have just been blinking in the dark. So many things might have happened, and yet there was only the deep black and silence of space. Until Delphi. They were almost there. . . .

Except not! Once again they'd drifted off course, and into an area that had not been mapped for potential refueling spots, since no one should have needed to at this point. They'd been lucky to find these comet fragments.

JEFF didn't know what was causing the course problems, though he had caught this latest one before it got too bad. He blamed the outdated computers on the Cosmic Cruiser, and the fact that the ship hadn't been built for such long journeys. Parts were corroding, calculations overwhelming the system, processors that were designed to be rebooted and updated far more often starting to fail. JEFF likely needed updating, too. But for now all they could do was refuel as quickly as possible and get back on course.

"Our target should be right above you," JEFF reported.

Liam checked the topside sensor, then twisted to look out the top of the canopy. "I see it."

"Can you get to it?"

"Yup," said Liam, but just then, another boulder nicked the starboard side of the drone, pushing him slightly off course. He tapped the thrusters and realigned himself, then edged through the maze of rocks toward his target. Another glanced off him; a scree of pebbles pinged off the canopy.

"Careful," said Phoebe. "Don't pull a Hans Buckle and let that grav-ball slip through your gloves."

"Very funny." Buckle was Liam's favorite player on his favorite team, the Haishang Dust Devils. He wore his lucky jersey beneath his suit right now. Phoebe had gotten it for him before they'd left Mars, even though she was a die-hard Meridian Canyon Bombers fan. Teams that no longer existed, from a planet that no longer existed. The stadiums with their pillow tops, the stands with their harnesses for when the gravity was turned off, the hum of the grav-balls: all of it gone now. There was supposed to be a draft for a new league on Aaru-5, but that was literally over a century away. A lot of things had to go right between now and then, when so far they'd been going horribly wrong.

Liam edged the skim drone closer to the target boulder. "All right, I'm going to grab it."

His fingers danced from one set of thrusters to the other, stopping the skim drone and rotating it until its underside faced the rock. He inched closer, then opened the large claw on the bottom of the craft. His seat vibrated as the claw extended—

CLANG! A smaller rock caromed off the back of the ship, knocking Liam sideways and offline. He cursed to himself and started realigning the craft. As he did, a light caught his attention.

The dial on his alien watch had started blinking blue. This blinking was never a good sign.

"Liam," said JEFF, "I don't want to rush you, but there's a particularly dense arrangement of objects drifting toward you from your eleven o'clock."

"I figured." Out of the corner of his eye, Liam saw a cluster of boulders tumbling around and over one another, making a cloud of dust like a schoolyard brawl. Some of the dust was ice, and it glittered like diamonds. Another beautiful sight out here, unlike anything he'd ever seen, but that also might kill him.

Liam flexed his fingers and gritted his teeth. The little thrusters on the top, bottom, and sides of the skim drone fired in white bursts until he had the claw back in position.

The watch blinked faster.

"It would be ideal if you could be out of the vicinity in ten seconds."

"Good to know, JEFF!"

The claw's metal fingers crunched into the sides of the boulder. Liam glanced one more time at the watch. Should he turn the dial and see what was going to happen? But the claw skidded for a moment, losing its grip, and Liam had to correct his angle.

"Liam, move," said Phoebe.

"Five seconds to impact," said JEFF.

The craft vibrated and rattled as the claw sank into the metallic surface of their target. He needed to have a firm hold—

A dim shadow passed overhead. Liam saw the gang of enormous craggy boulders nearly on top of him.

"Leaving now!" He burned the primary thruster on the bottom of the craft. It shook and lurched, and then shot back out of the way, the claw holding on. "Got it—"

But one of the boulders slammed into his cargo, sending it and the skim drone spiraling. The outside world spun. Flashes of other rocks, the blur of the distant cruiser lights, around again and again. He slammed into a smaller rock, then a larger one. There was a sharp cracking sound. Was that the canopy? Liam could barely tell, and his stomach was in his throat, but it seemed like he was spinning counterclockwise, and so he fired the port-side thrusters. The spin slowed, and slowed more, the labyrinth of comet fragments coming back into focus.

A yellow light began to flash on the controls. His battery had dropped to critical. How was that possible? He'd only been out here twenty minutes.

Another light flashed on a schematic of the craft, a section of the underside blinking red.

"Liam," said JEFF, "I think your battery compartment has been damaged, and I am detecting a chemical leak."

"Yeah," Liam said heavily. As he watched, the last three bars of battery power drained away, and the skim drone cycled down to dark.

3

The cabin became silent. Two boulders collided nearby, spraying the skim drone with dust but making no sound in the vacuum of space.

Liam shivered as the temperature plummeted inside the craft. He picked up the large helmet of his space suit from the seat beside him and fastened it into place. His breaths echoed inside it as he twisted around, looking for the Cosmic Cruiser. There it was, out beyond the curtain of rocks, a few hundred meters away. "So, wanna come pick me up?"

"We will have to wait until you drift to a more advantageous spot," said JEFF. "I'm afraid I can't risk flying into your current position. Our borrowed engine is particularly delicate."

"How long is that going to take?"

"I'm modeling the movements of the comet frag-ments now. . . . Based on these calculations, we should be able to reach you safely in three hours."

"*Hours?* What if two of these things decide to make me a sandwich filling before then?"

JEFF didn't answer immediately.

The watch was still blinking.

"How about debris pulses?" Liam asked.

"It would be far too dangerous to fire them into your vicinity. I simply cannot predict the potential chain reaction."

"JEFF, we don't have hours to spare!"

"Acknowledged. I will try to come up with another solution—"

"What if we push?" asked Phoebe.

"How are we going to do that?"

"I'll show you."

"Show me how?" Liam twisted to look at the cruiser before the rotation of the skim drone caused it to slip from his view. He didn't see Phoebe. Her tether hung there, snaking about without her.

"Phoebe, your connection must be loose," said JEFF. "I am no longer reading your suit vitals."

"Not loose," said Phoebe, breathing hard. "One sec, Liam. Uh!"

"Are you okay?" Liam asked.

"Fine, just . . ." She exhaled hard. "There we go."

"That is extremely dangerous."

"Phoebe? What are you doing?"

"Ah. This is nice."

The cruiser rotated back into view, but Liam couldn't locate Phoebe.

"Where are you?"

"You'll see."

Seconds ticked by. Liam turned this way and that, trying to keep an eye on the cruiser—something slammed against the canopy. Phoebe slid across the top of the drone and tumbled over the side, grabbing for the gold towing handles along the edge of the craft.

"What are you doing?" Liam shouted.

She just managed to snag a handle with two fingers of her thick white glove and dangled briefly off the side of the craft, her legs flailing in space. She smiled, breathing hard. "I'm here to rescue you, dummy." She held up an object in her other hand. It was shaped sort of like a silver turtle shell and had two straps: a booster pack. She wore one just like it. "Now get out and help me push—whoa!" She ducked as a meter-wide fragment drifted by, scraping her shoulder.

"Please be careful, Phoebe," said JEFF. "Any tear in your suit or loss of life support functions will expose you to the vacuum of space, which, in the best-case scenario, will be lethal after approximately sixty seconds."

"Why do you have to spoil all the fun, JEFF?"

"It is my duty to keep you alive. If exposed to the vacuum, it is vital that you exhale so that your lungs do not burst. Also, you must close your eyes—"

"All right, enough already! Jeez." Phoebe turned to Liam. "Ready?"

Liam looked back at the cruiser. "You flew over here without your tether?"

"Tether wouldn't reach. And actually I wanted to save fuel, so I just kicked off the side of the cruiser. Felt like a superhero! Flying through space."

"How did you not get hit by the rocks?"

Phoebe smiled in that familiar way. "Saw a gap," she said. "Went for it."

"You got lucky."

Phoebe rolled her eyes. "So? Luck counts. Now come on."

Liam surveyed the sea of boulders. He checked the watch; the blinking had slowed, but it hadn't stopped. Again he felt that urge to turn the dial, especially before climbing out into rock-strewn space. . . .

Phoebe rapped on the canopy. "Hello?"

"Okay, I'm coming." Liam reached beneath the rim of the canopy and pulled two emergency latches.

There was a hiss as the air sucked out of the cockpit, but it was quickly squashed to silence. His suit hummed to full power to compensate as a light sheen of frost instantly sparkled over the controls. He unbuckled and floated up, then pressed the canopy closed again. Once he was outside, he gripped a tow handle tightly; if he lost hold of the skim drone, he'd float off among the rocks with no way to get back.

"Here," said Phoebe, handing him the booster pack.

Liam hooked the front of his heavy boot under a tow handle and slipped the pack over his shoulders, yanking the straps tight and fastening the waistband. He pulled the thrust controller off one of the straps. It had a series of buttons that wirelessly controlled the pack's different directional rockets.

"Get beside me." Phoebe had moved herself to the front starboard side of the craft. Liam joined her. They each held on to two handles, Liam's hand over Phoebe's on the one that they shared.

Beyond the comet fragment being held by the skim drone's claw, there was nothing but utter blackness, and it was still strange to tell yourself that no, you weren't going to fall into it, and yet it went on forever in all directions, made the mere idea of *directions* almost pointless. It was still a disorienting sensation when you'd spent your entire life in the gentle embrace of gravity, where concepts like *up* and *down* seemed like certainties.

Liam found himself taking short, quick breaths, his heart racing, a tight, cramped feeling he'd had more and more, like: How could there be so much space? The farther they traveled, the bigger it felt. Maybe it would be better on the starliner; he'd heard that the artificial gravity helped you feel more like yourself.

"JEFF," said Phoebe, "we're coming to you. When's the next gap we can fit through?"

"Calculating. . . . There is one coming up in approximately twenty seconds."

"Watch out," said Liam. They pulled in their feet as a two-meter-wide rock drifted by.

Overhead, the biggest boulder yet cast them in shadow.

"Okay," said JEFF, "in five . . . four . . ."

"I don't see a gap," said Liam. The distant cruiser was nearly hidden by the rocks.

"It will be there if you go . . . now."

"Fire!" said Phoebe. Her main thruster burst in a jet of white smoke that immediately froze.

"Wait. . . ." Liam hesitated for a moment—because he still didn't see the space—and then he fired his thruster too late, and now the skim drone was lurching forward but also starting to spin.

"You were supposed to fire at the same time!" said Phoebe.

"Sorry!"

"You'll need to correct for that spin and move toward me more quickly," said JEFF, "or the gap is going to become a wall."

"Fire your port thruster," said Liam. They both did and the spin slowed. He could see it now, an opening appearing ahead, the cruiser in clear sight. But everything was moving and it would close soon—

"Forward again," said Phoebe. "Full power on three."

"Yup."

This time they hit their controls at the same moment and burst forward, arms burning as they pressed on the side of the ship, the thrust threatening to throw them over the top of the heavy drone.

"Please go faster," said JEFF.

"Burn again," said Phoebe. "Three-two-one-now!"

The boulders blurred all around them, far too close for comfort. A small rock clipped Liam's boot. Countless tiny ones pelted the sides of the skim drone, making no sound but sending vibrations up Liam's arms.

"It's closing!" said Phoebe.

The trapezoidal window to the Cosmic Cruiser shrank.

"One more burst," said Liam. They fired again, speeding up even more—

"Ah!" A rock hit Phoebe's arm and her hand slipped free and the force of her thruster pushed her headlong over the canopy of the ship.

"Phoebe!"

She got her bearings and stopped firing her pack, but Liam was still holding down his main rocket, and just in the second it took for him to stop, he'd accelerated more than Phoebe, overtaking her. The edge of the ship knocked her in the shoulder. She spun around, clawing for the tow handles, but the ship slid right over her and then she was tumbling along its underside.

"Grab the claw!" Liam said.

"I missed it!"

Liam pushed himself down, hanging on to the tow handle with the two free fingers of the same hand holding the thrust control. "I'm here," he said, reaching for her. Phoebe came somersaulting by his feet. His fingers scraped her leg, now her side. Her arms flailed, slapping into his. She was almost past him, into the boulders—

His hand caught her wrist and he squeezed as hard as he could, straining to keep hold of both her and the skim drone. "I've got you!" His shoulders burned. He wouldn't be able to hold on for long—

They sailed through the gap and out into free space.

"You are clear," said JEFF.

"Thanks," said Phoebe, breathing hard. Her eyes met Liam's.

"No problem," said Liam, gulping air and smiling.

Phoebe smiled back, but then her eyes widened. "We're going to hit the cruiser!"

Liam turned and saw the ship growing before them. "Come on!" He yanked Phoebe up and they scrambled over the drone, racing to the other side to provide a reverse thrust.

"We're not going to make it!" said Phoebe.

"Hold on," said JEFF. "I'm moving."

In a burst of white light, the cruiser's engine fired and the ship shot out of their way.

"Sorry, this engine is quite sensit—" JEFF's link cut out.

The cruiser was instantly lost among the dark and stars.

"JEFF?" Liam called.

"He'll be back," said Phoebe.

Liam craned his neck toward the comet fragments, the long band like a trail of smoke behind them now, so quickly reduced to little more than glints of light and holes of black against the stars. It spiraled in his vision, the only sign that he and Phoebe and the drone were not just moving away but also end over end. Liam winced, trying to find his center.

"You okay?"

"Fine," said Liam, but he gripped the tow handles tighter. The feeling was creeping up farther inside him. Not just dizziness, but the sense of being unattached. Not even boulders around them now, just darkness, *infiniteness* in all directions, nothing and nothing and more nothing.

"Liam, we're good. You got this."

He shut his eyes tight, took a breath, and then checked the watch. Its blinking had stopped. He wasn't going to die. Not now, anyway. *That doesn't mean you're not just going to float away until your life support runs out—*

"—ello, Liam and Phoebe."

"JEFF!" said Liam. "Where are you?"

"Right behind you."

The cruiser slid over them, its bright exterior lights creating an island in the dark, its retrorockets puffing lightly.

"I have matched your velocity," said JEFF.

Phoebe reached up and snagged her tether, which still dangled below the ship, a gold clip at its end. She hooked it to her waist.

Liam let go of the tow handles and flexed his sore fingers. He floated to Phoebe and took her hand.

She retracted the tether, and it pulled them up to the cruiser's main airlock door.

Liam opened a panel beside it and unspooled a second tether, which he clipped to his waist. He exhaled hard and pushed off the hull, floating to the rear underside of the ship, where the skim drone's dock was. There, he unhooked a thick black cable with a four-pronged metal plug at the end. He pushed down to the skim drone, sailing through open space for a moment. Funny how all it took was a little tether and he wasn't scared at all. Or at least not nearly as much. He still fixed his gaze firmly on the drone, not the infinite behind it.

He plugged the cable into a port on the back of the drone, which activated the power and allowed JEFF to slave its controls. The little craft blinked to life and rose toward its dock.

"I'll get the net." Phoebe moved to the midsection of the cruiser and activated a large hose, a half meter wide, guiding it out of its compartment. JEFF released the skim drone's claw, and Phoebe pushed herself toward the slowly drifting comet fragment. When she was close, she aimed the flat silver end of the hose at it.

"Please move to a safe distance," said JEFF.

Liam and Phoebe pushed back to the airlock door and hung on to long handles on either side. The hose flashed to life and a metallic net shot out of it, corralling the boulder. Once it was fully encircled, the net ballooned into a spherical shape, its triangular gaps similar to those of the colony dome back on Mars. The netting began to shimmer, and a rippling plasma field ignited. In a few moments, the boulder began to vent steam from all over as the plasma field heated it and melted the ice inside. Now, a series of drills on slim cables snaked out from the mouth of the hose, little rockets firing to guide their movements. They began to bore into the rock, and globules of water floated out, which drifted toward the hose and were sucked in.

"Hopefully that's the last time we'll need to do that," said Liam. He opened the airlock door and slipped inside.

"But we're getting so good at it!" said Phoebe, slapping his back as she followed him.

"Well, we keep not dying. That's something."

Back inside the cruiser, they slid out of their suits and hung them on charging hangers in the closet. Liam and Phoebe both wore black thermal tops and bottoms, Liam with his Dust Devils jersey over that. Phoebe slung her atmo pack over her shoulders and pushed the ends of the thin twin tubes into her nostrils, coughing lightly.

There was a crunching sound, and JEFF rolled

out of the short hallway that connected the cockpit to the main cabin. His wheels were magnetized so that he stayed rooted to the floor in zero gravity. His wide panda face in its permanent grin. "Refueling should be complete in about an hour," he said, "at which point we can finally complete our journey."

"If there's no malfunction," said Liam. "Any more info on why we drifted off course?"

JEFF's eyes flickered, a sign that he was calculating something. "Not much," he said. "I have run comprehensive diagnostics and updated a number of faulty circuits. But at this point, we are too close to Delphi for a similar course discrepancy to impact our arrival. I will be staying in active power mode for the rest of the trip, so unless something occurs that is—" JEFF's voice cut out midsentence, and his eyes flickered again. This had been happening, now and then, as if JEFF's processors were lagging. Of course he was nearly a decade overdue for maintenance. "—beyond my diagnostic parameters," he finished, "we will be fine. Shall we prep for stasis?"

Liam glanced at Phoebe.

"How about in a little bit?" she suggested. "We've got a couple things to do first."

"We are only three days over the minimum safe time period for stasis according to the Human Long Travel Protocol," said JEFF. "I would offer to let you stay awake for the final three minutes and use Tranquil to minimize the travel fatigue, but I'm afraid we don't have the food or oxygen rations."

"We were just thinking like an hour or two," said Liam.

"Acknowledged," said JEFF. "You will be pleased to know that because the stasis period will be so short, you will not need to eat slow fuel."

"Bonus," said Phoebe.

JEFF looked at her, and for a moment, his eyes flickered again.

"You okay there?" Liam asked.

JEFF turned. "Yes. If you need me, I will be spending the refueling time repairing the skim drone's battery."

"Sounds good." As JEFF moved to the supply cabinets by the airlock, Liam motioned toward the rear of the ship with his eyes and he and Phoebe floated that way. They passed the bathroom and entered one of the two smaller compartments at the back of the ship, where their parents' stasis pods were located.

The four pods were lined up side by side, their insides glowing a mellow amber, their back control panels blinking steadily with green and white lights. Liam and Phoebe visited them often during each waking period.

Liam floated between his parents. He rubbed

away the remaining frost on the flex-glass tops of the pods, left over from the ship being on low power during transit. Their expressions were peaceful, despite the red burn marks on their faces from the lab accident on Mars.

He double-checked their control panels: all systems stable. "Almost there," he whispered, and placed his hands gently on the glass above their faces. A lump formed in his throat. Phoebe sniffled, gazing down at her parents, too. She looked up at Liam and smiled.

"You want to go first?" He double-checked the doorway, but he'd heard the airlock open and close as JEFF went out to work on the skim drone.

"Sure."

Liam slipped off the alien watch and handed it to her. She put it on her own wrist, took a deep breath, and instead of clicking the dial to the right, which made time go forward, and where there was the danger of running into the Drove, she turned it two notches to the left.

Barely a second passed while she seemed unnaturally still; then she flinched and gasped, out of breath and blinking rapidly.

"How was it?" Liam asked.

"Amazing. Awful." A tear sprang free and floated away from her eye, a tiny trembling droplet. She pulled off the watch and handed it to him. "Your turn."

"Did you go to the playground again?"

Phoebe nodded. "And a few other places."

Liam slid the watch back on and gripped the dial. "See you in a blink."

He turned it two notches to the left, too. He felt a strange lurching, like a wind was kicking up through him, and he entered the timestream. If he looked down at himself, he could see that he was still on the cruiser, but he also seemed to be standing in a kind of foggy space, and outside of that, the world had started to clip along in reverse, slicing from one moment to the next, backward through time. Out into space, into the skim drone among the comet fragments and then back on board the ship and into a long, formless gray nothing.

The watch showed you the world from your own perspective, and this grayness was the years he'd spent in stasis. He clicked the dial another notch to the left. Time yawned backward even faster. Liam felt himself spreading out, thinning, as if space was opening between all the molecules in his body. He fought the wind and held himself steady against the strange, detached feeling. It scared him but also felt peaceful and made him smile. He liked it, maybe even craved it.

The first time he'd traveled backward with the watch had been at their first refueling stop after Saturn, three years into the journey. He'd finished pulling in the asteroid they'd targeted and was still disoriented from stasis. Hanging out by his parents' quiet pods with no word from Mina, he'd been overwhelmed by the desire to be home, to have anywhere that felt like it was his. He'd been wondering about the left hemisphere of the watch, and that was when he decided to try it out, learning that not only could it take him backward, but also that, for whatever reason, the Drove never showed up when he traveled in this direction. He'd shared it with Phoebe that very same day.

Lights began to flash, a brief period of activity— their last refueling, three years earlier—then more stasis void before that first stop. Light again, and soon after, Liam was back near Saturn, back in their solar system, and then in a flash of orange light he was on Mars.

He scanned the blur of passing time, and when he saw what he was looking for he clicked the dial back one notch toward the center. The wind and speed settled. Liam saw his apartment back in the colony, his room, and then the view from his balcony. Now he pressed the symbol in the left hemisphere, which had been blinking since he'd first turned the dial. But instead of releasing it, he held his finger down on it.

This was something else he'd learned about the watch since Saturn. When he'd first used it to view the future, he'd simply pressed the button and released it, which caused a message to appear in scrolling alien symbols before returning him to his present. It also gave him a whiplash feeling like his bones were separating, and nearly made him throw up. But if he pressed the button and held it down, time paused, frozen in the moment around him.

Liam suspected that, for some reason related to his human biology, the watch didn't work the same for him as it did for the dead alien from whom he'd gotten it. *Three-dimensional being with four-dimensional technology*, the metal-suited man from the Drove had said when Liam had run into him on Mars. When that alien had pressed the blinking button, he doubted that she got that flashing message, or that she was thrust back to where she'd begun. More likely, he guessed that she could move to a new spot in time and remain there. But while Liam couldn't stay where he traveled, this pause maneuver was a nice discovery.

Outside the timestream, it was a sunny afternoon on Mars. A frozen moment: he and Mina were sitting cross-legged on their balcony, playing a virtual card game called Pioneers of Andromeda on a slim video board between them. The sun gleamed through the dome overhead. Their parents sat by the large window just inside the balcony door, which was open, Dad reading on a holoscreen, Mom applying moisturizing electrodes to her bare feet. Her hair was down; Mom only ever wore her hair down on weekends.

He viewed it all out of his eyes as if he were back sitting right there. A still life of his family, some random weekend maybe six months before they'd left. Liam had stumbled upon it during an earlier time trip, and the scene had made him choke up. He wished he could actually be there again reliving it, hearing the bustle of the avenue below, the voices from nearby apartments, Mina's annoyed grumblings whenever he made a good play, feeling the heat of the Martian day, but those details were lost to him. From the paused timestream, everything was silent and still.

He'd been other places: to the field station tunnels, one time to school, another time to watch the classic grav-ball championship game of 2212 between the Dust Devils and the Canyon Bombers—Phoebe had gone back to that game, too, and they loved to debate the subtleties of that triple-time classic that had been won, sadly, by the Bombers—but most often he came here, to this moment on the balcony. He would look at his family, and at the colony skyline and the landscape and even the sun that had once frightened him so, and he would have a profound feeling that was sad but also calm. How many weekend afternoons had there ever been like this one, when Mina hadn't been off doing her own thing, and Liam and his parents hadn't been out at the field station? Would there ever be another?

He missed this so much.

Still, he had to be careful. Because the longer he stayed here, even with the world on pause, the more he felt that widening within, as if he was losing touch with the solid, physical version of himself that was still on the cruiser. Sometimes, he felt like he was more here than there.

He looked at his sister and parents, trying to memorize the image perfectly, and then he did something that he'd been practicing each time he came here, something he hadn't even told Phoebe about yet, mainly because he wasn't sure how to explain it. Even though the past version of himself on the balcony was frozen and focused on the game, Liam found that, if he concentrated with great effort, he could turn his viewpoint toward the circular window that led into his room. The watch was linked to his personal experience, but he'd been able to ever so slightly expand that viewpoint and see what past-Liam hadn't been looking at—his old bedroom, or the people paused in midstroll on the avenue below. There was something extra stretchy-feeling about doing this, and it made his head split with pain, but each time he could move a little further out of his own experience, almost like he was stretching a muscle.

This time he was able to make it all the way inside

the window and actually stand in his room. He looked around at the cluttered mess, the way it was before he'd packed everything up. Liam didn't understand exactly how this was possible, but then again, he barely understood how he could be seeing his own past in the first place. He wondered if he was somehow leaving his own body, or if he was actually moving *through* his own past, as opposed to just revisiting it. Like, if the past version of himself turned, would he see something like a ghost? But Liam didn't think so. After all, he had no memories of strange apparitions.

His head began to ache, and he relaxed and returned to his original position in the memory, and then counted down from five while looking slowly around. When he reached one, with a sad pressure behind his throat, he let go of the button on the watch. There was a grinding stop, the flashing alien message, and a jolting reversal, and all the past time blurred by him in a gut-wrenching instant, until he was back inside himself on the cruiser, floating between his parents' pods.

He blinked, fresh sweat on his brow and a headache like lightning bolts across his mind. He breathed in deep, flexed his fingers, and clenched his gut against the nausea.

"How'd it go?" Phoebe asked.

"Always makes me a little sick."

"I never know if I feel better or worse after," said Phoebe. She started to float out of the room.

"Yeah," Liam said, even though he was pretty sure that, once the physical symptoms passed, he always felt better. Grounded, even though there was no ground. He looked at his parents' faces and managed to smile. *See you guys soon.* Then he pushed after Phoebe.

"Wanna play *Roid Wraiths* for a bit?" she said over her shoulder.

"Sure." Liam floated past her to the galley, where he opened a drawer and got nutri-bars for both of them.

Phoebe buckled into the couch and loaded *Roid Wraiths IV.* A holoscreen rippled to life. Liam joined her and got controllers out of the compartment that served as a coffee table. He handed one to Phoebe, along with the nutri-bar.

As the system loaded, he pulled Mina's beacon out from inside his shirt. It was a small silver rectangle on a chain. He pressed the dome-shaped button made of green glass at the top. He still needed the tap code key Mina had sent to make longer messages, but he had memorized a few basic ones.

hi

There was still no chance she'd see it, months to go still before she'd wake, and yet he watched the beacon for a few seconds anyway before stowing it back in his shirt. He felt an ache inside, even as the trip back to Mars had helped a little. He wondered if she remembered that afternoon, too.

The airlock slid open and JEFF entered, ice melting off his plastic body and steam hissing out of his joints. He stepped into the holoscreen and the *Roid Wraiths* menu rippled over his smiling panda face. "I have patched the battery and it seems to be charging normally. I think it will hold, though I cannot be certain. Hopefully we will not need the drone again before we can get a replacement at Delphi."

"Nice work, JEFF," said Liam.

"Refueling is proceeding. If you need me I will be in the cockpit."

They sank into the game, currently on a level where they were stuck in a particularly intense wraith hive inside a derelict tanker.

"We can definitely beat these guys before stasis," Liam said right after they'd been ripped limb from limb by the wraith babies for the third consecutive time. And yet, there was another feeling that was urging him to postpone stasis a little longer.

He looked over at Phoebe. When they woke next, they'd be at Delphi, back with everyone else on the *Scorpius*, back to their old life with their parents and friends around. It wouldn't be just the two of them anymore, out here, doing their own thing. Not that being off in deep space on their own was anything he would have wished for, with all the danger, and the way it made him feel lonely and sick, but still . . .

"What?" Phoebe was eyeing him eyeing her.

"Nothing." Liam turned away, his face burning.

"You just got completely wrecked by those wingers again," she said. "I told you: you have to use pulse cannons."

"Oh. Yeah." Liam felt like his heart had started clawing its way up his throat, and he had a spinny upside-down feeling, and he sort of had to pee and now he wasn't breathing and he'd been thinking about something now and then and wasn't sure so ahhhh he leaned over and kissed Phoebe on the cheek.

Phoebe flinched away. "Hey!"

"Sorry," said Liam, darting away himself. Her skin had been cool and tasted weird, sort of like salt and plastic . . . but—oh no. She hadn't wanted him to do that and he was an idiot! Why had *he* even wanted to do that? "I didn't mean to, I . . ."

Phoebe paused the game. Her fingers traced slowly down her cheek, almost like she was checking to see if he'd given her a rash. She was staring straight ahead. Sort of grimacing, too. Then she slowly turned toward him with an odd expression. Except she was smiling, sort of? "Thank you."

Thank you? What could that possibly mean? "I'm

84

sorry," said Liam. "Uh, it's all this zero gravity. I just—"

"No, Liam. . . ." She reached out and patted his knee, probably like you did to someone you definitely didn't want to kiss you ever again. "You're the best."

"Okay."

"No, I mean, my best. Friend." She touched her cheek again, running her finger up and down it. "I like that you did that. I was just surprised. You mean a lot to me, too."

What came next? If she liked that, did she want to do . . . more of that? Did he? This was horrible.

"Don't tell Shawn," said Liam, looking at his hands.

Phoebe laughed, but it almost seemed like she was fighting tears. "I won't." She stared across the room.

"So . . ."

Phoebe clicked her controller. "Let's play one more level."

"Okay."

Was that it? Was everything fine between them? Liam had no idea.

After that, they only really spoke to point out creatures and hazards to each other. Two levels later, JEFF told them to hang on, and their bodies strained against their buckles as the cruiser made its final burn for Delphi.

"We should probably get into stasis," said Phoebe.

"Yeah."

They shut down the game and stowed the gear. Liam used the bathroom and floated to his stasis pod. Phoebe was perched on the edge of hers, her heels hooked beneath it.

"Aren't you getting in?" Liam asked. He realized he sounded sulky. He wasn't, or was he? The memory of kissing her, but also of Mars and his parents and Mina—it all felt like a lot right now.

Phoebe smiled. "I've got a couple things to do."

"Like what?"

"Just girl stuff."

"Oh. Um, okay, well . . . see you soon."

"May Ana wake you from pleasant dreams," said Phoebe, as she always did before stasis.

"You too."

"And I meant it. Thanks for the, you know . . ." She touched her cheek.

Liam looked away. "Right."

"Thanks, too, for saving my life so many times."

"Well, you too. It's been fun, you know, when it hasn't been terrifying."

Phoebe nodded and smiled but also turned away quickly and floated out of the compartment.

JEFF arrived to attach the muscle stimulators and the fluid line, and to connect Liam's link, and then Liam lay back and buckled in. The clear panel lowered over him. As it clicked shut, he checked the beacon and the watch one more time—no flashing, no blinking—and then closed his eyes and breathed deep. The pod began to hiss and cool. His heart sped up for a moment, thinking of the months of dark to come, of Barro and the attackers stealthily pulling up to their ship while they were defenseless. It made this box feel too small, and the space around the ship too big again.

He shook his head and tried to imagine seeing Mina and Shawn on the starliner, or visiting his parents as they recuperated in a hospital compartment, and yet he kept picturing Phoebe instead—her smiling face through a helmet visor, or sitting next to him on the cruiser couch, just the two of them all these days. . . .

I'm an idiot, he thought.

Liam closed his eyes and settled on the memory of his balcony back home, the view of the distant canyons and mountains, and of the giant sun that had scared him daily, and that he now missed impossibly, as the stasis gas tugged him under.

4

Why would you run off like that?

Mom loomed over him, taller than he ever remembered her. Liam sank into his bunk, but he was also wearing a pressure suit, the mask clouded by his breath. Rusted light filtered through the windows of the small, dome-shaped living quarters at the research station on Mars. *We specifically told you not to leave,* Mom went on, glaring down at him. She wore a pressure suit, too, but hers was scorched with burn marks. Black soot streaks covered half of her helmet's clear mask.

You never trust me! Liam shouted, which caused a

tremor of guilt even in his dreaming mind. *You're the ones who sent us out to the air vents. We were trying to help you!*

Mom laughed in a way she never did, a sort of cackle. Meanwhile, the floor had become the molten surface of the sun.

Why would we ever send you to the air vents? That doesn't make any sense. Don't be stupid. Mom had become Mina now. No pressure suit, one fist on her hip, wearing her favorite retro Moon Junkies T-shirt, black hair hanging down across half her face. *Come on, already.*

Something flashed. With her other hand, Mina was tapping her necklace with her thumb. *Liam, hurry!*

"Welcome back, Liam."

Icy gray, a damp pressure in his chest . . . Liam's eyes fluttered open. He squinted in the overhead lights.

"We are arriving at Delphi." JEFF loomed over him, grinning. "Remember to breathe slowly, and please count down from thirty before you attempt to sit up."

Liam blinked, counting to himself.

"Also, you are receiving a message." JEFF slid away.

"Wait, what?" Liam strained to lift his head and

saw that the necklace was floating just above his chest, blinking in green flashes. "JEFF, why didn't you tell me sooner?"

"I only became aware of it when I opened your pod."

Liam lurched up, taking the necklace in his hand, trying to catch up to the series of fast and slow blips. He needed the tap code key from the link Mina had sent him—

Splitting pain tore through his head, and his stomach lurched. Sweat breaking out all over—oh no. Liam had floated halfway out of the pod. He grabbed the side, hands clammy, arms shaking, tried to push himself toward the bathroom—

Too late. He spun and vomited into the stasis pod. The liquid burst from his mouth in wobbling brown globules, some splashing against the foam insides of the pod, some floating free around the room. Gasping at the sour, metallic taste, Liam slammed closed the top of the pod, containing nearly all of it.

"JEFF!" he croaked. The necklace drifted up into his view, still flashing. He breathed deep, spun himself around, and—ugh!—felt his bare heel collide with one of the warm vomit bubbles still drifting around the room.

He pushed over to the cabinets on the wall and pulled out the link Mina had sent him. Weirdly, it

opened to that video that Mina had made for him—
there was Shawn's face on pause. Liam didn't remember watching it since they'd first received the link. He
clicked to the menu and opened the file with the picture of the tap code key, a simple pattern that used
sets of dots, or in this case flashes, to indicate letters.

His head still ached as he watched the beacon, trying to catch up. How long had she been sending him a
message? It might have been seconds, or it could have
been minutes. She might have tried a few times over
hours, even days.

Tap code was slow and arduous. The beacon went
dark momentarily, which indicated the end of a letter.
Then four taps, another space, and two more taps,
which all together meant the letter *U*. Four and four,
that was an *R*. Now an *I*, then a *B*. Now a longer space
indicating the end of a word.

u-r-i-b

What was that? Must have been a fragment. Or
he'd gotten a letter wrong. But there was no time to
check because another word was starting. He ran his
finger over the code key.

h-u-r-r-y

Liam smiled. They were so close! He couldn't wait
to see Mina, to give her a hug and have her scowl at
him. The beacon stopped blinking and he started his
reply.

delayed but close now

"How long until we get there?" he shouted.

"Forty-one minutes," JEFF replied from the cockpit.

less than one hour

He wished there was some way to send an exclamation point, or include a smiley face, anything to convey his excitement. But Mina would know. He stared at the beacon, but it didn't blink again. She was probably busy in the social center, or maybe down on Delphi itself.

Liam tucked the beacon into his shirt. There was a soft splooshing sound, and he saw one of the vomit bubbles pop against the wall, spraying into smaller ones. Some of them were heading right for Phoebe's pod, which was already open and empty. He darted over and closed it before he floated out of the room. He peeked in at his sleeping parents, their pods still warmly lit, and then pushed through the ship to the cockpit.

He was just passing the airlock when the world seemed to slide in his vision. He felt like a door had opened, a great breeze blowing through him, and everything blurred—

Suddenly, the sun appeared before him, swollen, red, hurling furious solar flares around itself. Liam saw the skim drone cockpit, his hands in the gloves of a space suit, working the controls. The sun was enormous, its waist bowed out like it would explode at any second, and for some reason, he was flying directly toward it—

Splitting pain in his head. Liam flinched and found himself tumbling backward in the cabin of the cruiser.

"You okay back there?" Phoebe called.

He had flipped upside down and now grabbed the wall and righted himself. His head ached, and he vaguely remembered hitting it on the cabinets near the cockpit entrance. He rubbed the bump already growing there and felt that strange, spacey feeling inside once more. He checked the alien watch. Had he touched it by mistake? But it wasn't blinking or flashing. So why did he feel like he'd just used it? The burning-bright image of the enormous sun flashed in his head again. He had been dreaming about being back on Mars when he'd woken up, and he was always a bit disoriented after stasis, but he also wondered, not for the first time, if the trips he made with the watch were messing with him. After all, the watch wasn't meant for humans.

Liam took a deep breath and waited for his vision to stop swaying, then pushed into the cockpit.

"Hey," he said. "Sorry, just a little out of it after stasis— Whoa."

Out the cockpit window, a dim gray-blue orb glowed faintly in the distance, not much bigger than a fingertip.

Delphi.

"Finally!" Liam buckled into the seat behind JEFF and stowed the link with the tap code in the side pocket.

"Decelerating to two percent velocity," said JEFF. Retrorockets on the front and sides of the ship fired in short bursts.

"JEFF, I, um, sorta threw up in our compartment. It's mostly in my pod, but . . ."

"Acknowledged." JEFF stood, and Liam thought he heard a tiny sigh. "Autopilot is engaged; I will return in just a moment." He rolled past Phoebe, who was in the copilot's chair, and then swiveled to look down at Liam. "You'll"—his eyes flickered in that lagging way—"see to the controls?"

"Sure." Liam unbuckled and moved to the pilot's chair. He surveyed the panels, everything blipping along. "There's nothing really to do, though, right?" he asked over his shoulder.

JEFF didn't answer and Liam figured he'd already headed out, but then he heard the hum of JEFF's increasingly stubborn joints. Liam turned and saw the bot looking at him and Phoebe, or maybe the controls, eyes flickering again. "Of course," he finally answered. "We just want to be sure, as landing procedures are delicate."

"Relax, JEFF," said Liam, turning back around and feeling a rush at the sight of the dim planet. "We're in the home stretch."

JEFF rolled out. Phoebe was staring at Delphi, her expression serious.

"Nervous?"

"I'm fine," she said quietly, picking at her thumbnail.

"Don't worry, they're still here."

Delphi grew rapidly before them. It was a rogue planet, about one-quarter the size of Earth. At some point, long ago, it had likely been part of a solar system, but whether due to a supernova, an asteroid collision, or its star simply dying out, it now floated without a home through the void.

Though it appeared dark and cold, Delphi had an intensely active geothermal core and, above that, large oceans that were encased in a kilometer-thick layer of ice. The heat from the core caused massive plumes of steam to jet skyward, creating a dense cloud of ice fog that enshrouded the planet.

As Liam remembered from countless viewings of the virtual tour, the waypoint station was built on one of the rare land formations that jutted out of the ice. It was powered by the geothermal energy, and from there, the oceans were mined for fuel same as humans had once done at Saturn Station on Enceladus. Delphi had a far weaker gravitational field than even Mars, so the *Scorpius* could dock directly above the station, which made refueling easy.

By the time JEFF returned to the cockpit, Delphi had grown to the size of a fist, but it was still murky, almost like a smudge on the black. Liam could just make out the faint swirls of the clouds. His relief and anticipation were briefly dampened by a flash of worry: They hadn't been near a planet in so long, and what better place for an ambush from the Saturn attackers? But then wouldn't the middle of deep space have actually been easier, with no one else around? It was more likely that Barro and his people were far behind somewhere. Or, with any luck, they hadn't even gotten out of the way of the supernova in time.

"Well, that was involved," said JEFF, buckling back into the pilot's chair as Liam returned to the seat behind him. "Everything normal up here?"

"Looks good," said Liam. "I would have told you if not. I still remember how to fly this thing, you know."

"Of course. I will now put us on a landing vector."

Liam and Phoebe shared a look. "Everything all right, JEFF?" Liam asked.

JEFF's eyes flickered. "Hopefully we will have that answer very shortly, upon our safe arrival."

"Okay." Liam tapped on the beacon:

i see delphi

Still no reply, but that didn't matter. They were only moments away now.

"We will be entering the atmosphere a few thousand kilometers from the station," said JEFF. "I would advise that you remain in your seats. The descent through the ice fog is reportedly quite turbulent."

A countdown on the navigation screen gave them thirty minutes to arrival. Liam slowly spelled out another message to Mina:

only a half hour until we are there

He eyed the beacon, waiting for a response, but it remained dark. Liam noticed Phoebe watching him. "She's probably with Arlo," he said. "Maybe they have a show or something." Mina was the singer and guitarist in a band called the Gravity Minus. They were supposed to have played the launch party on the *Scorpius*, but Mina had said in her video message that the show had been postponed after the attack at Saturn.

And yet, was there some other reason why she wasn't answering back? Why she wanted him to hurry? A tremor of worry rumbled in his belly. He tried to force it down, because there was no reason for it; well, except for ten years of accumulated uncertainty. Or maybe it just bothered him that Mina wasn't monitoring the beacon more closely. Wasn't she as anxious to see them as he was to see her?

"Yeah," said Phoebe, turning away.

Liam was about to tap her shoulder, except he wondered if he could just tap her shoulder anymore after he'd kissed her or if now everything *meant* something. Still, he managed to say, "You okay?"

She nodded but didn't turn around.

"The station should have us on their scopes by now," said JEFF. "They will try to hail us shortly over long-range com, but even though that won't work, they will still be able to identify the ship."

"How soon until we can reach them over link?" Liam asked.

"A few minutes. Because of the atmospheric interference, we'll need to get closer than we did at Saturn," said JEFF.

Liam's stomach growled, and he floated to the galley and grabbed nutri-bars for himself and Phoebe. When he returned, Delphi had grown to fill most of their view. Its swirling gray-blue ice clouds spread out beneath them, a wide semicircle, its lower hemisphere out of view. Soon, instead of flying at it, they were flying above it.

"I wonder if this is what it looked like to fly over

Earth," said Liam. "You know, before it was burned out. Like when our parents were kids."

"Sparkling oceans," said Phoebe quietly. "Glittering cities."

"It must have been really pretty," Liam agreed.

Phoebe sniffled. Liam wondered why she didn't seem more excited. He wanted to ask, but he also felt weird about talking to her too much, because: Had she liked that he'd kissed her? Was she crying about that? Was there any chance that this sadness was due to that same thing that he'd been thinking before stasis, about how their time together was going to be over? Or was it not about that at all, and she was actually feeling awkward around him because she'd thought about it more and decided the kiss was gross and now was counting down the seconds until she could get away from him? Maybe she was planning to spend the next century on the starliner avoiding him. *Stupid,* he thought, *you never should have done that.*

They slowed, their angle of descent growing steeper, and the curved rim of Delphi began to flatten.

"Entering atmosphere," JEFF announced.

There was a flash of fire and a series of bumps, and they were thrust down against their seats. Liam felt aching throughout his body, like his bones were being jammed together. All at once, sound returned from outside: the screaming whoosh of air, the buffeting of wind gusts, the creaking and rocking of their boxy craft. It was all so loud after their time in space, an assault on Liam's ears.

"Taking the fusion engine offline," said JEFF. He tapped a series of buttons. "Bringing up the thrusters. They will take a moment to cycle up, but our entry angle is confirmed."

They skimmed the tops of the clouds. Ice crystals hissed against the hull. The cruiser began to shudder.

"Brace yourselves," said JEFF.

The cruiser's forward lights reflected off the crystal-line tips of the clouds. They seemed close enough that you could reach down and run your fingers through their whipped, frosting-like edges.

With a wicked bump they submerged into the inky fog. The stars disappeared, and millions of tiny crystals flashed through the lights and sheeted against the cockpit.

Liam gripped his seat as the cruiser rocked back and forth. Outside the cockpit was a void; a graphical overlay on the windshield mapped their descent through the nothingness. An alarm chirped on the console.

"Rear thruster has shorted out again," said JEFF, quickly tapping a holoscreen and swiping through the hardware controls.

"Is that a problem?" Liam asked.

"It would be if we needed to take off again, but hopefully this is the last trip this vehicle has to make."

"What's that flashing?" Phoebe pointed to a yellow light in front of her.

"Checking diagnostics," said JEFF. "A segment of the thermal shielding has failed, but we've already reentered the atmosphere, so that should also be fine."

"We're trashing this poor ship, aren't we?" said Liam.

"HA HA HA," said JEFF.

"That's only funny if it's not going to trash us, too."

"Acknowledged," said JEFF. "So far, none of these problems are fatal."

"Good to know." Liam rolled his eyes, trying to catch Phoebe's attention, but she just stared out into the dark, her arms crossed tight.

Yet another sensor began to blare, this time on the windshield display.

"We are nearing cruising altitude," said JEFF. "Hang on as we level off."

All at once, the cruiser dropped beneath the frosted clouds and into a dim, nighttime world. JEFF fired the remaining thrusters at full power and Liam was shoved back against his seat. Gusts of wind rattled the cruiser, rocking it back and forth.

Below, a buckled and folded vista of gray-and-purple ice stretched in all directions, punctuated here and there by the spines of black mountains. There were moments of inky smooth ice, and other places where the ice had cracked and heaved to such extremes that it jutted up like enormous, curving crystal fangs, with black edges and aqua-blue crevices that glimmered in their lights. Here and there, these fangs resembled great jaws, waiting to snatch the cruiser. In the distance, massive plumes of steam billowed from the ice, welding the ground to the dusky cloud layer. They swayed like snakes in the whipping wind. According to the virtual tour, there were primitive, fishlike creatures living in the hidden ocean, with something like antifreeze for blood and bioluminescent features. There was a spot for viewing them at the Delphi station.

Liam checked his silent beacon again. "Are we in range yet?"

"Almost," said JEFF, tapping the link connection screen. "Lots of interference, but we should be picking up the station's signal any moment now."

Liam peered across the forbidding twilight landscape. Was that a light? No, just his eyes playing tricks on him. "How far to the station?"

"Two hundred and thirty-six kilometers," said JEFF.

He tapped a message on the beacon:

really close

"Shouldn't we be able to see the starliner by now?"

"It is likely to be at least somewhat hidden by the cloud layer."

Liam winced at a flash of light-headedness. Maybe it was just leftover nausea. He eyed the beacon. Why wasn't she writing back?

"What's that?" Phoebe pointed ahead.

A spire of black rock thrust out of the ice like a claw. On its tip was a geometric structure, gray and metallic, glinting in their lights.

JEFF's eyes flickered. "According to my Delphi schematics, that is a mining relay station, one of the locations where they drill into the ice for water. It should also be functioning as a guidance beacon, but it is not appearing on our link."

"Why not?" Liam asked.

"I do not know. It is possible that my files are outdated and it has been decommissioned, as we are the last fleet to need fuel, or it has malfunctioned."

As they raced closer, their lights revealed the irregular shape of the walls. Liam leaned forward and squinted. There were jagged metal edges, black streaks . . .

"It appears to be damaged," said JEFF.

"What kind of damage?" Liam asked.

They passed overhead and saw that the roof had been torn open in a gaping, perfectly circular hole. Inside was only blackened wreckage. There was debris scattered on the ice far below.

"Or completely blown up," said Phoebe quietly, still hugging herself tightly.

"Why would you say that?" JEFF asked, his head swiveling toward her.

"I don't know." She glanced nervously at Liam. "Look at it."

Liam watched out the side window as the tower retreated behind them. His heart raced. "You mean like, attacked?"

Phoebe just stared ahead.

"Blown up by what?" JEFF asked. Liam noticed that JEFF was still looking at Phoebe.

"How should I know, JEFF?" Phoebe snapped.

JEFF's eyes flickered, and he turned back to the windshield.

Crosswinds buffeted the craft. On the link screen, the same words kept blinking:

Searching for signal.

"We should have made contact by now," said Liam.

"There must be a problem with station communications," said JEFF.

"What about comms on the *Scorpius*?" said Liam. "Or other private ships trailing behind? Mining stations? Why isn't anyone on?"

"I do not know. I agree that it does seem improbable. Perhaps there is an issue with our link transmitter." JEFF brought up a new screen. "I will run a diagnostic."

They sped over the ice, the hull of the cruiser shuddering in the crosswinds. Liam swallowed, tight, metallic. His fingers had started to shake. He kept looking for the great shape of the starliner through the clouds, the glow of its giant egg-shaped engines, its six core cylinders arranged like the chambers of an old Earth revolver, the X-shaped array at its front that held the solar sails.

"Our link is functioning normally," JEFF reported.

Geometric designs began to light up on the windshield screen, a schematic showing the outlines of structures that were still too far away to see in the fog and twilight. No one spoke.

"We have visual on the station."

The buildings began to take shape on the horizon but remained silhouettes. No lights.

"We should definitely be able to see the *Scorpius*," said Liam. *Unless it's gone.* He didn't want to say it, but they were getting so close, they should have been nearly under it by now, but there was nothing.

Searching for signal.

Liam looked back at the beacon. Mina had said *hurry.* . . . "Something's wrong."

"I calculate that you are right," said JEFF.

"We should go," said Phoebe. "Back into space. We should get out of here."

"We can't," said Liam. "Not yet."

They could see the station plainly now. It was a large complex of buildings perched on a craggy island of rock and spreading down its one gradual side. Metal and rectangular structures surrounded a wide white dome in the center. All the buildings were dark, veiled in Delphi's eternal gloaming. . . .

"Oh no," said Liam as he spied the first wide blast hole in one of the walls.

"Sensors report no signs of life-forms," said JEFF. "And I am picking up strong radiation signals."

They passed over the outskirts of the station, watching silently, in shock. Liam felt stuck to his chair, frozen with disbelief. All the buildings were burned out or collapsed, the walls charred with black streaks. The dome, and other main buildings, had been punctured with more giant, perfectly circular holes, almost like they had been drilled, except that the edges were warped and melted. Tatters of fabric and paper stuck to twisted metal teeth, swirling and blowing and strewn across the ice in all directions—

And there, on the icy plain below the station, something golden, in long jagged shards scattered over the ice floes.

"A solar sail," said Phoebe.

But Liam's eye had already traveled beyond that, far out across the vast ice sea, nearly to the horizon, ten or more kilometers away. Something enormous and dark, rounded and geometric, like a great, exhausted serpent, kinked and bent and blackened, with one central section thrusting high into the sky, nearly to the clouds.

"Is that . . . ?" But Liam couldn't finish. He knew what it was.

A starliner core. A home for millions of people, crashed, destroyed.

Part of the *Scorpius*.

Liam fumbled for the beacon and started typing:
are

"We should go, right now," said Phoebe.

"That is unadvisable," said JEFF. "I'm afraid we do not have enough fuel to depart and make the journey to another suitable refueling station."

you

"It doesn't matter," said Phoebe.

ok

"We must also consider the damage we sustained while entering—"

"We have to go, JEFF!" Phoebe shouted.

"And why exactly are you so certain of this course of action—"

"No!" said Liam, his throat tight. He stared at the crash. "We have to know which core that is, and where the rest of the starliner went. . . ."

"Core numbers are printed on the docking bay doors at each segment," said JEFF.

They flew past the station, out over the ice wastes, the great wreckage looming ever larger. Liam barely breathed. There was a light now, far off on the horizon beyond the crashed core. JEFF highlighted it on the windshield screen and zoomed in. It looked like an enormous torch had been stuck into the ice: a starliner engine, spewing blue-and-white firelight up into the sky. The radiation warning beeped faster.

"We cannot stay out here long," said JEFF.

They closed in on the great core wreckage, reaching its near end, which was lying flat on the ice. The upthrust section was still over a kilometer in the distance, but it towered so high that it seemed like it might topple onto them at any moment.

Even just this end was impossibly large: nearly a half kilometer in diameter, dwarfing their ship.

Liam saw that the long side stretching away from

them was peppered with precise holes, like it had been strafed with gunfire. Sections of it looked completely intact, but others were collapsed and charred. As they neared, Liam spied another of those wide circular holes, and through it he could see the vague, shadowy outlines of balconies, as well as one of the social centers, everything smashed and covered with frost that glittered in the cruiser's lights.

"Do you think it was . . . attacked?" said Liam.

"I cannot be one hundred percent sure," said JEFF, "but that seems most likely."

"It was," said Pheobe.

"How do you know?" asked Liam.

Phoebe motioned with her chin. "What else could have happened?"

"There is a hangar airlock," said JEFF. They neared the side of the core, and the cruiser's forward lights illuminated the giant doors.

Liam didn't want to look. He had to look. *Please don't be . . .*

"It is Core Three," JEFF announced quietly.

Liam froze. He remembered Devon, the virtual assistant in his *Scorpius* tour, the one he'd taken so many times he'd memorized it.

You have been assigned to Community Twenty-Two, in Segment Eight of—

Core Three.

His heart tripped over itself. He couldn't move, couldn't breathe. He could only keep looking at the giant number.

Mina. Shawn. No.

Tears welled in his eyes.

The beacon remained dark.

5

Liam sobbed, head in his hands but still checking the beacon in his palm, and yet it didn't blink, didn't blink, didn't blink. His amazing, annoying, perfect sister. His funny, brave, scared friend. And all the others. So many millions of people on board.

Phoebe pushed onto his seat beside him and put her arm around him. "I'm so sorry," she said. "It hurts so much."

"You don't know," said Liam, but then hated that he'd said that—Phoebe had people on that ship, too: their classmates, teachers, neighbors, so many different faces from their apartment buildings and all their classrooms over the years—and yet he couldn't help

111

it. He would never see his sister or his friend again, would have to tell his parents that their daughter was gone, and how had she died? What had those final moments been like? Had she been terrified, scream-ing for help? *Hurry*, Mina had said. . . .

But they were too late.

Phoebe breathed deep, like she was going to say something, but didn't. That was when Liam remem-bered that she'd lost her brother, years ago, and her grandparents, and he felt awful for being so selfish on top of how awful he already felt. "Sorry."

"Don't be."

JEFF raised the cruiser away from the doors, up and up, to the top of the fallen core. He flew along its side, bringing up a schematic overlay of the structure and tapping it at various points. Liam didn't know what he was doing and didn't care.

"As we suspected, these larger holes appear to be blast points," said JEFF. "Both the size of the holes and the metallic fusing around the edges suggest a particle weapon, but one whose power would only be theoretical to the colonial military."

"What does that mean?" said Liam.

"This weapon is more advanced than any human technology."

"You mean it's alien?"

"Yes."

"Those attackers at Saturn," Liam muttered to himself. "It has to be them." It could also have been the Drove, but they hadn't attacked before, unless you counted turning the sun into a bomb. He rubbed his hands over his face, sinking into a cold well of grief once again.

But after another terrible moment of silence, JEFF said, "It is possible that this is not as bad as it appears."

Liam looked up, brushing at his eyes. "How?"

JEFF pointed at the wreckage. "Do you see how those smaller holes are in uniform lines? In the event of an emergency, the starliner cores can eject their stasis pods, which have batteries that allow the pods to operate in space for an extended period of time. Then they can be salvaged with a magnetic tethering system."

Liam sat up. "Do you think that's what happened?" He scanned the cylinder, pocked with rows of holes, and then the ice beyond. "I don't see any pods."

"Yes, that is also a good sign."

The radiation warning had become a steady drone. JEFF put the cruiser into a tight arcing turn and headed back toward Delphi station.

"Sensors are still picking up no life-forms or heat signatures," he said. "There is also no sign of further starliner wreckage, nor of the ship itself in the nearby atmosphere, though the range of our scan is limited to our link."

"So . . . what do you think?"

JEFF brought up the rear camera on the holo-screen and pointed to the upended section of the core that towered into the clouds. "In order for the core to impale itself in the ice like that, it would most likely have to have fallen from a great height, perhaps even from low orbit. Together with the lack of stasis pods and any further wreckage, I would theorize that the *Scorpius* was able to move itself out of the atmosphere before ejecting the passengers from Core Three. This would have been quite advantageous, as the pods could be retrieved in zero gravity, before they could fall to the surface and sustain damage. Since the *Scorpius* had lost an engine, they may have then ejected the damaged core to reduce weight. Both the core and the engine are so large that they would have fallen out of orbit rather quickly."

Liam sat up. "Do you really think that's what happened?"

JEFF's eyes flickered for a moment. "I calculate that this is the most probable outcome without more information."

"What kind of information?" said Liam.

"A scan of the entire planet and nearby celestial vicinity for wreckage, direct communication with the *Scorpius* or any other members of the fleet, and a log of what happened here."

"And we don't have any of that."

"No. We could conduct a full visual sweep of the planet ourselves, but that would take many hours, and I think we would agree that we don't have time for that."

"No," said Phoebe.

"So they might have escaped," said Liam, "or they might be crashed on the far side of the planet, or wrecked out in space somewhere."

"Correct."

"And the ejected stasis pods could be on the *Scorpius*, or they could be floating out in space, too."

"Again, we cannot know."

"Where would they even go? Did they have time to refuel?"

"We will need more information."

"Well, how are we going to get it?" Liam held the beacon between shaking fingers and slowly tapped a message.

we see crash are you ok please

"We need to access the station's long-range scanner," said JEFF. "It is not working currently, so our first task is to assess its condition. Clearly, there has been a station-wide power failure, and it is likely that control centers have been damaged. We will have to investigate."

"We should just leave," said Phoebe again.

"As I have stated before, departing now commits us to a statistically fatal outcome, given our fuel supply and the damage we've sustained. We must land to address those issues at a minimum before we depart." JEFF rotated slowly toward Phoebe. "Unless you have some information that suggests otherwise?"

JEFF's tone was strange. There seemed to be something more in his simple question to Phoebe. Liam didn't think he'd ever heard JEFF sound that way before.

Phoebe glanced at Liam, her face stony, then back at JEFF. "All I know is this place was attacked and we don't know if whoever's responsible is still around."

Liam checked the sky in all directions. Were the Saturn attackers chasing down the *Scorpius*? Or were they still here? Maybe they had many ships, an entire army, enough to attack all the starliners and still wait here to mop up the stragglers at the back of the fleet. But the watch wasn't blinking. And the beacon remained dark.

JEFF was still looking right at her. "And do you have a theory about *who* might have done this?"

Phoebe slid back into her seat and crossed her arms. "Liam's right: it's probably the Saturn attackers. Don't you think?"

JEFF didn't answer right away. His eyes flickered. Finally, he said, "I do," and turned back to the controls. Liam was left wondering: *What is he thinking?*

And yet a surprising thought flashed in his mind: all the way back to the underground lab on Mars, their parents lying there, injured, and Liam's mom saying, *It was sabotage, Liam. They . . . You need to go, right now.* In his search for an explanation, Liam had wondered for a brief moment if Phoebe's parents were behind the turbines exploding, before he'd dismissed the thought. It was Barro—he'd admitted as much—and Phoebe had shot his ship down in the rings of Saturn.

But JEFF definitely sounded suspicious, as much as a bot could, anyway. When Liam thought about it, he realized this wasn't the first time JEFF had acted oddly toward Phoebe, going back to their previous refueling stop. Then again, maybe his circuits were as fried as the cruiser's. Liam remembered hearing about robots that got really old, and their perception and conduct filters would start to break down and they'd say and do inappropriate, almost human things. It wouldn't take much: a corrupted line of code here, an out-of-sequence fact set there. That might explain the processing logs, too.

He looked at the core wreckage on the rear camera and thought about the attack at Saturn Station. "Is this a war?"

"What we've seen, from Mars to here, does suggest an organized, large-scale offensive," said JEFF. "Someone seems to be trying to sabotage the human mission to Aaru."

There's that word again. "But why?"

"For the moment, their purpose is beyond calculation. We should know more once we access the long-range scanner, which is right— Oh." They had reached the station again, flying to the side of the large dome at its center. JEFF banked around a tall communications tower. The array of circular dishes had been blown apart.

"That doesn't look good," said Liam.

"There will be a backup scanner," said JEFF. He tapped the console, and schematics appeared on the holoscreen beside him, displaying a multilevel complex. A dot blinked on the lowest level. "I have located it: sublevel six. It will be in a blast-shielded compartment and have its own battery backup system. This is also where the backup data recorder is located, which should contain at least partial logs of what happened here." He pointed to the schematic, then out of the cockpit. "The main command and data center has been destroyed. You will need to turn on the scanner and retrieve the logs manually."

"You mean we have to go down there ourselves," said Liam.

"Correct. You should also be able to reboot the station's power system from there, or at least what's left of it. In the meantime, I will work on repairing and refueling the cruiser. Once the scanner is operational, we can search for the *Scorpius* and hopefully contact it."

Liam's stomach churned as JEFF brought them over the central complex of the station. Collapsed buildings, their insides burned.

"There's no smoke," Liam noticed. "How long ago do you think this happened?"

"The lack of heat signatures suggests that the attack occurred soon after the *Scorpius* arrived. It would have been at its most vulnerable when docked."

"So the attackers might have left by now," said Liam, peering out across the ice. Then he sat up. "But I was getting that message from Mina barely an hour ago, and it said to hurry. So if the attack was a few days ago, that definitely means she survived it, right?"

"That is possible," said JEFF. "Though if we assume the starliner was not destroyed, then it likely executed a burn and left the system. Her message might be time delayed by the distance they've traveled since the attack. It may only mean that she was alive to send you a message in the recent past."

"But it would be less than four days ago," said Liam.

"Yes," said JEFF. "The scanner data will tell us more."

"It probably means she got out of here alive," said Phoebe, giving Liam the first hopeful look he'd seen on her face since they'd woken from stasis.

"Yeah, if they were able to pick her up." Liam imagined Mina alone in her pod, sending him a message as she tumbled through space. If she activated stasis, she could survive out there for years. But in stasis, she wouldn't be able to see his messages, so how would they ever find her?

JEFF flew toward the front of a long, curved building just beside the main complex. It was half collapsed, its garage-style doors cockeyed and burned. "This is the main hangar for local transports. I will see if I can salvage the parts to aid with our repairs while you two head down to the sublevel."

JEFF lowered the cruiser onto a landing pad outside, but it was cratered in multiple spots. "Hang on. We still have damaged landing gear from our crash on Mars." The cruiser crunched down on the rubble-strewn pad and its back wobbled, jolting them hard in their seats.

"If we are lucky," he added, "I will be able to tap into the water systems from here to refuel as well."

"Our luck would have to change," said Liam.

"We've been pretty lucky," said Phoebe. "What if

we'd arrived here two days ago like we'd planned? We might be part of the wreckage— *What?*"

JEFF was gazing at Phoebe again, his eyes flickering, his head cocked slightly.

Liam felt a nervous tremor. "What's going on?" he finally said.

Neither of them answered.

"JEFF?" Liam spoke again.

But the bot swiveled back to the controls. "You should get into your pressure suits. Delphi's atmosphere is slightly more suitable to your bodies than that of Mars, but the temperature is quite cold at the moment, nearly fifty below zero. Yet another reason why it is in our best interests to stay here as briefly as possible."

"Sounds good," said Phoebe. She unbuckled and strode out of the cockpit.

Liam looked at the back of JEFF's head. "Am I missing something?"

JEFF swiped the holoscreen, flipping through different schematics. "I do not follow. Can you clarify?"

"Something between you and Phoebe."

JEFF paused for the briefest moment before replying. Again, Liam had the sense that JEFF was choosing his words carefully. "I believe we are all in agreement regarding our current plan. You should get going. The sooner we have eyes and ears, as they say, the better."

"Fine." Liam got up. As he left the cockpit, though, he glanced back at JEFF and was surprised by his next thought: *I don't believe you.* Could JEFF be lying? Was that even possible? And what exactly was he lying about? Something to do with Phoebe. Like he didn't believe what she was saying. All she'd talked about was being worried they'd be attacked if they stayed around, and that they'd been lucky to not get here sooner. Both things seemed totally reasonable; in fact, Liam felt the same way.

But whatever it was, JEFF didn't seem willing to say, and he was right that they needed to hurry, for so many reasons.

Liam left the cockpit, and his first step in Delphi's low gravity sent him careening into the wall. He grabbed a nearby handle for support and took smaller steps toward the main cabin.

Phoebe was zipping up her black pressure suit. She stopped halfway and removed her atmo pack, tossing it on the couch. Liam unhooked his suit from its charger and started sliding the thick, rubbery fabric over his legs. Compared to the space-grade suit, it was much easier to move around in. "Everything okay?"

"Not really. How about you?"

"Yeah, not really. But better than when we first found that core. Hey, um, it seemed like JEFF was giving you a hard time."

Phoebe huffed. "Who cares about JEFF? He's a bot. Do you know what he's *not* feeling right now? Scared. He's calculating probabilities and protocols while we're worried about everyone we know dying."

"True," said Liam, but the worries still needled in his mind. "Is there anything else?" His insides tied in knots as he asked it. He was barely sure why. "Things seemed weird."

Phoebe pulled the soft helmet of her pressure suit over her head and zipped it closed. She clicked her link into the port on her sleeve and activated the suit's controls. Then she looked back at him, through the dissipating puff of fog on the inside of her visor. "I'm with you," she said through her suit's tinny speaker. "We're a team. Best in the galaxy. Okay?"

Liam nodded. "Okay." He pulled up his suit, and as he did, he felt the impressions of the two objects in the hip pockets of his thermal wear: the orange crystal and the Phase Two data key. He and Phoebe would never have made it this far without each other.

He checked the beacon one last time: nothing. "Hold on," he said to Phoebe. He ducked back into the cockpit and grabbed the link with the code key, then quickly tapped out:

back soon

Maybe all his messages were still traveling through space. Or if Mina was receiving them but was still injured, maybe someone could tell her later that the beacon had blinked. That is, if she wasn't dead from the attack, or in her stasis pod floating in space. He shook his head, trying to clear those buzzing thoughts. Had to focus on what he could do right now.

He took off the alien watch, slid his arms into the sleeves of his suit, and put the watch on over his gloved hand. Then he zipped himself in and clicked his link into place. The heating and breathing systems hummed to life. Liam watched the readings rise to 100 percent. He ran his finger over the patch on his leg, the one covering the tear he'd sustained in the cave on Mars. Still holding.

Liam's link flashed and JEFF spoke in his ear. "The access door to the sublevel will have a security lock, but with the power out, you will need to open it with a magnet drill."

"Got it," said Phoebe. She opened the closet by the airlock and hauled out a heavy metal box. She flicked open the latches and pulled out the magnet drill—a bulky, meter-long tool with a trigger, a second handle off the side, and a curved metal cup at its end. Phoebe slung it over her shoulder by its thick yellow strap.

"I have sent you the schematics of the station," JEFF continued, "and highlighted the route down to the backup scanner. You can enter through the doors directly off the bow of the cruiser."

"Okay." Liam tapped his link and the map opened. Two blue dots blinked at the bottom of the screen for Liam and Phoebe, a red dot in the upper corner, which was the backup scanner, and a green line leading them to it.

Phoebe opened the map, too, and they both stepped into the airlock, Liam closing the inner door behind them. They stood shoulder to shoulder, both breathing hard in the cramped, quiet space.

"Ready?" said Phoebe.

"Yeah." Liam pressed a button, and the outer door slid open and stairs lowered to the ground. They were greeted by howling wind and a wicked chill. Liam's suit hummed to compensate.

"Wonder what kind of distance we can get," said Phoebe, and she leaped out of the hatch, sailing on a long, gradual arc, much farther than they had on Mars. "Whoa!" She slammed into the side of the hangar building, dropped, and staggered on the rubble-strewn ground.

"You okay?"

Phoebe flicked on her headlamp and looked over her suit. "Yup. Very low gravity!"

Liam activated the closing cycle on the outer door and then hopped gently down from the airlock. Even this little movement sent him five meters from the craft, his boots crunching on the black rock. It was chipped and splintered, similar in composition to the volcanic glass they used to encounter in the lava tubes on Mars, only more crumbly, like walking on dry cereal, and coated with ice. He turned on his headlamp, leaned into the relentless wind, and started toward the building beyond the cruiser. Ice crystals thwicked against his suit. A slight chill seeped in, and Liam shivered, thinking *please be okay*, meaning Mina and Shawn, but also meaning him and Phoebe, now that they were outside the ship, exposed.

As he walked, it dawned on him that he was standing on another planet, far off in space, and that this planet had once had a solar system, was perhaps many billions of years old. It felt as solid as Mars once had, and yet he'd seen it from a distance and knew how small, how infinitesimal it was compared with the years of black around it. The thought made him feel dizzy, and with each arcing step he feared he might fall right off the side of the planet and back into endless space. He shortened his stride until he would have been barely shuffling along on Mars.

He peered through the sheeting ice, back at the damaged hangar, its doors yawning open like crooked teeth, and then out across the dark plains of ice, toward the core wreckage, and the engine burning far in the distance. No signs of movement, of attackers. Or of survivors.

They reached the shadowy entrance to the main complex, ducking out of the vicious wind into a doorway. Liam heard a distant crunching sound behind him—but it was only JEFF, rolling across the crumbly ground, a bright light on his chest spearing through the ice into the dark hangar.

The control panel beside the door was burned out, and the door was slightly open, askew in its track. The edge of the door and the wall beside it were strafed with black streaks, like an explosion had blown out from the inside. Liam gripped the edge and strained to pull it open, but it wouldn't budge. Phoebe slid into the narrow gap and pressed her back against the door, using her legs. It groaned farther open, enough for Liam to step around her. The inner airlock door was in the same state, blown slightly ajar. They dragged it open and entered a dark hallway. The once-white walls were striped with black burn marks here, too, and frosted over with a layer of ice that sparkled in their headlamps. The ice was tinged purple, thick here and thin there, whipped into points and curves like frosting, but also like gnarled fingers, reaching for them.

They moved down the hall in loping steps, trying to keep from hitting their heads on the ceiling. Their boots crunched through the ice coating like breaking glass and clomped on the metal floors. If the power had been on, there would have been a gravity field in here like back in the colony. As it was, it took them only a handful of long, half-floating strides to reach the hall's end.

They entered a large square room with a balcony around the upper level that had collapsed in multiple places. Wind howled through a huge, circular hole in the roof, the metal melted and twisted around its perimeter. A light snow of ice drifted through. The circular hole also extended into the lower levels, the remaining floor warped and sloping toward it.

Liam leaned back against the wall and moved his headlamp slowly around the room, over the frosted piles of computer banks, broken beams, and fallen chunks of ceiling. There was an odd pile in the far corner, and before his mind had even registered what he was seeing, his heart jumped and adrenaline surged through him.

A body. Legs sticking out from the twisted metal of a collapsed staircase. The head and most of the torso hidden, wearing the maroon fatigues of colonial personnel. Liam held his breath, trying to control it, the sound loud in his helmet. The body was so still, like another piece of the wreckage. . . . Phoebe saw it too. Liam switched over to the local link with shaking fingers, afraid to use the intercom, afraid to make a sound.

"Should we check it?" He took a tentative step toward the body.

Phoebe held her arm out across his chest. Her eyes were wide, and Liam could hear her fast breaths over the link. "Let's do what we came to do first. I don't think we can help her."

Liam felt a sickening pull inside him to look more closely, but he forced his gaze away. "Where is everybody else?"

Phoebe shrugged. "I guess there wouldn't have been many people here before the starliner arrived, just a small maintenance crew." She checked her link and pointed past him. "Stairs are that way."

They left the central room and moved in arcing strides down a long hallway, picking their way around rubble, fallen beams, tangled guts of wires and ducts that spilled out of walls. Liam tried to only look straight ahead. Every shadow, every dark doorway, might hold another victim. The slightest sound made him tense up—a shriek of wind, the groaning of wrecked structures. They couldn't be sure there weren't still enemies here, somewhere.

The hallway opened into a vast room, the central space beneath the main dome of the station: the Silver Pearl casino, sister to the Rings of Gold back on Saturn. Most of the roof had been blasted off and the wind howled through it. The floor was scattered with rubble, half covering the frosted hulks of slot machines and gaming tables. Glints of the polished silver surfaces reflected their headlamps. To either side, archways led to smaller gaming rooms. Here and there were the twisted forms of bots lying on the ground, as well as various animal shapes, and though Liam tried to ignore them, he also noticed limbs that looked much more human, all coated in frost.

"It's on the other side." Phoebe led the way, threading through the wreckage, their boots leaving footprints on the frosted carpet.

They reached another large set of airlock doors, half open, and stepped through to a wide walkway that was surprisingly intact. On either side, full-length flexglass walls curved in toward them: a series of oblong bubble shapes, like they were walking between clear balloons. These walls, cracked here and there but not smashed, were the sides of enormous oval capsules, like giant frozen water drops, held in place by thin silvery scaffolding. The great containers were lined up on either side of the hallway, one after another, and when Liam looked down through the floor, which was also glass, he saw that there were five or six more walkways and rows of bubbles below these, and all of them were connected by rounded openings, so that the entire complex resembled a hamster habitat.

"What are these?" Phoebe wondered.

"The baths." Liam remembered them from the orientation guide. "The minerals in the Delphi oceans makes this really dense steam that's almost like a gel. Then with the low gravity, being in these things is sort of like floating underwater, except you can still breathe. People think it's good for your muscles and lungs after stasis. You had to sign up months in advance of leaving Mars to get an appointment down here, and they were super expensive."

They passed between ten sets of the giant bubbles. Liam imagined them full of laughing humans, the way he'd seen in the guide, darting and bobbing around in their bathing suits, or just relaxing along the railing that spanned the midsection of each container, wearing their virtual glasses as they soaked. Now twisting, purple-tinged icicles hung from the tops of the capsules, and feathered ice patterns were smeared across the sides.

They stepped through the airlock at the far end of the walkway and entered a smaller corridor where sets of elevator doors hung crooked.

Something crunched beneath Liam's boot. He lifted it to find the smashed exoskeleton of a cockroach, brittle and dead. "Hey, look," he said, pointing it out to Phoebe.

"So much for leaving them behind." She turned to keep going but paused and pointed her headlamp into a crevice near an elevator door. "There's another one."

Liam couldn't help smiling for a second. How

many times had he heard the warnings to check all personal items for roaches, and been reminded of the strict protocols for keeping them out of the space elevators and cruisers? But the creatures had found a way. At least this far.

"Stairs are over here." Phoebe vaulted ahead.

Liam pushed off into his next long stride—

Everything slipped again. A blur, and he felt a yawning emptiness and found himself once more staring at the enormous sun, boiling, moments from exploding, and still he was flying toward it in the skim drone, only now there seemed to be lights dancing in the nearby dark to either side of the cockpit. Flashes, like explosions. And Liam was counting to himself, pushing the skim drone toward its maximum speed, and yet worried it wouldn't be fast enough, while also watching his rear camera, something about the starliner. He heard himself saying, *I got you*—

"Liam, hey." Phoebe was tugging his arm. Liam was almost surprised to find himself in the elevator hall and not in the skim drone. "What's up?"

He shook his head. When he blinked, it almost seemed like there were green echoes of the sun behind his eyelids. "Sorry. I'm having these weird flashes, almost like dreams. I think it's stasis sickness or something."

"Well, shake it off," said Phoebe. "We gotta hurry."

"Yeah, sorry," said Liam, but his head still felt foggy, his insides weirdly hollow. What was with these visions? Such a weird thing, to be back at the sun, and yet it felt less like a dream and more like something he knew, almost like a memory.

Phoebe pushed open a door just past the bank of elevators. "JEFF," she said. "We've reached the stairs."

"Acknowledged." His voice clipped in and out. "I am fix—thermal tiles. All is go—well so far."

Liam stepped through the door and peered down the switchbacking flights, his headlamp making the ice-coated railings sparkle. "How far down?"

"Six levels," said Phoebe, moving her finger over the map on her link. She jumped lightly and sailed down the first flight to the metal landing below.

Liam followed, and they dropped through the dark. As they descended, the sound of the wind and that constant flicking of ice faded. Liam's breathing grew louder in the silence, punctuated only by the clanging of his boots on the landings. With each level, he felt the weight of the blackness beyond his headlamp. He tried to keep his gaze straight, didn't want to check any corners but kept checking them anyway.

At the bottom of the stairs, they reached a thick metal door with a security panel, which, like everything else, was dark. Phoebe pressed the magnet drill against the door frame, beside the panel. The wall rumbled and vibrated. Liam felt it in his feet and teeth.

There was a thud from inside the door. "Got it." Phoebe dragged the drill sideways, straining, and the door slid open with it. Then she turned off the drill and slung it over her shoulder.

They slipped through the half-open door into a narrow, low-ceilinged corridor with black metal walls and a carpeted floor.

Phoebe checked her link and turned down a side corridor. "Backup power for the station should be this way." The short hall ended at a computer panel covered by a shallow bubble of clear plastic. Phoebe slid open a compartment on the wall beside the panel and lifted a red handle. The plastic unlatched. She swung it up and pressed a large green button on the panel. "I hope this works," she muttered. A second passed . . . Something rumbled through the walls. There was a hum and a series of rhythmic clicks and the panel in front of them blinked to life.

"We found the power," Phoebe reported to JEFF.

"Acknowledg—ly partial lighting up here. Some of the circuit—must have been destroyed."

They returned to the main corridor. The door through which they'd entered had slid closed. Amber lights had illuminated in the ceiling, and warm air hissed from vents. Liam checked the readings on his link and unzipped his helmet. "Still a little chilly," he said, "but the air is normal." Phoebe reemoved her helmet, too.

They headed to the next intersection, passing sealed compartments that contained various control systems for the station. Many lights were flashing red, likely due to the damage. They stopped where the corridor split left and right.

Phoebe zoomed in on the map. "The backup scanner is that way," she said, pointing in one direction, "and the data recorder is this way. They're in separate compartments for fire safety. Why don't you turn on the scanner and I'll get the recorder."

"Shouldn't we stay together?" said Liam.

"Well . . . I think we get this done as fast as possible so that we can find the *Scorpius*."

"Yeah, or before someone finds us."

Phoebe started down the passage. "Let's just meet back here."

"Okay." Liam headed in the other direction—

But after a couple steps, he paused. He turned and watched Phoebe walking the other way. A strange feeling, like he needed to be there with her . . . but of course she'd be fine. Except that wasn't exactly what he'd been thinking. Instead, JEFF's words ran through his mind: *Unless you have some information that suggests otherwise?* And Liam was surprised to find himself wondering: *Can I trust her?* He thought again about Phoebe's parents, the way he'd suspected them on Mars.

Except JEFF's strange behavior might be due to him malfunctioning. Still, for the moment, maybe he should go along with Phoebe to the recorder, just to be sure—

Stop it! he thought. Because Phoebe was right, they needed to hurry, and here he was standing around wasting time questioning his only teammate. *Best in the galaxy*, she'd said.

He turned back and continued down the passage, tapping his link as he went. He zoomed in on the backup scanner and brought up a detailed guide to its operation.

The hall ended at a thick door with a clear central panel. Liam pressed the button beside the door and it slid open. Inside, he found a cone-shaped structure in the center of a tiny room with smooth black walls. A cluster of wires led from the cone's top into the ceiling. He checked the scanner instructions again and knelt beside it, opening an access panel. He threw the main power switch and the device hummed to life. Then he used a small screen to calibrate the scanner's signal. He boosted it to maximum, and it whirred to a higher pitch.

"JEFF," said Liam, "I think I've activated the scanner."

"Acknowledged, I see it," said JEFF. "Good work—should ha—results in a few minutes."

"Phoebe, how's the recorder coming?" Liam asked.

"I've almost got it," said Phoebe. "I'll meet you in the hall in just a second."

"I'll come to you." Liam stepped around the scanner and back to the door. "I'll be there in a—" Liam froze. He held his breath, listening—

There it was again. An echo from down the hall.

Voices. Liam checked his wrist. The circular band around the face of the alien watch had begun to blink—only this time it was red instead of blue. He'd never seen it blink red before, had no idea what it meant, but the watch never activated when anything good was about to happen.

More voices. Louder this time.

Liam's heart pounded. "I don't think we're alone down here."

6

Liam edged to the door and peered into the corridor. No signs of movement.

But there were definitely voices.

"Do you hear that?" Liam whispered to Phoebe.

"Hear what?"

"The voices!" It sounded like two people arguing. He stepped into the corridor and started cautiously back the way he'd come. The voices were muffled, but he could now hear that they sounded young. Almost like they were his age. The watch blinked faster.

"*—can't believe it!*"

"*It's not what you think!*"

A boy's voice, and a girl's.

"Phoebe, they're coming from your direction," Liam whispered. He moved as quietly as he could, nearing the intersection.

"Hold on," said Phoebe. "I don't hear a thing."

"I'm not going to let you hurt anyone else!"

That was the boy. Clearer now, but still somewhat muffled, as if Liam was hearing it through a wall.

"Don't!" the girl shouted. It sounded like Phoebe.

"Don't what?" whispered Liam.

"Huh?" Phoebe replied, right there in his helmet, different from that other voice, which seemed to be in the corridor somewhere.

"What's going on over there?" Liam asked, peering down the hall.

"Nothing!" Phoebe hissed. "I told you! I'm almost done."

But Liam had reached the intersection, and the sounds were definitely coming from straight ahead, from the compartment at the far end of the hall where Phoebe was. How could she not hear them? There were lights flashing around in there, too. Like her headlamp, but more than one.

"Phoebe—"

A light burst out of the doorway, and Liam froze. At first he thought it was Phoebe, but this was some kind of glowing figure. A person Liam's size who was shimmering from head to toe in a strange amber light, but he was also translucent, almost like a hologram, or the way things looked when you first entered the VirtCom, before you settled into the illusion; Liam could see the outlines of the walls through him. The figure was bounding right at Liam while frantically zipping up what appeared to be a pressure suit.

Another figure appeared at the doorway, also suiting up. "*Wait!*" the girl yelled, sticking out her hand. And Liam saw for certain that it was Phoebe standing there, but also glowing strangely. Was she shouting to him? Or to this figure who was coming right at him?

Now Liam saw the flashing on the suited boy's wrist. A watch blinking blue. And the boy turned back around—but it made no sense. The glowing boy looked like Liam. It *was* Liam. Had his alien watch and everything. But how could he be seeing himself running right toward him?

Suddenly light bloomed from behind the glowing version of Phoebe and there was a terrible crash of sound and air.

"Phoebe!" Liam yelled.

She was erased by a fireball exploding out of the doorway. It rolled down the hall, right at him. There wasn't time to move—the blast hit the flickering version of him and sent him flying through the air and right through Liam. But Liam barely felt it because here came the fireball and what had happened oh no he needed to run—

Liam shut his eyes. A deafening roar, the rumbling and tearing of the blast enveloping him—

Except he could still hear himself breathing.

"Liam? What's up?" Phoebe asked over the link, as if she had not just blown up.

And he realized that he didn't actually feel any heat or wind, no scalding pain. Liam opened his eyes. Blinding light all around him. He was in the center of a firestorm, an exploding star, flames and melting steel and wind and coils of black sooty ash and smoke. Was this part of that vision he'd been having? But no, that had been in a skim drone. . . .

Chunks of ceiling toppled onto him—no, through him. He looked down and saw himself standing there as if nothing was happening, his pressure suit intact. The watch was blinking, but still red, and not nearly as fast as it had at other times when he'd been in danger. Definitely not as fast as it should have been given that he was standing in the middle of an explosion.

Okay. . . .

This wasn't really happening. So what was it? He turned and saw the other Liam lying on the floor behind him, still glowing and translucent like he was made of light. His pressure suit was singed and smoldering, his version of the watch pulsing blue. The visor on his helmet had melted, and he was moaning and clawing at his scalded face.

Liam's fingers jumped to his own visor, and for a moment he was sure he felt a stinging sensation on his cheeks, but no, his visor was perfectly intact. He was unharmed, and the explosion-that-wasn't had begun to die down around him, its flames giving way to the lights on the ceiling, and Liam could see that the walls and the floor were still there, undamaged, as was the far doorway. There was still so much smoke and ash, but it was fading away, too, dissolving as if he'd been watching it in the VirtCom and was now lifting the virtual glasses from his eyes.

"Hey."

Phoebe appeared, walking down the hall toward him and looking this way and that as she did. "What were you talking about?" she asked quietly. "Is there someone here?"

Liam shook his head. The fire had faded completely, just echoes when he blinked, the smoke and collapsed walls gone. The hall was back to normal. He looked behind him again. The body—*my body, that was me, dying in an explosion*—was gone, too, and the watch was no longer blinking red. "I guess not," he said.

"But you heard voices?"

"I thought I did. It, um . . . I must have just been

freaking out." Liam felt woozy, a metallic taste in his mouth. He put a hand against the wall. It was strange; this feeling reminded him of those moments right after he'd used the watch. Also of those times recently when he'd pictured the sun about to go supernova. What was going on with him?

Phoebe rubbed his arm. "You all right?"

"Sorta. I'm not sure. Did you activate the recorder?"

"Yeah. It seems to be transmitting, so JEFF should be able to connect to it. But . . ." Phoebe narrowed her eyes at him. "You're not telling me something. Did you use the watch just now?"

"No. I saw something, though, like a hallucination. I don't know."

"What was it?"

"I thought I heard voices, but it was, like, you and me, fighting about something, and then I saw this version of me running away from you and there was this massive explosion and it killed us both."

Phoebe looked around. "You saw that here? Just now? What were we fighting about?"

The details were hazy in his mind. He could barely recall it, like it was fading from his memory the same way it had faded from the hallway. "I don't know. I wasn't going to let you do something."

"That is usually what we fight about."

One fragment bubbled up in his mind: *I knew I couldn't trust you,* the other version of him had said, but Liam kept that to himself.

Maybe it really had been some kind of hallucination. Maybe an aftereffect of using the watch, coupled with disorientation from stasis, and multiplied by the stress and fear since they'd arrived on Delphi. All of that was bound to confuse his brain, taking his worries and making stuff up. Except the watch *had* been blinking; he was pretty sure he hadn't imagined that. What did that strange red color mean?

"We're under a lot of stress," said Phoebe, patting his shoulder. "Finding out what happened to the *Scorpius* should help. Can you make it back up to the cruiser?"

Liam nodded. Phoebe took him by the arm. He looked back one more time, but the corridor was silent and still.

The stairwell was fully lit and full of rapidly warming air. As they climbed, their steps became shorter and heavier, and by the top level they felt the full effect of the artificial gravity field. The lights were on in the elevator hallway, and the airlocks had shut at both ends of the baths.

Inside the bubble-walled corridor, the air was stifling and damp. Orange heat lamps glowed overhead. Liam saw that the big, clear containers were flooding with purplish steam, the melting ice sparkling in the multicolored lights that ringed each bubble and blinked on and off in slow, soothing patterns. A couple of the containers had cracked, and lavender clouds seeped out into the hallway. Phoebe coughed, slipped her helmet back on, and zipped it up. She stumbled as she took her next step. Liam caught her by the arm. "You all right?"

"Yeah, just—*cough*—it's hot in here. Messes with my lungs."

They stepped into the airlock at the far end of the baths and peered through the small, thick windows. The power was still out to the casino and beyond. Liam put on his helmet and Phoebe pressed the button to open the door. They were greeted by the stiff, frigid wind, and pinpricks of ice.

"JEFF," said Liam, "we're almost back."

"Acknowledged. I have finished replacing the thermal tiles and am now analyzing the data from the scanner." There was a click and then JEFF continued. "Is everything all right?"

Liam tried to catch Phoebe's eye, but she was just gazing straight ahead. "Um, yeah. Why?"

Phoebe cocked her head. "Huh?"

"Just making sure," said JEFF. There was a pause, and Liam could almost picture his eyes flickering. "I will see you on board."

"He's being weird," Liam said.

"What do you mean?" Phoebe replied absently.

"I don't know, maybe it's nothing." Except as they retraced their path through the complex, Liam wondered if Phoebe had heard JEFF. The way the signal had clicked: Had JEFF only been talking to him?

"I call bathroom," Phoebe said the moment they'd climbed back on board the cruiser. She hurried straight to it, not even taking her helmet off.

Liam pulled his off and checked the beacon, but it was silent as ever. He peeled off his pressure suit, hung it up, and found JEFF in the cockpit analyzing a three-dimensional holoscreen that showed a spherical map of space. "How's it going?"

"Unfortunately there are no available parts for repairing the rear thruster, or the antenna. And we still need to refuel. But I have also been analyzing the data from the scanner."

Liam studied the holoscreen map. Delphi was a large ball at its center. Objects blinked, rotating in orbit around it.

Liam's heart skipped a beat. "Is that—"

"No," said JEFF, "these objects are far too small to be the *Scorpius*. They do appear, however, to be wreckage. One is a transport ship like the kind that would have been stationed here. Another is emitting an extremely strong radiation signal; I believe it is another of the *Scorpius*'s engines. There are also pieces of its front array, which would explain the solar sail we saw out on the ice. There is further evidence of radiation in the atmosphere, which may indicate warhead detonation—perhaps the *Scorpius* trying to defend itself."

"What does it all mean?"

"Most likely that the *Scorpius* was in a significant battle," said JEFF, "but managed to escape. That said, its condition is not promising, but it could be worse. The front array holds most of the navigation and communication systems, but as long as the remaining engines and cores are intact, the ship could still fly. In theory."

"So then where is it?"

JEFF tapped the menu on the side of the screen, and the view changed to a wider map of space, with Delphi now just a small point in the center, surrounded by concentric circles almost like shells, getting larger and larger from the middle. Every few seconds, the map refreshed, adding another shell, and shrinking the spaces between the existing ones. "The scanner is progressively mapping more and more of the local region, but as the signal is limited by light speed, it is a slow process."

With the next refresh, the circles shrank significantly, and a large white dot appeared far beyond where the scanner had mapped. JEFF tapped it and checked its readings. "That is the *Starliner Saga*," he said. "It is broadcasting its normal call sign and status information. It seems to be unharmed and functioning normally." The circles scaled smaller and a second dot appeared, even farther out. "There is the *Rhea*," said JEFF, "also transmitting normally. They are both part of the second-to-last fleet."

"Shouldn't the *Scorpius* be closer than those two?" said Liam.

"Yes. The fact that we cannot yet see the *Scorpius* likely confirms that its comms are down. That makes sense, tactically speaking. Whoever attacked the ship tried to take out its ability to move and to call for help, to keep the rest of the fleet from knowing about the attack. And now, since it is not transmitting, we must wait for our scanner to find it."

"How long is that going to take?"

"Calculating. . . . If the *Scorpius* was indeed attacked upon its arrival four days ago, and if it could depart at something close to its maximum speed, then it would currently be about nine light-hours away. Which means nine hours for our scanner signal to reach it, and nine more hours for that reading to return to us."

"Eighteen hours. . . ." Liam felt himself deflating. "We can't wait around that long."

"Likely not."

"Got anything?" Phoebe asked, joining them.

"Other starliners," said Liam. "And wreckage, but no *Scorpius*. Can we use this backup scanner to reach anyone?" he asked JEFF.

"Yes, I sent a message on the all-colony frequency, identifying us and explaining our situation. But that message will not reach the *Saga* for nearly six weeks."

"But how come we can see its signal now?" Phoebe asked.

"That signal we see is five weeks old. The *Saga* has been transmitting continuously in this direction since its departure. Same for the *Rhea*, which is a week farther ahead. We are also picking up an all-colony emergency broadcast, which I wanted both of you to hear."

JEFF tapped the console and a message blared over the speaker. "*—will be needed to assist with passenger reassignment and possible military actions. Please send your modified course corrections to tactical command on this frequency, and safe travels. End message. Begin message. Attention all colonial craft: this is an emergency message priority urgent. Reports indicate destruction of Delphi station and significant damage to* Starliner Scorpius. *Limited data points to a hostile attack of unknown origin. We have lost contact with the* Scorpius, *but their last transmitted message and trajectory indicates that they are making for the emergency rendezvous point. Therefore all*

colonial craft, fleet-wide, are ordered to make an emer-
gency course correction to Destina, for triage and defensive
maneuvers. Repeat. All colonial craft are ordered to disre-
gard Human Long Travel Protocol and initiate the latest
emergency protocol, received on eleven, twelve, twenty-
two. Proceed immediately to Destina. All ships will be
needed to assist with passenger reassignment—"

JEFF clicked off the message.

Wind buffeted the cruiser. Ice raked across the windshield.

Liam gazed at the screen, the dot of Delphi with circle after circle of space. All the nothingness around them, like they were marooned on the tiniest island. The map refreshed again. A new small light blinked, a few concentric circles away from Delphi.

JEFF checked the reading. "A military cruiser. Destroyed, I'm afraid."

"Where is Destina?" The last time Liam had seen an updated map of the route to Aaru-5, none of the waypoints past Danos had been officially named yet, but those maps were a decade old now.

JEFF's eyes flickered. "The name Destina does not appear in any information about the journey. The third waypoint had a proposed name of Fortuna but had not been officially added to the logs, as second-ary scanning satellites had not reached it yet by the time of our departure from Mars. The message refers to an emergency protocol sent last year, but with our antenna down, we were unable to receive it."

"It could be anywhere," said Phoebe, gazing at the map, her expression similar to how Liam felt.

"What was the fourth waypoint supposed to be?" Liam asked.

"It was unnamed, but its planned location was the second planet of Proxima."

"Proxima," said Liam. "It sounds familiar." He tried to remember their space studies back in Ms. Avi's class.

"It is a red dwarf star, part of the Alpha Centauri system."

"Wait." Liam thought back to the message from Mina that he'd awakened to. Before she'd said "hurry," there had been those other letters. U-R-I-B. "Alpha Centauri is a binary star, right?"

"Correct. The two stars are Centauri A and B."

"Centauri B," said Liam. "That's where they're going. That's what Mina was trying to tell me. I bet that's where Destina is!"

"That calculates," said JEFF. "Centauri B is not too far from Fortuna, but perhaps it has some greater strategic or tactical value as a rendezvous point."

"Okay," said Liam. "So what did the backup recorder say? Do we know who we're up against? Who the Saturn attackers really are?"

"Here is what I found." JEFF tapped the console and a second holoscreen appeared. Below a series of readouts, a message flashed, green letters on a black background:

NO DATA.

"The backup recorder has been erased." JEFF pointed to the top lines of the readouts. "You can see that it is fully online, transmitting correctly, but its hard drives are empty."

"Was it the power outage?" Liam asked.

"The box is built to withstand power outages and surges and is shielded from an electromagnetic attack. I'm afraid someone must have erased it manually."

"So all the records of what happened here and who did it . . ."

"Gone." JEFF swiped the screen away.

Liam turned to Phoebe. "Did the recorder look like it had been tampered with?"

"I couldn't tell," said Phoebe. "All I did was turn it on."

Liam found JEFF looking at him. He shrugged. "I didn't see anything." But the scene from down in the corridor flashed through his mind. That other version of him shouting at Phoebe. *I'm not going to let you hurt anyone else!* But that had just been his mind messing with him, spinning his worries.

The scanner map refreshed again; more darkness.

"Well, it doesn't matter who they are," said Liam. "We have to head for Destina. How far is that from here?"

"Calculating." JEFF's eyes flickered. Kept flickering. "Thirty-three years."

"Thirty-three . . ." Liam trailed off.

"I've run some calculations, and the good news is that, if we adjust our burn for maximum efficiency, and with proper power-saving routines, I believe we can make the trip with only five to six stops for refueling and three course corrections."

"If we don't drift off course again."

"I believe I now know how to keep that from happening," said JEFF.

"Thirty-three years," Liam repeated. "Will we even be okay in stasis that long?"

"It should be fine. That said, there is no data yet on the effects of such a trip. Even the First Fleet hasn't traveled that far."

"It's just so long." Imagining it made all the space between here and there feel heavy, crushing.

"Back at Saturn, you said our parents were going to be in trouble if it really took us twenty-five years to get here," said Phoebe. "Now it's been ten, and we're talking about thirty-three more. Are they going to be okay?"

"It does increase the risk," said JEFF, "but I'm

afraid we have no other choice."

Liam checked the scanner map again. "What about the *Scorpius*? Are we sure they can make it there?"

"Well, we've already scanned a few hundred thousand kilometers in all directions and there's no sign of them, which does suggest that they were able to execute a burn, and the colonial message said their last known trajectory was Destina. If they do indeed have four of their engines intact, they should be able to make it."

"Can we catch them?"

"I will have to make a more in-depth calculation. We will be following an essentially identical flight path. We may be able to find them along the way."

Liam looked at Phoebe. "So that's it, then? Get out of here and make for Destina?"

Phoebe's arms were crossed tight across her chest, and she stared at the map. "I guess so."

"Liam," said JEFF, "I have collected additional information that indicates that it is not that simple."

"Why, because we still need fuel?"

"Forgive me while I search for the most tactful wording. . . ." JEFF's eyes flickered. "Before we can depart, I am afraid that we must make some choices that you will find extremely difficult."

"What are you talking about?"

JEFF rotated toward Phoebe. She looked up, and

when she found JEFF facing her, her eyes widened, the color draining out.

"I'm sorry," said JEFF. He raised his right arm and pointed at Phoebe.

"Wait! You don't—" She started toward the doorway, but JEFF pressed his finger against her shoulder and a bright blue flash sparked there. Phoebe's eyes fluttered and she slumped into the copilot's seat.

"JEFF!" Liam shouted. "What are you doing?"

JEFF's hand flipped back to reveal a set of holes in his wrist. Red plastic cable shot out. JEFF grabbed it with his other hand and quickly bound Phoebe's wrists together. He then straightened her up, looped more cable around her and the copilot's chair, and tied it off behind her.

"JEFF, stop!" Liam gaped, frozen in place.

Phoebe groaned, her head lolling, and as the stun effect wore off, she looked around groggily. "What was that?" She felt the restraints and started to writhe against them. "Hey! Let me go!"

Liam instinctively moved to help, but JEFF held him back. "I am sorry, Liam. Given your emotional connection to Phoebe, I calculated that it was in your best interest to delay this until we reached the *Scorpius*, but at this point I must follow my primary safety protocol, which is always to protect the lives of the humans on board."

"Don't listen to him, Liam! He's malfunctioning!"

Liam stepped back. "JEFF, what are you talking about?"

"I believe," said JEFF, "that I have gathered enough evidence to reasonably suspect that Phoebe is in fact working to sabotage our journey, and may be acting on direct orders from the enemy who attacked Saturn, Delphi, and the *Scorpius*."

"He's lying, Liam!" Phoebe's eyes were wild and red. "Don't listen to him! You stupid bot!"

"What kind of evidence?" Liam stammered.

JEFF tapped the console, and the holoscreen between them changed to a wide-angle view of the cockpit. There was JEFF, in the pilot's chair, not moving. Phoebe appeared, floating in behind him.

"It's always been deactivated for convenience, but this ship is equipped with a basic security system. This is from three months before our most recent refueling stop."

As Liam watched, Phoebe stuck something to the back of JEFF's neck, then sat in the copilot's chair and brought up a holoscreen. In the dim, distorted picture it was hard to tell what she was doing, but Liam felt a terrible sinking inside.

"The digital fingerprints are extremely hard to detect, but after much analysis, I was able to determine that Phoebe is the one who caused the course errors on our journey, resulting in our late arrival at Delphi."

Liam peered at Phoebe. "You made us late? On purpose?"

Phoebe's lip trembled like she was about to say something, but a tear fell instead.

"Liam, please check the left leg pocket on Phoebe's pressure suit."

"Why?"

Phoebe stared hard at him. "Liam, please . . ."

Liam knelt and unzipped the pocket, his fingers shaking. He pulled out a small, silver cylinder with a tiny screen, a red button on its side, and a black suction cup on its end.

"That is an electrical dampening device," said JEFF. "It could be used to disable my systems briefly, as well as to erase a hard drive like the one in the backup recorder, destroying any evidence of who or what attacked the *Scorpius*. Is that correct?"

Phoebe didn't answer. She looked away, staring at the floor and sniffling.

"Phoebe." Liam thought of his suspicions, of the strange vision down in the sublevel. "Did you?"

"I . . ."

A warning beeped on the console and the security feed blinked out, replaced by the map showing the space right around Delphi. A new light was blinking there, close.

JEFF tapped the light. "There is a spacecraft inbound for our location."

Liam's heart raced. "What kind of ship?"

"A Nebula Class Comet H-6."

"One of ours?" said Liam. "It could be someone who stayed behind to watch the supernova. They could help us—"

"I don't think so," said Phoebe quietly. She held up her link. A white light was flashing there.

"What's that?"

"Liam," said JEFF, "any other ship would have received the emergency bulletin we heard and changed course by now."

"It's a message," said Phoebe. "It's from *them*."

The watch had started blinking, too.

Liam looked at the map, at the ship getting closer. "What are you talking about? Phoebe, tell me what's going on."

"Liam, you have to let me go and then I'll explain."

"Negative," said JEFF. "Liam, it is against my protocols to put your safety at risk."

"I need to know," said Liam. "Are you . . . ?" He didn't even know where to start. "Are you a traitor? Your parents, too?"

Phoebe shook her head emphatically. "I'm on your side. I can prove it, just—"

Far off in the distance, a flash of rocket engines: the sleek Comet dropping from the clouds, racing toward them across the sea of ice.

"It's them, isn't it?" said Liam, adrenaline boiling his nerves. The watch was blinking faster. "It's Barro."

Phoebe nodded, tears falling. "You have to let me go."

All at once he remembered back at Saturn, as he made ready to fly away in the skim drone, seeing Barro and Phoebe talking through the window. Liam had assumed that Phoebe had been stalling, but was she . . . ? *No.* Phoebe had shot them out of the sky before they could get Liam! Didn't that mean she was on his side?

"We have to get out of here. JEFF, do we have enough fuel to take off?"

"Yes, and to break orbit, but not enough to get much farther than that."

"Liam, please trust me," said Phoebe. "We should stay and—"

"Stop it!" Liam shouted. "How can I trust you? Is it true? Are you working with them?" More thoughts cascading down now. "Did you sabotage the turbines on Mars? Is it your fault my parents are injured?"

"No! Mine are hurt, too, remember? I just—"

"Are you the reason my sister's in danger?"

"Let me explain!"

A distant roaring reached his ears now. The approaching ship's engines.

"I suggest that we take off," said JEFF. "Perhaps we can outmaneuver them and then return for fuel." He moved into the pilot's chair and buckled in.

"We can't outrun them!" said Phoebe. "Liam, we can trick them. I have an idea—"

"I would advise that you not listen to her," said JEFF, firing up the main thrusters.

Phoebe glanced at her link, the strange light blinking there. "Liam, you have to believe me. I wasn't sabotaging us. I was *saving* us!"

Liam fell back against his chair. He glared at Phoebe and felt himself shaking with hate, and yet she was crying and she was still Phoebe and what was he going to do?

Out the windshield, the brilliant glow of rockets drew closer.

7

"Initiating liftoff sequence," said JEFF. "Liam, I suggest you buckle up."

"No!" Phoebe struggled against her restraints. "Liam, please! Trust me!"

The Comet was gaining on them. Liam looked from Phoebe to JEFF. His heart pounded and his guts were doing somersaults.

He considered the dampener in his hand.

"Red button," said Phoebe, her eyes wide.

"Do not listen to her," said JEFF.

Liam gritted his teeth and thought he might explode. Phoebe was his friend, even if all this was true, but there wasn't time to figure it out!

Unless . . .

He looked down at the alien watch, blinking furiously. Put his fingers on the dial. The mere touch of the cool metal made his head swim. If Phoebe had really betrayed him, he needed to know for sure. Needed proof.

"Hold on." He clicked the watch dial to the left. The world halted, slipped, and lurched backward, all the movements unnatural, like they were being pulled on strings. Their words being sucked back into their mouths, JEFF zipping out of his chair and back in, Liam and Phoebe jerking backward from the cockpit, putting their helmets back on, reverse-jumping from the airlock and retreating into the station. . . .

But at the same time, Liam also standing there in the cockpit, that strange double sensation of two realities at once: where he was physically, and what he was seeing in the timestream. It made his head ache. He could feel his chest rising and falling in his present but could also hear the electric sound of his backward breathing through the pressure suit speaker as they reversed their way into the station, past the steam chambers, down the stairs, and into the sublevel where the recorder and scanner were located.

Now Liam backed down his corridor, Phoebe down hers. Liam watched her going in reverse to undo what it was she had done to the recorder, either simply starting it up, as she claimed, or also erasing it. He needed to know, and to do that, he had to somehow follow Phoebe. He studied the watch—its left hemisphere symbol was blinking, as it always did when he traveled into the past, but he didn't want to pause time like he did when visiting his apartment on Mars. He wanted to move with time, just not his *own* time. Was that possible?

Liam concentrated as he had on his apartment balcony. He focused on Phoebe and pressed forward, trying to reach her. To move down the hall, even though that wasn't part of *his* past. But it didn't work. He kept retreating, following his own timeline, into the scanner compartment where he knelt and turned it back off. He tried again to push out of himself, this time through the wall—that didn't work either. His past self stood and backed into the corridor once more. Liam kept pushing. If he didn't get to Phoebe soon, he would miss it—

Do I trust her? That thought appeared in his mind—it had been right at this moment, as they'd first separated in the hall, when Liam had paused, felt a sliver of doubt and considered following Phoebe—

Suddenly, his vision seared with pain, and it seemed like he was being pulled in two. The world lit up in white for a moment, and then he was moving down the corridor toward the door where Phoebe had gone, walking forward instead of backward. Liam's head ached, and he realized that he could no longer see the present-time version of himself in the cruiser cockpit. Instead, he had an uncanny sensation of moving in two directions at once. One version of him was still backing up the corridor, as he had in the past, but now this other version was walking *forward* through the doorway to where Phoebe was, and somehow, he was seeing both realities as if from his own eyes. Neither felt quite real, and yet both felt like they were actually happening.

Liam entered the recorder compartment and found Phoebe kneeling by the controls, which were in a console on the wall. "How's it going?" he heard himself say. It felt like he had really said this, and yet also like he was hearing someone else say it.

She started. "What are you doing here?"

"Just, um, figured we should stick together," this other Liam said.

"No, Liam, you shouldn't. I, um—" Phoebe moved quickly, tapping at the recorder controls, but her body was blocking what she was doing.

Liam stepped beside her. He saw that silver dampener stuck to the control panel. A yellow light flashed on it, and a string of numbers on the panel display was rapidly counting down. "What are you doing?"

"Nothing—"

"Are you sabotaging it?" he said. "I can't believe it!"

"It's not what you think!" said Phoebe. "I did it for us. I'm on your side!"

Liam lunged toward the control panel. "I'm not going to let you hurt anyone else!"

"No, Liam— Don't!"

He tore the dampener off the controls. An automated voice blared in the compartment:

"SECURITY BREACH DETECTED. SELF-DESTRUCT SEQUENCE INITIATED."

"What did you do?" Liam shouted.

"I didn't mean to—I— You're not supposed to be in here!"

Liam looked from the recorder to the dampener in his hand. He felt thoughts coming together that seemed to be new to this version of him—his suspicion on Mars, the way Phoebe had talked to Barro, JEFF's strange behavior, thoughts the real version of him (and yet it was getting quite hard to tell which one was real, or even what might make one more real than the other) had already figured out, except technically wasn't that in the future from this point? He felt dizzy trying to fit it all into his head.

Meanwhile the version of Liam in the recorder compartment spun and ran out the door.

"Wait!" Phoebe called from behind him.

And then there was a whump of air, and that explosion that Liam had sort of experienced before erupted behind him, bursting through Phoebe and storming down the hall, grabbing him and hurling him forward. He was thrown to the ground, fire everywhere—searing pain all over but especially in his eyes.

And yet at the same time the other version of him was still reversing through time, meeting back up with Phoebe and retreating up the hallway before any of that had ever (or never) happened. Liam felt like he was being pulled apart, split down the middle. A wind blowing between his eyes, through the middle of his chest—

And then all at once, everything stopped. It was as if the universe itself had been put on pause.

Liam gasped but also found himself feeling whole, like he was back in his body and had returned to his present—just one of him, not two—and yet he wasn't in the cruiser cockpit at all anymore. No Phoebe, no JEFF. Instead, he was standing in the sublevel corridor. Silence around him.

An orange light flickered in the corner of his eye. Liam turned and froze. There was someone just down the corridor, kneeling and shining a light against the wall. At first, Liam feared it was the metal-suited man from the Drove, but this being wasn't wearing a space suit of any kind. It was taller, spindly, dressed in black robes, and had dark blue, translucent skin, and milky white eyes. The light was dim, but Liam thought he saw the outlines of four legs folded beneath the robe, and more than five fingers on each hand.

The being was holding a round orange crystal just like the one Liam had in his pocket, and examining the wall in the crystal's light, running its fingers up and down the panels there. The being was also wearing a watch just like Liam's.

This creature looked like the one he'd seen in the observatory on Mars. More than that, it looked identical. But could this really be the same alien? She'd been very much dead—

And now she saw him. She turned off the orange crystal, stood, and walked toward him, gliding like a spider on her many legs. As she moved, Liam had a strange sensation that the alien was blurry. She was here in the corridor, but she also rippled like she was a hologram, or, many holograms together. One moment her face looked smooth; another, it looked wrinkled, older.

She stopped before Liam, towering over him. The only sound was her breathing, slow and reedy, coming through two noses, one above the other. She held her orange crystal out toward him and cocked her head as if trying to tell him something.

Liam stood there, fingers tingling, heart racing.

The alien looked at her crystal, then back to him again. She had large, pearlescent eyes with no irises or pupils.

Liam reached into his pocket, removed his own crystal, and held it up. The being nodded. Her mouth opened and she spoke in long, whispery sounds. For a moment, Liam couldn't begin to understand, but then both of their crystals glowed brightly, pulsing in bursts of light that increased speed and also synced up, such that soon they were blinking rapidly together.

Her whispers began to untangle into words.

"You're wearing my watch." The being's translated voice sounded the same as the voice on the recordings that were inside Liam's crystal, the ones about the infected stars and the supernovas that he and Phoebe had listened to on Mars.

Liam looked from his wrist to hers. "How do I have this if you still have it?"

"Where did you get it?"

"Uh, I got it from you? Or someone like you."

"There is no one like me. When did you get it? What location?"

"Oh, um, Mars. It's—I mean, it *was*—a planet in our old solar system. We found your observatory, and you were inside it."

The being made a sound like a sigh. "Ah, the red planet, in that single-star system. That explains it.

You found me after my death."

"I—I guess so, yeah. I wasn't stealing it, I just thought, since, well, it seemed like you'd been dead awhile."

She blinked.

"I'm Liam. Who are you?"

The being still didn't answer. She glanced at her version of the orange crystal sphere, studying it. "I'm running a diagnostic on your conceptual capacity."

"Like, you're scanning my brain?"

"In order to determine if you can comprehend the answer to your own question."

"What's that supposed to mean?"

The being studied the flickering light. "Well, it's worth a try. I am a chronologist. I manage this sector of the galactic."

"A chronologist?"

"We are tasked with recording the long count of this universe."

"Okay. . . ." Liam looked around. "Where are we? Is this the past? Because I have to get back to my present. We're in danger and—"

"I have constructed a brief bubble within spacetime so we could meet. Time is 'frozen,' as you might say."

"So I'm here? Or I'm back there?"

"Yes."

"Um, okay." Liam decided to move on. "But if you were dead on Mars, how can you be here now?"

"*Now* and *then* are constraints of three-dimensional beings. You also have my recorder."

Liam held up his orange crystal. "This one is that one?" The chronologist nodded again. "There was a message," said Liam. "It translated into our language—is that what the crystal is doing now? Translating between us?"

"One of the recorder's functions is to bridge communication. What did the message say?"

"That we should take the crystal to the nearest regional manager's office."

The chronologist sighed again. "I see."

Liam cocked his head. "You sound disappointed."

"You cannot exactly get to my office."

"Well, no. We looked it up; it's pretty far away."

"That is putting it mildly."

"Yeah, so we decided to take it with us, because we need the information about the stars, what the Drove are doing to them, so we can show it to—"

"Hold on. The who?"

"The Drove. You know, the guy in the— Oh."

"What?"

"I was going to say the guy in the metal suit, but . . . he, well, I don't know if I should tell you."

"You should tell me."

"He's the one who kills you. On Mars. Or already did?"

"I haven't gone there yet. It is in my future. So you took the crystal because of the message. And you took my watch because . . ."

"I wanted proof about you. None of my people have ever seen an alien before. Or we hadn't, as of then. I'm not sure what's happened since." Liam held out his wrist beside the crystal. "Do you want them back?"

"I am going to need that crystal, and you *shouldn't* have taken the watch, but I cannot take either of them at this moment, because I already have them. That would likely cause another superposition, and you've already created enough of those."

"Superstitions? What do you mean?"

"Do you even know what a *superposition* is?"

"Not really."

"You have been using the watch."

"Just a couple times," said Liam.

"And what made you think that was a good idea?"

Liam shrugged. "It helped me see what was going to happen, so I could save people I know from dying. And . . . I've also used it to go back in time a bit."

The chronologist focused on her crystal for a moment. "According to your nuclei, you have made twelve discrete arc-lines in space-time. That is no small amount for a being of your composition. You're fortunate that you weren't torn apart into your base particles."

"I, um, I guess. So you mean I really have been traveling in time?"

"Of course. Are you aware of how my chronometer works?"

"Your what?"

"My watch."

"Oh, sorry. It shows you the future and the past."

"The watch creates a dilated time transit field around its wearer."

"Does that mean it shows you the future and the past?"

"For you, yes. And what were you trying to do here, just now?"

"I came back to see if I could find out what my friend was doing when we were down here."

The chronologist checked her crystal. "You are having a curious interaction with the watch. How have you been feeling since you began these trips?"

Liam felt like he was at the doctor. "Kinda weird, I guess."

"Have you experienced anything unusual?"

"You mean like in addition to time traveling? I usually feel pretty sick afterward."

"Have you experienced any anomalies in your perceived timeline?"

"My perceived . . ." Liam thought of the weird dream, or vision, he'd had. Seeing himself back at the supernova in the skim drone, feeling terrified by it. "I've seen something that scared me, that felt almost real, more real than a dream anyway, kinda like a memory, except it never happened."

"I see. And have you been able to deviate from your own timeline?"

"You mean, like, see stuff that I didn't see at the time?"

"Possibly."

"How did you know about that?"

The chronologist just looked at him.

"Fine. I can sorta push into other spots. Like move away from myself in the past. That's what I was trying to do down here, to see something I didn't see the first time. But then it got strange."

"Strange how?"

"Like I saw another version of me, or something."

"That likely explains it." The chronologist began tapping her version of the watch. "Thank you. I will release you now and return you to your native space-time coordinate."

"Wait, hold on! What's going on? You have to tell

me. One of those supernovas destroyed my solar system, and now we're in a war with some mysterious group of people, or aliens, or something. I don't know what to do next!"

The chronologist paused. "Supernovas?"

"Yeah, the ones you were monitoring from Mars."

"*Will be* monitoring. These supernovas you speak of haven't begun yet."

"For you, maybe, but they have for us."

The chronologist thought for a moment. "Fine. Tell me, then; what did you see just before I isolated us?"

"Well, it was like there were two of me. One was doing what I remember doing, but then I saw this other one that was doing something different." Liam thought of that moment where he'd wondered about following Phoebe. That slight mistrust. "Actually, I think maybe the other me was doing something I *thought* about doing at the time but then didn't. And they got all mixed up and it felt like both were happening at once."

"You perceived two experiences at the same time."

"Well, sort of, except I only did one."

"You only did one in this reality."

"What's that mean?"

The chronologist looked around the room. "Again, it would be hard for you to understand."

"All of this is hard to understand."

She consulted the crystal.

"Tell me," Liam pleaded.

"Just a moment. I am scanning your brain to find a suitable reference point. Okay, this should work. Imagine that you had a . . . are they called nutri-bars?"

"Um, yeah?"

"Good. Imagine you have a nutri-bar and you are deciding whether or not to eat it. You weigh your hunger against how you'll feel after, or whether you want something else. In that moment, both futures—the one where you eat it, and the one where you don't—are possible. There are even more futures, like where you choose to eat something else, or drop the bar on the ground, and when you bend over you accidentally hit your head and pass out, but for the moment let's just focus on the two basic choices. They both exist, in a sense, superimposed on each other in space-time. When you have used the watch to go into the future, you have been in moments of choice, where multiple outcomes were possible. The watch followed the future that was most probable at that moment, and alerted you to a negative outcome, as the watch is designed to protect itself from damage."

"I thought it was trying to keep me alive," said Liam.

The chronologist continued: "So let's say you

choose to eat the bar. The moment you do that, only one reality becomes *your* reality, and the other reality, the other possible outcome, no longer exists in your universe. But even though it is lost to you, it is not gone. That other outcome—you *not* eating the bar and everything that happens after that—moves along in its own reality, same as with every other choice you ever make or don't make."

"So . . . you're saying there's a version of me not eating the nutri-bar in, like, an alternate universe?"

"Essentially."

"But I've made billions of choices in my life. And so has every other person and animal and . . ."

"Yes, yes, it's a lot of universes, but we're talking about infinity, after all, so this is really just normal operating procedure. Sometimes, realities recombine later, so there's some conservation there. Eventually, this universe will have expended all of its energy and reached a point of maximum entropy, and that will be that. No doubt it's an overwhelming idea to a mind like yours. And there's no way you could ever really perceive these multiple realities, though I would imagine that your scientists have seen some evidence on a quantum level. But ultimately, you can't help but see yourself as a fixed center of your single reality. Unless, of course"—the chronologist seemed to perform her version of a smirk—"you borrowed another being's watch and used it to do things that you other-wise couldn't."

Liam tried to keep up. "Okay, so . . . you're saying that, down here, I saw the other possible outcome of the moment when I thought about following Phoebe. I saw what would happen if I did follow her. Like in a parallel universe. And I was able to see it because I've been using the watch?"

"Yes."

"But that doesn't make sense. I also saw it in the hallway *before* I used the watch, like when I was down here for real."

"Again, that's a linear way of looking at it. By trav-eling back in this direction along your timeline, and by then trying to follow an alternate decision, this *later* version of you caused the reality overlap that the earlier version of you saw."

Liam shook his head. "Sure. So, if I had chosen to go follow Phoebe in my real timeline, I would have caused an explosion that would have killed us both."

"You did cause that explosion, in another reality. Then there is another reality where you nearly caused that explosion, but didn't, and so on."

"But why was I able to see it? I thought you said that you couldn't see the other possible outcomes of choices?"

"Yes, well, you're not *supposed to* be able to. And

now we have finally gotten to the real reason why I'm here. By pushing out of your own timeline and following this other probable outcome, you inadvertently created a tear in your reality at a probability node, and that other reality bled in."

"I didn't mean to."

"Of course you didn't. Beings like you don't mean to do a lot of things." The chronologist gestured over her shoulder. "I was just working on patching it up, but I'm not sure yet if it will hold. As you would say, time will tell, which, by the way, is humorous."

Liam looked past her down the hall. "Is a tear bad?"

"In a word: yes. But what's curious is that this is not the first time this has happened in this location. This specific area of space-time is a bit of a weak point in the boundaries between realities, it seems. I am still trying to determine what originally caused that weakness."

"It wasn't . . . me, was it? I didn't, like, break space-time?"

"Ha, no. The energy required to create this kind of damage far exceeds anything you are capable of. But the point is, it was extra dangerous to attempt to leave your timeline in this particular spot."

"I didn't really know—"

"This kind of tear in space-time can cause realities

to bleed together, which could lead to a paradox cascade."

"A what?"

She checked her crystal again. "Okay, imagine a whirlpool, or a tornado. Imagine so many of them converging that they form a giant spiraling system that sucks up everything around it to the point where it even sucks up itself. Then imagine that happening in a chain reaction on a multi-universe-wide scale."

"You mean like a giant black hole?"

The chronologist made a snorting sound, perhaps a laugh. "Black holes are adorable. Paradox cascades are catastrophic."

Liam glanced at the watch. "So I should stop using this."

"Well, the watch was not meant for you, and you were not meant for it, so, probably. It's more that you should stop trying to follow realities that aren't your primary one."

"You said this isn't the first time this has happened."

"Correct," said the chronologist. "This is one of a few locations where these weak points in the fabric of the universe have appeared. It's an ongoing inquiry. I suspect that it is related to the data you have from my observatory, and these Drove that you mentioned, but I won't know for a few more millennia. Which reminds me, I should release you and get back to work."

"Oh." Liam tried to push aside these enormous thoughts. Phoebe was still back in the cockpit, maybe a traitor, with Barro and that Comet closing fast. "Yeah, I guess."

"Scans indicate that you are unsatisfied with our conversation."

"It's just that I came back here because I needed answers and I still don't know what to do."

"Answers are the easy part. Finding the right question is often much harder."

"Maybe for you."

The chronologist peered down at him. "May I ask, what exactly were you trying to discover on your alternate timeline?"

"It will probably sound silly."

"You might as well try me."

"I was trying to figure out if I can trust my friend or not."

"Hmm. . . ." The chronologist checked her crystal. "A friend is a companion organism."

"Yeah."

"I see. You gain advantages by cooperation."

"You make us sound like ants."

The chronologist shrugged. "And you did not observe enough to answer your question?"

"I'm pretty sure she was doing something here

that she was keeping secret, but I wasn't able to find out why."

"You do not have the proof you sought. Do you believe in her?"

"In Phoebe? Well . . . yeah, I guess I do. I'm just not sure."

"Trust is a powerful adaptation of three-dimensional beings. The hope or belief in something. It's your engine for still making a choice when you don't have all possible information. Even a four-dimensional being such as myself never has all the answers. Seeing what happens tomorrow or three million years ago doesn't always tell you *why* it happened." She consulted her crystal. "You have these expressions, *follow your heart*, or *go with your gut*. I don't think trust actually has anything to do with your internal organs, but either way: maybe this is a good time to employ that strategy in making your choice."

"But what if I'm wrong?"

The chronologist's face wrinkled into something like a smile. "I'm sure you will have an opportunity to make a new choice and correct for it, assuming this choice doesn't immediately kill you."

Liam's heart raced. "I know you said no time is passing here, but I still feel like I need to get back." He held out the crystal. "You sure you don't want this now?"

"This is not when I acquire it."

"But how will I get it to you?"

The chronologist paused. It seemed to Liam like her face shifted for a moment, the skin somehow withering. Then she was back. "You will have to experience that for yourself." She tapped her crystal. "Good luck."

"You believe in luck?" said Liam.

"Not really."

Everything around him began to blur. The corridor faded, swirled, and all at once Liam found himself in the cockpit of the cruiser again, back in his present.

He blinked at white spots in his eyes. Clenched his stomach to keep from throwing up. Phoebe was gazing at him, still bound to the chair. JEFF was still at the controls. Outside, the enemy ship was getting closer, its engines lighting up the dark.

"Liam . . . ," said Phoebe.

He shook his head, the encounter with the chronologist like a recent dream, already hazy in his mind. He thought of what he'd seen in that moment when he'd followed Phoebe into the room with the backup recorder. She'd used this dampener that he was holding in his hand now. JEFF was right—she'd sabotaged the recorder, or it had seemed that way. And yet she had said she was on his side, that she'd done it for them. Could that be true? Or was it a traitorous lie to cover up other traitorous lies?

Do I trust her? Liam bit his lip.

He slapped the dampener's suction cup against the back of JEFF's head and pressed the red button.

"Liam—" JEFF began.

There was a whump of magnetic charge. JEFF slumped over. Liam reached around him and powered down the thrusters. The cruiser settled onto the ground.

Fresh tears fell from Phoebe's eyes. "Thank you."

Liam couldn't quite look at her. He wasn't in any mood to be thanked. "Now what?"

"Cut me loose. We need to get back inside the station."

8

Liam hurried into the main cabin and grabbed a pair of utility scissors from a drawer in the galley. He returned and sawed at the red plastic cable that JEFF had tied around Phoebe.

"Hurry," said Phoebe.

"I'm trying!" Her link was still blinking with that white light. "What is that?"

"We have a special program that lets us communicate."

Liam grunted, slashing at the stubborn cables. "Who's we?"

"Them." She motioned out the cockpit. "And me.

I'll explain later. We have to get back inside before they land."

Liam estimated the Comet was ten kilometers out, maybe less. "So you knew them," he said angrily. He remembered that same light now on Phoebe's link, all the way back at Saturn, just before they'd made contact with Mina and the *Scorpius*. He was so stupid! But there had been so much going on that he hadn't even given it a thought. "When that guy Barro was at our door back at Saturn. You *knew* who he was and you acted like you didn't."

Phoebe nodded. "I couldn't tell you. I'm sorry."

"No." Liam stepped back. "You *could* have, but you chose not to."

"I said I'm sorry. And I wanted him to keep thinking that I was doing my job, that I still had my cover—"

"So, what, you're like a spy? For who?"

"I'm not a spy! Not exactly. But Barro had to think I was still on his side so he wouldn't suspect that I'd betray him. Which I *did*, remember?"

"How do I know that wasn't part of the plan, too?"

"Because I'm telling you it wasn't! Also, how could shooting my own people down and leaving them behind be part of the plan? Now finish cutting. If they catch us, they'll . . ."

Liam crossed his arms. "What?"

Phoebe sighed. "What do you think? Look what they did to this place, and to the *Scorpius* and Saturn Station."

Liam pointed out the window. "So Barro did this?"

"No, we have another ship. Our main transport. It's way more powerful. But those two won't think twice about killing you or anyone else, no matter what I say."

"What the heck did we ever do?" said Liam.

"It's a long story. I swear I will tell you everything later."

"Why didn't you tell me before now?"

"Because I was waiting for the right time."

"And when was that going to be?"

"I have no idea!" Phoebe's head dropped. "It's all been crazy, and I hoped maybe I wouldn't even *have* to tell you until we were safe! I was wrong, okay? I did my best but I screwed up!" she motioned out the cockpit window. "They don't know what we know, about the Drove, and they don't understand what I do. . . . But Barro will never listen to me. You heard me try back at Saturn. So we have to get to the *Scorpius* and get our parents treated. My parents will listen, I know they will."

But Liam felt frozen in place. "Did your parents sabotage the turbines?"

"I . . . think it was an accident—"

186

"Phoebe. Look, I believe you, okay? But I have to know. My parents almost died."

Phoebe's mouth scrunched. "They didn't tell me everything, not the details. Their plan was to try to get the final data, I know that. And then we were supposed to leave on the *Scorpius* and meet up with Barro and Tarra—she's the commander—out at Saturn. My parents got hurt down there, too! They definitely didn't mean to cause the meltdown. Well . . ." She sighed. "They did send us out to those air vents, though. Really far away from the explosion. Maybe they knew whatever they were planning might be dangerous, but I don't know, because I swear they didn't tell me! They barely told me anything, except . . ."

"Except what?"

Phoebe checked out the cockpit again. "Please, I'll explain more later."

Liam thought of his parents, their faces through the stasis pods, the radiation burns on their cheeks, of them lying injured down in that cave . . . He shook his head. "Fine. But I swear I might still leave you here."

"Maybe I'd deserve it."

Liam knelt back down and dug at the cables with the scissors. Finally, a few lengths frayed apart and Phoebe was able to wriggle free. She jumped up, shaking feeling back into her hands.

"Okay, we have to put on the space-grade suits

and then get back into the station." She darted into the main cabin, yanked open the closet, and pulled out the suits. She handed him one.

"Why these?" said Liam. "Won't they just slow us down?"

"Just trust me, okay?"

Liam glared at her. "I already am trusting you, a lot."

"I know." She reached back into the closet for two stun rifles and handed one to Liam. "You'll need this, too."

Liam gripped the cool plastic, a bolt of fear shooting through him.

"And you have the Phase Two data, right?"

He felt his pockets for what seemed like the hundredth time. "Yeah. But what about our parents?"

"They'll be safe here. Barro and Tarra will be more concerned with the data."

"So what are we going to do, run?" said Liam, thinking back to Saturn's rings. "They're not going to fall for that a second time."

"That's why you're taking me hostage."

A rumble grew outside, and the whine of slowing thrusters.

"They're here." Phoebe plunked the large helmet over her head. "Come on!" She punched the controls on the airlock and stepped through the inner door.

Liam put down the rifle and started tugging the suit over his thermal wear. He got it up to his waist and then paused, looking down at his Dust Devils shirt. He grabbed the bottom and yanked it over his head.

"I understand if you want to trash it," said Phoebe, looking back at him.

Liam frowned. "No." And now he wanted to put it back on, or not; oh, whatever! Either way there wasn't time, so he balled it up and threw it in the closet. He shoved the helmet on and was just sealing it up when Phoebe popped open the outer airlock door without bothering to close the inner door. She leaped out as the cabin depressurized and a torrent of wind swirled around Liam. He grabbed a wall handle to steady himself, picked up the stun rifle, and stepped toward the door, but then, after checking to see that Phoebe was out of sight, he doubled back into the cockpit and yanked the dampener off JEFF's head. He hurried back to the airlock, stowing the device in a pocket. He shut the inner door, hit the closing cycle on the outer door, and jumped out too.

The moment he landed, Liam had to throw himself to the ground. The air roared with light and heat. He rolled onto his back to see the sleek silver side foils of the Comet lowering right above him. Its landing gear crunched against the black rock. Liam scrambled out of the way and vaulted after Phoebe, who

189

was bounding toward the station. It was harder to run in these bulky suits, but Liam could still cover many meters with each step in the low gravity. Behind them, the Comet's engines cycled down.

They ducked through the half-open door, and Liam slowed as his thick sleeves scraped against the sides. A suit tear now was not an option. They ran down the dark, frosted halls back into the wrecked casino. Phoebe led the way straight toward the baths. The airlock windows glowed bright orange. As the doors slid open, a massive cloud of gelatinous steam burst out. It froze on contact with the air, instantly creating delicate folds of ice that shattered against them. Phoebe pushed her way inside. Liam followed, and she shut the door behind them.

Their suits began to hum, cooling this time, instead of heating up, and the outsides of their helmets were immediately covered with condensation. Liam wiped it away with his thick sleeve. To either side, the bubble-like glass walls had fogged up, and the baths had filled with the purplish vapor, roiling and folding in heavy billows. Here and there, it jetted through the cracks in the containers, clouding the hallway.

"Now what?" he asked, following Phoebe as she hurried through the steam.

She stopped midway down the hall, at the control panel beside a clear door that opened into one of the baths. This was one of the containers that had cracked in a few places around its curved wall. Steam hissed out of the jagged fissures. Standing this close to it made Liam's link flash: *WARNING. UNSTABLE ATMOSPHERE. USE CAUTION.*

"First we're going to crank this up," said Phoebe. She pressed the touchscreen temperature dial for the bath and raised it to maximum. There was a loud series of hisses and the steam grew thicker inside the bath. Phoebe pulled open the door and steam clouds tumbled out, the viscous consistency making a slippery hiss across their suits.

Phoebe motioned across the walkway. "Go do the same thing with that one."

Liam moved to the other side in a single leap. He found the temperature dial on an identical panel and slid it to max; then he pulled open the door. The gelatinous fog thickened, and their suits chirped complaints about the worsening conditions.

Phoebe was blinking rapidly and tried instinctively to rub her eyes, her hand hitting the glass of her helmet.

"The heat was getting to you before, too," said Liam, feeling sweat beading on his own forehead, despite his suit's best efforts.

Phoebe nodded. "If I'm right, those two will read the Delphi atmosphere and come after us in simple pressure suits. They won't—*cough*—be enough in here."

"What do you mean?" Liam checked his link. "It's really hot but not, like, lethal."

"You'll see," said Phoebe. "Go in there." She pointed to the bath he'd turned up. "When they come in, you call them toward you on your link. *Cough.* They'll track you to the bath." She held up her stun rifle. "I'll make sure they end up inside with you. Then you stun them, too, and while they're out of it, we'll pull off their pressure suit helmets and lock them in."

Liam looked up and down the hall. "Why would they fall for that? They're going to see that we're in different places."

"If I'm right about them wearing pressure suits, this heat is going to make it hard for them to see and hear. And I'll turn off my link completely so they can't track it."

"And what if they're in their space suits?"

Phoebe shrugged. "Then we'll need a new plan. *Cough.* Trust me, this will work."

Liam almost protested. *Trust her.* . . . But it was too late to turn back now. He had made his choice, and she was all he had, for better or worse.

"Okay." He waded through the gelatinous fog and ducked through the door into the bath container.

The strange steam pressed against his suit, which hummed at max power. He grabbed the inner railing and stepped down onto the rounded inside. The far side was barely visible.

He half walked, half swam to the other end, then turned and leaned against the curved wall, breathing hard, the stun rifle in his gloved hands, his palms slick with sweat.

"Liam," said Phoebe over the link.

"Yeah."

"I'm going dark. *Cough.* Watch for them."

Liam checked his link settings and saw Phoebe wink out. He peered out of the tank, at the blurry chambers to either side, at the hallway. Steam jets hissed all around him, but otherwise there was silence.

He crouched there—

But then he slipped again in his mind, and found himself back in the skim drone. The great boiling sun far too close, tossing its flares in a tantrum. A fear crept up inside him that he'd be too late, that he was going to miss something. And now he was opening the canopy top of the skim drone as it hurtled through space, strange flashes of light all around him. There was so little time! And yet it was almost like he wanted to get closer to that inferno—

Back in the tank. Liam had fallen over on his side. What was happening? That weak point the chronologist had mentioned: maybe it was still affecting him. His head swam but he shook it off and righted himself. He checked the watch. It had started blinking blue.

His link was also flashing. Liam saw a familiar name on the screen: *Simon Onatu*. This was the name that had appeared back at Saturn, when Barro had tried to board the cruiser. It was from a stolen link, presumably the owner of Barro's last ship. Liam's heart raced. He breathed deep and tapped the name.

"Hey there, kid," said Barro. His deep voice sounded like he was always grinning. "Fancy seeing you on this rock."

Liam didn't answer. He wanted to shout something, as mean as he could. At the same time, he also wanted to ask Barro about Phoebe.

"Not feeling chatty? All right, I get it. So, we're doing this again, huh? You've got the data and we're supposed to come find it?"

Liam swallowed hard, shaking all over. "I've got Phoebe, too. I know she's working with you and I'll kill her if you don't leave us alone."

"Well, I have a hard time believing that, and yet it would certainly be a very *human* thing for you to do. When in doubt, just kill 'em! Yee haw! Sorry, had some time to kill on the flight here and finally watched that show that Phoebe was always talking about, *Raiders of the Lost Planet.* Space cowboys and explorers and all that. Pretty fun stuff, I have to admit."

There was a distant hiss. Through the sea of steam, Liam could just make out the airlock doors sliding open and a figure stepping in, wearing black—a pressure suit, just as Phoebe had predicted.

"From what I saw in those old movies," said Barro, "before you slaughter all the helpless villagers, you're supposed to fall in love with the beautiful girl. I'm betting that's what's happened to you, and you're just bluffing about killing our dear Phoebe. Would explain her recent behavior, too."

"Don't come any closer, or you'll find out."

Barro didn't respond. Liam ducked to get a slightly better view and saw him standing just inside the hallway. He seemed to be fiddling with his suit. He took a step and stopped again. It looked like he was rubbing at his mask.

"Man," he finally said, breathing hard, "you humans—*cough*—have some weird preferences. But here's the catch, *Liam.* You're right, I'm not going to come any farther, because you're going to come out. Otherwise, my associate, Tarra, who is currently on board your ship, is going to open up your parents' stasis tubes and toss them out onto this icy nowhere, and then we can watch them shrivel up and die."

"No!" Liam shouted before he could stop himself.

Stupid! Of course they'd split up. Why hadn't he thought of that? Why hadn't Phoebe?

Or had she?

"So why don't you bring me my girl, right now, before I give Tarra the signal. She's not really the patient type. Might just kill them anyway if she gets bored. I'd say it's best not to keep her waiting."

Liam cursed to himself. His heart sank and he nearly punched the glass beside him. He peered across the way and saw Phoebe crouched inside the door of the opposite chamber. If she'd powered down, she wasn't hearing any of this. Unless . . .

No! She's not working with them! It was just that Barro had outsmarted them. Had JEFF had time to power back up? Even if he had, would he be any match for Tarra? Liam couldn't be sure, which meant he had no choice now, with his parents' lives at stake.

"You win," he said. "I'm coming." Liam floated across the chamber, shaking, and climbed back out into the hallway.

"Good. I'll just—*cough*—be waiting right outside these doors."

Liam caught Phoebe waving her hands furiously at him as if to say, *What are you doing?* Liam mouthed back, *My parents!* Phoebe cocked her head like she didn't understand, but Liam just motioned to her to come along, and started up the hall. Maybe she could convince Barro to let them live.

Liam could just make out Barro's silhoutte through the billowing steam. He'd turned and was stepping slowly to the side of the hallway, moving carefully, with his hands outstretched. When his palms hit the curved glass of one of the baths, he started, shuffling his feet and turning so that his back was to Liam. Almost like he was trying to find the door.

He can't see, like Phoebe said. Liam looked at his link and saw that the temperature in the chamber had passed one hundred and fifty degrees. If Barro really was blinded . . . Liam picked up his pace, raising his stun rifle and readying to pull the trigger. He hadn't ever actually used one, other than in the brief orientation his dad had given him one time at the research station, but as he remembered it, all he had to do was aim and pull the trigger.

Barro was just a few meters away. Liam raised the rifle. You had to be pretty close, Dad had said.

"Kid, you forgot," Barro said over the link, his back still to Liam. "I've got you—*cough*—on the link screen here." He spun around, a rifle of his own trained. His mask was completely fogged up. "So don't think you can sneak up on me."

Move! Liam thought, but too late. A bolt of blue energy shot out of Barro's rifle. With his sight impaired, Barro's aim was off, but the charge still just caught Liam in the arm, and fingers of shocking white spiderwebbed around him. Liam felt a jolt throughout his body and was thrown onto his back, his helmet banging against the floor. His eyes burned, his teeth gritting reflexively, arms and legs twitching, but the space-grade suit dispersed the energy just enough that he didn't lose consciousness, and he was still able to see and hear, albeit through tears and a wicked ringing in his ears. And yet he couldn't quite move, and he'd lost track of his rifle.

Barro stepped over him, his face still hidden by steam. He aimed the rifle again, not quite at Liam, but close enough, and jabbed it at him as he spoke. "You have no idea what your people have done, do you?" He was shouting now. "Just imagine—*cough*—when we kill your parents and then imagine it a thousand times over—*coughcough*—and even then you *still* won't know what it felt like. What it's felt like every day since—"

Phoebe came at him from the side. She jammed her stun rifle directly against Barro's neck and fired. Barro spasmed, jolted briefly off the ground by the threading bolts, and was tossed a meter to the side, slamming into the flex-glass wall. He made a choking, gasping sound as he crumpled in a heap on the floor.

Phoebe stared at him for a moment, chest heaving, before turning to Liam. "Why did you move?"

she said, back on the link. She offered her hand. Liam had to really focus on which muscles were which to reach her, and she dragged him up onto wobbly feet.

"He said Tarra is with my parents. She'll kill them."

Phoebe frowned. "I'm so stupid. Yeah, she might."

"We have to get back."

Phoebe turned for the door but then paused. "Oh, wait. . . ." She darted over to Barro, rolled him onto his back, and pulled his helmet off. He moaned slightly, his head lolling back and forth.

"Why are you doing that?" Liam asked.

"Because it will help keep him down. Ready?"

Liam found his stun rifle and they made their way out of the baths, back across the casino, and through the halls, emerging outside in the dark, a wicked wind strafing them with ice flecks.

"Hey," said Phoebe as Liam started bounding toward the cruiser. "We should have a plan. We can't just walk in there."

Liam kept going. "We're out front," he said into his link, hoping against hope. "What's the status in there?"

"Who are you talking to?" Phoebe asked.

They reached the cruiser and the airlock door slid open. JEFF appeared. "There was an intruder," he said. "I thought it would be best to incapacitate her. Are you okay?"

Liam sighed with relief. "Thanks, JEFF." He turned to Phoebe. "I reactivated him, in case anything happened."

Phoebe eyed JEFF with a frown.

"It is my duty to restrain her again," said JEFF.

Liam unzipped the pocket on his sleeve and pulled out the magnetic dampener. "JEFF, I need you to override that command, or I'm going to have to use this. Phoebe's on our side."

"I do not believe there is enough evidence at this point to—"

"I believe her. And technically, I'm in command of this ship, right?"

The bot's eyes flickered. "Acknowledged. But in this case my protocols state—"

"JEFF"—Liam waved the dampener—"you're not allowed to incapacitate *me*, are you?"

"No."

"So . . ."

"Would the captain like me to amend my security protocols to make an exception?"

"Yes, JEFF."

"Are you sure?"

Liam paused. Was he? But he'd just seen Phoebe stun Barro, once again choosing him over them. How much more did he need?

"I'm sure." He turned to Phoebe. "You better

explain everything once we're out of here."

"I will. Let's get Tarra and take her in where Barro is. And then we go."

"Can you get us ready to fly?" Liam asked JEFF.

"Acknowledged. But I have to say, the arrival of this Moon Racer has provided us with a very convenient fuel source, not to mention a place to salvage parts."

Liam peered at the underside of the craft. "Same thrusters?"

"Yes, though I am less sure about their antenna."

"Can you fix that stuff fast? We need to get out of here."

"I can salvage the parts now, and then make the repairs once we are on the journey. Only the thruster will be a challenge during takeoff, but I calculate that we can make it, if we are not being immediately pursued."

"Okay, get to work."

Liam and Phoebe leaped up through the door and found Tarra lying stunned on the floor of the living area. Phoebe grabbed her arms. Liam bent to grab her legs and paused.

"What?"

"Nothing."

"What is it?"

"I just thought . . . It's really nothing."

"Liam, tell me."

"It was bad, but, just for a second, I thought that maybe we should kill them." He looked up to find Phoebe's eyes wide. "Sorry, I didn't mean it. I couldn't—" He was going to say he couldn't *imagine* doing it, except that he had, vividly. Pictured dragging them out into the cold and tearing open their suits just like Barro had mentioned doing to his parents. Even now, the idea of it made his jaw clench and his hands close into fists. That's what they deserved for all this.

He figured Phoebe would be mad, but she spoke quietly. "Please, no more killing. I know they've done terrible things, but they're like family. And I don't have much left." Tears welled up in her eyes.

"Sorry." Liam grabbed Tarra's legs. She wasn't very heavy in Delphi gravity, and they carried her swiftly back through the complex to the steamy bath hallway.

Barro was still there, rolled over on his side, his chest rising and falling slowly. Liam could only see the back of his head and worried for a moment that he might be pretending to be unconscious, but he didn't move. They dropped Tarra beside him, and as Liam backed away, Phoebe pulled off Tarra's helmet. She stood and crossed her arms, staring at them.

"Are they really family?" Liam asked.

"No. They were my dad's coworkers."

"Like in the army or something?"

"They're scientists. . . . They used to be."

Liam fought another swell of anger inside. He knew the urges were wrong, to shout at them even though they were unconscious, to kick them while they were lying there. He balled his fists and shook it off. "We should go." He stepped toward the door and pulled on Phoebe's arm.

She didn't move. Still gazing at them. "Phoebe."

When she turned, she was unhooking her helmet from her space-grade suit. Her eyes were wide, fearful, her mouth small.

"What are you doing?"

"Before we go back on board, I should show you. I don't know how else to do it, and now is as good a time as any." She pulled her helmet off, bent, and placed it on the floor. When she stood, her face was beaded with sweat from the scorching, dripping air, her eyes swollen and red. "This way, if you decide you want to leave me with them, you can."

"Phoebe," said Liam, his pulse speeding up, "I'm not—"

"Just . . . listen, Liam. This is going to be hard. You've known this person for three years, spent all kinds of time with her, at school, at the field station. You kissed her once on the cruiser."

"What do you mean—"

"Shh. Let me finish. The thing is . . ."

Liam was about to interrupt her again, but he stopped because a strange thing had started happening to Phoebe's face, like it was softening somehow, getting shiny, in a way he couldn't quite understand.

"That was Phoebe," she said. "And Phoebe's real, but she's not the whole story. I *had* to lie to you, and I don't want to anymore. So before we leave, you need to know who you're really leaving with."

She stood there, helmet off, trembling in spite of the heat, and ran a finger down her cheek. The motion left a thick purple streak there, spotted with black, but no, that wasn't quite what had happened. More like her skin had been rubbed away and Liam was seeing something beneath it.

Tiny black dots began to appear all over Phoebe's face, prickling up through her skin, as drops of sweat swelled all over—except they were more than just sweat: glistening, opaque beads, as if her skin itself was bubbling. Phoebe's entire face seemed to slide, to droop, like it was becoming liquid, her skin thinning into channels and running down onto her space suit, leaving behind more of the lavender with black spots. Melting and melting, until the person standing before him no longer had human skin at all. She pinched at her eyes and they changed completely, then fiddled around on her scalp and pulled off her pale red hair: a wig. Beneath it was a long, slim braid of silvery, silk-like hair that spiraled around the top of her head.

"This is the real me."

Phoebe blinked her blue-and-black eyes, her pupils sparking gold.

"My name is Xela."

9

"I can't actually see you like this," said Phoebe. "The star where we came from is a red dwarf, so we mainly see by infrared. Without the adapters on my eyes, all this steam is making everything a big bright blur. It'd be like if you stared up at the sun."

Liam rocked on his heels, and the thought that flashed through his mind was: *Run*. Get out of here while she couldn't see. Back to the ship, shove her parents' pods out the door and take off, run for it and never look back. Get back to his people, his world. . . .

Except he had no idea where his people even were. And his world was long gone.

He exhaled hard, hands fidgeting at his sides. "Are you an alien?"

Phoebe risked a slight smile. "Aren't we all?"

"I guess, but you're not human."

Her smile faded. "Do I look it?"

"No." Liam turned to Barro and Tarra. Streaks had appeared on their faces too, the purple, spotted skin showing through. Back to Phoebe. His heart was racing, his nerves ringing. It seemed impossible that what he had just seen had really happened, and yet in some ways it felt as much like a relief as a surprise. *But she's part of the enemy—*

"Are you still there?"

Liam took a deep breath. Her nose was still the same. Her mouth the same shape, her lips a sort of pink, and her teeth humanlike, or were they also a costume? He wanted to ask, but maybe now wasn't the right time.

"Yeah. I'm here."

Phoebe cleared her throat. "We even had our vocal cords surgically altered, to make learning your language easier."

"What did your old voice sound like?"

Phoebe's throat moved up and down. "I can't really do it anymore. It was sort of like human sounds, but also I remember one time we watched a video in class about the rain forests on Earth, and there were these big birds? We made noises like that, too. More musical, I think."

Liam had a million questions knocking urgently on all the doors in his head. Where to even start? And he had to ignore that voice that was still saying *Run!* "Where are you from?"

"A planet called Telos." Phoebe blinked over and over. "Can we talk about this once we've gotten out of here? It's weird talking to a blob, and seriously, if I stay in this steam much longer I might pass out. Our bristles are heat-sensitive too."

"Bristles?"

Phoebe ran a finger over the black dots on her cheek. "We shave them down from time to time, but yeah. Bristles. Plenty of Earth animals have them."

"Does that hurt? Shaving them?"

Another half smile. "It all hurts." She held out her hand. "Help me toward the door?"

Liam looked at her hand. Over her shoulder toward the doors. *This is your last chance—*

But he reached out. Nothing weird about her hand, at least through her space suit, and he reminded himself that, technically, Phoebe wasn't even the weirdest alien he'd seen in the last hour. Still, he'd thought she was one thing and now she was something else.

Except she was still Phoebe . . . wasn't she?

He stepped beside her, put his hand on her shoulder, and turned her toward the door. Bent and grabbed her helmet and raised it over her head.

"Just a sec." Phoebe pressed the adapters back into her eyes, one at a time, and blinked until they were set. "Okay."

Normal-looking eyes made a big difference, Liam found, but he still gritted his teeth and held his breath as he leaned closer to her and lowered her helmet into place. Seeing the bristles on her skin up close . . . like he had to keep telling himself that she wasn't going to bite him or something.

Her fingers fumbled around the helmet. "Everything's still a little fuzzy."

"I got it." Liam attached her clasps, then took her by the wrist and tapped her link, setting the suit controls to maximum to compensate for the heat and steam.

"Can you grab their links?" Phoebe asked. "We don't want them letting the others know about this."

"You mean on the main ship," said Liam. "How many of them—of you—are there?"

"Fifteen, including me and my parents and Barro and Tarra."

Liam stepped over to them—they were stirring a

little now; a brief moan came from Tarra. He tensed as he neared them. "You guys don't have any, like . . . alien powers, do you?"

Phoebe frowned. "Yes, we have lizard tongues that shoot acid."

Liam paused. "You're kidding."

"Liam!"

"Sorry. I just . . ."

"It's okay. You get a pass . . . for like five more minutes."

Liam knelt by Barro and gingerly lifted his arm. Barro twitched just a little and Liam flinched, but Barro's eyes remained closed, his head on the ground. Liam unclipped his link and slid it free. He turned—

Tarra's eyes were open wide. She blinked over and over. "Who's there?" she said groggily.

Liam shuffled closer to her, held his breath, and snatched the link from her suit. She grabbed at him, but too slow, as Liam jumped back to his feet.

"Don't do this, Xela," said Tarra. "Don't betray your own people."

Liam started to shake. He couldn't tell if it was from anger or fear. He wanted to shout at her, felt the urge to kick her again. "Sorry," he said through gritted teeth, and he didn't even know why or what for, but he hurried back to Phoebe. "I got them." He took her by the arm and opened the airlock doors.

They stepped out through the instantly freezing folds of steam. Liam shut the airlock doors and guided Phoebe through the casino wreckage. "Getting any better?"

"Yeah, almost there."

Liam tried to think of what else to say but nothing came out, and they ended up walking through the casino and the halls without speaking.

"Just a sec," said Phoebe as they returned through what had once been the station's comm center. Phoebe stepped around the giant hole in the center of the room, to where the body they'd seen when they first arrived was pinned under rubble. She pulled a piece of ceiling panel free and tossed it across the room. Liam joined her, yanking away twisted lengths of carbon bar and wall sheeting. The body was in a human pressure suit, but when they uncovered the face, Liam saw lavender, bristled skin, and eyes with gold pupils frozen and staring.

Phoebe's head dropped.

"Did you know her?"

"No. She was with us on the way to Mars, but I never talked to her. I'm sure my parents did."

"Do you want to bring her body with us?"

Phoebe shook her head. She pulled away a cracked section of the body's mask and reached inside. "May Ana keep you," she said, trying to push the eyelids down, but they were frozen solid. She spun away and hurried across the room.

Liam took a last wary look at the body—it seemed to stare at him, almost accusingly.

Outside, the wind howled, smaller flecks of the black, rocky ground joining the ice that pattered against their suits. Liam's link flashed; the temperature was dropping fast.

JEFF was outside, rolling between the cruiser and the Comet, his chest lamp illuminating the sleeting crystals. He'd attached a thick hose between the two ships.

Phoebe stopped and turned away from JEFF. "I don't want him to see me," she said quietly over their link channel.

"JEFF," said Liam, summoning his courage. "You heard what I said about overriding your security protocols."

"Acknowledged."

"You're not allowed to change that, no matter what, you understand me?" He tugged Phoebe's arm and she turned back around.

JEFF studied her, eyes flickering. "Acknowledged."

"It will be all right," Liam said to Phoebe.

"I don't know about that, but thanks."

"How's it going with the fuel and parts?" Liam asked JEFF.

"Nearly complete. I've siphoned all of their remaining fuel and salvaged the thruster that we need. I also tried swapping in their long-range antenna, but it is sadly not compatible. Still, our pursuers will have quite a bit to do before they can lift off."

They leaped on board while JEFF stowed the fuel hose.

Phoebe began to pull off her suit and surveyed the streaks of melted skin putty around the collar and down the front. "I guess I should have brought some towels or something."

"Oh, it just looks like a usual face-melting," said Liam. "Happens all the time."

Phoebe smiled. She scraped at the suit with her still-human-looking fingernail, causing flecks to drift to the floor. "Mom would kill me."

"For leaving those two?"

Phoebe laughed darkly. "I just meant about the suit. I don't even know what she'd do if she knew about *that*." She headed for the bathroom.

Liam pulled off his suit and hung both on their chargers, put the stun rifles away, and then went to check on his parents. He paused in front of the four pods and stepped between Phoebe's parents first. Their sleeping faces looked as normal and human as ever. He peered closer: Could he tell that their skin was fake, knowing what he now knew? He felt a fresh surge of anger inside, an electric sensation, thinking of how he'd never really liked them, how they'd seemed mean and strict, and now it made sense: they were the enemy, evil . . . except maybe that wasn't exactly what he felt. Maybe it was more like a kind of sadness, but he wasn't quite sure why.

He moved to his parents' pods. Their faces were the same, readings the same. He tried to imagine what they would say if they knew: that their research partners had been aliens, had meant to steal the work they'd spent their lives on, that the entire human race was depending on. He could imagine Dad getting furious, and Mom . . .

But then he thought that actually, she'd probably be sad like he'd felt a second ago. Angry too, but he remembered what she'd said to him back on Mars: *We'll take it one unknown at a time.* She would want to know more before she made up her mind. About Phoebe. About all of it.

Liam pressed his palms against the glass above their faces, waited a moment until his skin had warmed the smooth surface beneath his touch. "I think I'm doing the right thing," he said quietly. "I hope you're not disappointed." Then he returned to the cockpit.

JEFF was back in the pilot's seat, firing up the thrusters.

"Are we good to go?"

"We have fuel," said JEFF. "I calculate that we can get out of the atmosphere without any catastrophic problems."

"That's not very reassuring."

"I doubt that much about our situation is." He brought up the navigation overlay on the windshield and loaded a departure vector.

Phoebe entered. She'd replaced her wig and put the covering back on her face. She smiled. Same old Phoebe, the girl he'd known for years—except for a purple streak on her neck just below her ear.

"You didn't have to do that," said Liam.

"I thought it was best—what? Did I miss a spot?"

"Yeah." He touched the same spot on his own neck. "You're really good at that. I mean, like a professional makeup artist or something. You could work for VirtCom entertainment." He couldn't help studying her face, looking for signs that it was a mask.

"Well, it's not exactly makeup. It's a smart polymer that conforms to your face. I guess it's technically alive, or something? But I did practice every morning before school for three years, with my mom's help. It didn't look this good at first, but nobody looks at you closely when you're the new kid."

"I thought everybody was pretty nice to you."

"Kinda. But remember at the field station how you and Shawn used to go off, just the two of you, and play with your Raiders figures?"

"Oh. I don't think we meant to ignore you. We just didn't really know what to say."

"I had to map those first couple lava tubes myself before you guys finally started paying attention. And school you in grav-ball."

"Yeah, right."

Phoebe grinned momentarily. "So now what?"

"We will depart and set course for Centauri B," said JEFF."

"Can we catch the *Scorpius*?" Liam asked.

"Even if they are still able to achieve their maximum velocity, our engine is slightly faster. We should be able to make up a four-day head start. And if they have sustained further damage, we should come upon them along the way."

A silence passed over them.

"Is it still going to take thirty-three years?" Liam asked.

"Give or take a month."

Liam felt a sensation like a balloon filling in his head. "But what if the *Scorpius* is being attacked right now? Or next week, or even next year?"

"I know it seems like an impossible time span given the situation, but there is nothing we can do to shorten the distance."

Liam turned to Phoebe. "You said they had another

ship. Do you know what the Teloses' plan is?"

"Telphons," said Phoebe. "That's what we're called. I don't know any specifics. My parents were only tasked with the Phase Two data. We've barely been in contact with the rest of the team these last three years. The mission was all need-to-know, for safety. Maybe my parents knew more, but they never even told me what Barro and Tarra were doing."

"But you knew about this attack," said JEFF. "Which was why you were delaying our arrival."

"After the attack at Saturn, I figured this was their next move based on what I'd heard."

Liam felt his anger boiling up again, thinking of Mina, of Shawn, the *Scorpius* exploding around them. "What good did you think it would do for us to be late?"

Phoebe shrugged. "I wasn't even sure. I was just trying to keep us out of harm's way."

"That didn't really work."

"You and your parents are still alive, aren't you?" Phoebe glared at him momentarily but then held up Barro's and Tarra's links. "I checked them for messages, but there's nothing. The communication system we use doesn't save anything, for security. Clearly the two of them were looking for us, to get the data. But I don't know what the rest of our—*their* team is planning next."

"And what do you know about this ship they have?" said JEFF. Liam thought he could hear a tone of disapproval. "Its weaponry appears to be extremely advanced."

"We borrowed it," Phoebe said carefully, "from the Styrlax. It can travel much faster than anything humans have."

"What's a Styrlax?" said Liam.

"Another alien," said Phoebe.

"You've got to be kidding me."

"No. And they have these ships that can make wormholes. That's how we—they—"

"You can just say *we*," said Liam. "I get it."

"Okay. Well, yeah, that's how we got to Mars so fast. But like I said, I haven't been with the rest of the team since I was ten years old. I'm sorry I don't know more."

"It seems logical," said JEFF, "that with such a small force and only one ship, the Telphons bided their time to obtain the completed Phase Two data, and then waited until humanity was scattered in order to attack, utilizing the element of surprise. By attacking the fleet from the rear and disabling communications, they could create as much confusion as possible. Does that sound about right?"

"I guess," said Phoebe.

Liam eyed Phoebe, thinking again about how if

she had erased the backup recorder, that still fit with this plan JEFF was laying out. . . . He gazed back at the station. "We should have questioned those two."

"They wouldn't have told us anything," said Phoebe. "They'd rather die."

"What about you?"

"I made my choice, okay? We should just go."

"I agree," said JEFF. "Initiating launch sequence."

The thrusters rumbled and the cruiser lurched from the ground. Its headlights swept over the dark station buildings, dead and frosted. Liam wondered how many years or centuries these ruins would sit here silently, looking exactly the same. He wondered if Barro and Tarra would die here, freezing to death or starving, or if they'd be able to get the Comet off the ground and escape. Liam thought that he hoped for the former, and yet his very next thought was that Phoebe would be sad, and also that it was cruel to just leave them here, and yet what other choice was there?

As they rose, he saw the baths beyond the casino dome. Steam was pluming out of those buildings now, catching the wind as it froze and leaping away in strange geometric clouds. The bases of the clouds glowed orange with the light from inside. It looked primal, like the videos Liam had seen of volcanoes back on Earth. There would be nothing warm in space. Thirty-three years of cold and dark awaited them.

The cruiser bucked and hopped in the whipping winds. JEFF accelerated beyond the station and out over the frozen expanse. Ice flashed and blurred in the ship's lights. The hulking wreckage of the *Scorpius* core towered above, the arcing teeth of ice and rock. A rare gap had opened in the cloud layer, revealing a brilliant field of stars. Liam looked from the core to the stars and played with the radio beacon between his fingers, tapping it now and then. He wished it would blink, just once.

"Buckle up for escape thrust," said JEFF. Liam and Phoebe got into their seats as JEFF angled the ship steeply toward the sky, and the frozen wastes of Delphi disappeared behind them.

The cruiser started to rattle and buck, almost like it was skidding on the air.

"Is that okay?" Liam called over the racket.

"It is not ideal," said JEFF. "But we only have to ascend a little bit farther. . . ."

And a moment later they were up and out, the rumble of wind and their engines snuffing to silence, bodies floating against their restraints in zero gravity.

They circled the planet, a slingshot to increase their speed. Along the way they passed the spinning hulk of the starliner's second fusion engine, glowing futilely as it tumbled along in orbit, as well as some other twisted debris, including the wrecks of at least one military cruiser. Liam felt fresh worry, imagining Mina, Shawn, all of them, floating in space. But thankfully, there was no sign of stasis pods.

"Switching off thrusters," said JEFF. "Bringing the fusion engine online."

Liam watched the scanner map with Delphi at the center of many circles. They were merely a dot now too, still nearly on top of the planet.

"Calculating final course vector. And . . . initiating primary burn."

The engine lit up, and Liam felt the hard press back against his seat. The cruiser rumbled around them, making Liam's teeth vibrate, and then shot away from Delphi, into the endless dark once more.

The map flashed off, replaced by a message: *SIGNAL LOST.*

"We are out of range of the backup scanner," said JEFF.

"On our own again," Liam said quietly.

The engine burned for thirty more minutes, a gradual increase until they'd reached their maximum velocity. Then JEFF cut it, and the silence of space engulfed them.

10

Liam gazed out into the empty dark, glittering with distant stars, and tried to keep his feelings steady. A pit had opened in his stomach and he felt himself welling up. Everything was so far away again. It would be thirty-three years before they saw another object that could trick them into believing in solid ground, thirty-three years without setting foot in a place that wouldn't immediately kill them. Thirty-three years with what increasingly felt like merely a thin shell of technology between them and death. Of course it wouldn't feel that long, being in stasis, and yet stasis did its own strange thing to time. He might have only been awake for what amounted to a week now since

Mars, but it felt so much longer, like the ten years had seeped into him in some way that he couldn't quite quantify. And this next journey was more than three times that long.

Phoebe unbuckled and left the cabin. Liam fished Mina's link out of the seat pocket and sent her a message with the beacon.

we think you are headed to destina

we are coming

see you in thirty three years

Of course the beacon didn't blink back. Of course she was in stasis. Hopefully on the *Scorpius*, not tumbling endlessly through the dark. Not among drifting starliner wreckage. If that was the case, he could only hope that her pod was fully functional, that at least she'd be peacefully asleep until her batteries ran out. . . .

Liam felt dizzy, his mouth dry. He shut his eyes tight. Tried to imagine him and Mina together somewhere, but he didn't know where to put them. The balcony on Mars again . . . and yet he could only think of how that spot, that entire planet, didn't even exist anymore.

"I would recommend we prepare for stasis shortly," said JEFF.

Liam unbuckled. "Okay. Give me a minute to talk to Phoebe, okay?"

"Acknowledged." JEFF swiveled around. "Liam, I hope you do not mind me inquiring: If Phoebe is part of the hostile force, have you calculated the odds that she is not being honest with you?"

"I believe her."

"And what about the odds that she is telling you what you want to hear only until she can reunite with her people—"

"Yeah, JEFF!" Liam snapped. "I have *calculated* that, actually. And those odds are still better than any other chance we've got. She's my friend. I don't expect your circuit-board brain to understand, so do me a favor and leave it alone." He thrust himself out of the cockpit.

"Liam," JEFF called from behind him. "I did not intend to anger you—" but Liam just kept moving.

He found Phoebe in back, floating between her parents' pods. "Hey."

Phoebe didn't turn around. "I've been getting up early at every stop and fixing their faces. The putty gets brittle over time."

"You want to tell me more about it?"

Phoebe sighed and spun around. "I do. I'm so sorry . . . but also so mad, and sad. I don't even know how to start."

"I don't either. Maybe tell me about Telos?"

Phoebe's mouth scrunched. "Let's go sit." She

pushed toward the door. They floated back to the main cabin and buckled into the couch.

Liam sat there, not sure what to say. Phoebe stared across the room. Finally she pinched her sleeve and pulled up the fabric tab in the crook of her elbow, where the fluid line went. She ran her finger over the three faded black circles there. The skin covering had cracked beneath them.

"We only put the putty on up to the shoulders," she explained. She dug her fingernail into her elbow and scraped the covering away, exposing the purple and bristled skin beneath. Three permanent black dots were tattooed there.

"I told you my brother and grandparents died in an accident. It's true. Nearly everyone on Telos died. Me and my parents and Barro and Tarra and only like two hundred other people survived."

"That's horrible. What happened?"

Phoebe bit her lip. "We weren't violent people. I mean, there were wars on Telos. Not so much when I was growing up, but there had been big ones in the past. Telos was a little younger than Earth, but we were pretty similar, like our technology and stuff. I don't know. Anyway, it was a mostly peaceful place at the end. There were whole cultures that we lost in the attack."

"You were attacked?" said Liam.

"Sort of. It's . . ." Phoebe rubbed her legs and started to cry. "Remembering is hard."

Liam put his arm around her. He tensed as he did it; again, feeling that weird uncertainty about what she even was that he hated feeling. It was fear, wasn't it? Because he couldn't begin to understand her yet. Except that he knew her pretty well. Didn't he?

"I wish you could see it," said Phoebe. "I wish I could take you there and show you."

Liam pulled his arm back.

"Sorry, am I leaking skin on you? This is why Mom was always so severe. Showing our emotions might literally give us away."

"It's not that." Liam ran his finger over the watch dial. "I just wonder if you could show me with this. Like maybe the watch could take us both back."

"I thought it only worked for the person wearing it."

"Me too. I learned some new things about it when I went back to see what you were doing with the backup recorder. You did erase it, didn't you?"

Phoebe nodded. "I was afraid if the details of the attack got out, colonial would somehow figure out that *we* were Telphons, and then they might not help my parents on the *Scorpius*, or they might just kill us when we got there or something."

"Why didn't you tell me this sooner?"

"I swear as soon as we were safely off Delphi I was going to. That's probably hard to believe."

Liam shrugged. "So you weren't, like, acting on orders?"

"No! The only orders I've ever gotten are to play along, stay out of the way, and not get found out.

"If you'd been able to see me down there, you would have seen me freaking out and yelling at myself and not knowing what to do."

"I did see you," said Liam. Phoebe looked at him oddly. "You looked like you were quietly working."

"Well, yeah, but I was a mess inside. It's been like that the whole time. I have to maintain this perfect exterior, while inside, I'm losing it. I've had to think three times about every single thing I've said, worrying who I'm betraying."

"That sounds hard," said Liam.

Phoebe just nodded. "How did you see me down there? We weren't together."

"I sorta broke from my own timeline. It didn't go well. Turns out if I had followed you, it would have led to the recorder self-destructing. Also I guess I almost caused reality to collapse."

"What are you talking about?"

"I met that alien that we got the watch from, and she told me."

"You mean the scientist alien? She wasn't dead?"

"She's called a chronologist. I guess for her, it was earlier in time."

"That's confusing."

"It got worse. She was fixing a weak spot in space-time. She said it was already there, and I kinda ran into it when I pushed out of my own timeline."

"How exactly did you leave your timeline?"

"I can't really do it. Just sort of. She said I've been altered by using the watch, or something."

"None of that sounds good, Liam. Maybe we shouldn't use it anymore."

"She just said I shouldn't try to push out of my own timeline again. But it mainly had to do with being in that spot. Here's the thing: she said what the watch does is create a time field around the person wearing it. So I wonder if we could get it to create a field around both of us. Then we could see things together."

"How would we do that?"

"I don't know. Maybe if we held hands or something." Liam pulled off the watch and held it out to her.

Phoebe raised an eyebrow at him.

"It's just a theory. But if it works, you could show me where you're from."

"All right." Phoebe slipped on the watch and took his hand. Her fingers and skin still felt human.

"Here goes." She turned the dial backward.

Liam felt something. A sort of nauseous swaying, like he'd suddenly lost his balance, or the belt holding him to the couch had come undone. Echoes in his head like backward voices, him and Phoebe talking, the shouting back on Delphi, and Liam thought he saw the steam baths kind of appear around him.

Then he rushed back to the present. Phoebe was blinking at him. "Did it work?"

"I think it almost did, but I only saw back a little ways."

"I went all the way to Telos. It seemed like maybe you were there but then I couldn't see you." Phoebe unbuckled and floated up. She slid her toe under the edge of the couch so that she was in a standing position. "Maybe we need to be closer. Get up."

Liam unbuckled. "What do you mean?" He hooked his toe like Phoebe so that he was standing, facing her.

"Hug me," said Phoebe, glancing quickly away as she said it.

"Hug?" Liam's mouth was instantly dry, his armpits sweating.

"Yes, duh, a hug. Don't make it any more awkward than it already is, okay? But maybe if we're that close, the watch will take us both."

"Um . . ."

"Just come on." Phoebe pushed toward him and wrapped her arms around him. "This is another thing that if you ever tell Shawn—"

"I know already, just try it." Liam put his arms around her.

"Okay." She craned to see over his shoulder and her chin rubbed past his neck and he thought of how her skin wasn't her real skin and how he'd even thought it was strange when he'd kissed her that time. *I kissed an alien.* He could feel her fiddling with the watch, heard it click, and he held his breath—

They started moving, together.

The world slipped and lurched out of gear, into reverse. Liam could still see himself hugging Phoebe in the cabin, but he also saw a backward view first of the Delphi baths, then off the frozen planet into space.

"Ooh, shut your eyes!" said Phoebe, her voice breezy and distant but also seemingly inside his ear.

"Why?"

"I'm going to the bathroom!"

Liam saw the cruiser's bathroom door close—he really was seeing Phoebe's version of history around him—and he shut his eyes tight.

"Okay, you can open them." Liam saw a long, gray period of just dull shadows, with little blooms of color here and there. "Just boring old stasis," said Phoebe.

She pulled away and stood beside him.

"Wait—" Liam began, but then he saw that back in the cockpit, they were still hugging.

"I think it's okay. Hang on, I'm going to speed things up." She clicked the dial two more notches.

Liam winced, a headache slivering through his mind. He felt himself wobbling on his feet, but not really on his feet. More like wobbling in reality, and there was that hollow feeling again, like all the tiny spaces inside him, right down to his cells, were expanding. Outside, they left stasis, zipped around—Liam briefly saw them flying through the comet fragments, and then he saw the skim drone from a distance as Phoebe would have seen it, but it was going by so fast he could barely tell—then back into stasis again.

He felt like he might throw up. "I'm closing my eyes," he said. "Just tell me when we get there."

The hollow wind of the timestream grew louder around him. Liam started to feel like he was a breeze, not quite all in one place, his thoughts having to cross wide distances.

"Phoebe, this is too fast!"

"I know," Phoebe said dreamily. Liam peered out his squinted eyes and saw that the version of her here in the timestream had her arms out, her face serene: that same expression she'd had on the roof of Vista, back on Mars.

Liam felt spread out, dangerously so. He shut his

eyes again, tried to focus on himself. Needed to stay in one piece, whatever that meant.

And then all at once, everything halted. There was a wild swirling sound, as if a dust devil had wrapped around them. Liam felt like he'd been stopped, crushed, and then everything became silent and still.

"We're here," said Phoebe.

Liam opened his eyes and saw that time had reversed, moving at a slight fast-forward.

Outside the timestream, they were standing in a patch of crimson-colored grass, its blades short and thick and rubbery. The sky was lavender colored, and a series of rings sparkled faintly like a rainbow high above sienna-colored clouds. It seemed to be evening, and yet the sun was directly overhead, a small orb the color of a penny, casting a mellow glow.

"This is Telos," said Phoebe. The scene swayed back and forth, and Liam realized this view through Phoebe's eyes was taking place from something like a playground swing that she was sitting on, except instead of hanging on chains, the seat was humming between two parallel bars that seemed to be magnetized.

Phoebe pointed across the wide lawn. It was crisscrossed by a series of gray stone paths, and surrounded on all sides by triangle-shaped buildings, their surfaces glittering in a black covering woven with gold circuitry. There were taller buildings in the distance, also in triangular shapes and glistening black. "That's my house," said Phoebe, singling out one of the closer structures.

There were other kids around Phoebe on a collection of playground equipment. Each device moved like it was powered by magnets: spinning, spiraling, and looping.

"This is the place you always come to," said Liam.

"Yeah." Now a younger Telphon ran up in front of them and spoke. He had the same lavender skin and bristles and cloud-blue eyes with black irises and gold pupils like Phoebe's, only his silver hair was short and gathered into spikes sticking this way and that. Like all the kids around, including Phoebe, he wore a short-sleeved shirt made of some kind of metallic fabric. His was white, with a design of arcs and symbols that Liam guessed might be Telphon language.

The little boy waved his arms and spoke in sped-up bursts.

Beside Liam in the timestream, Phoebe started to cry.

"Is that your brother?"

Phoebe nodded. "Mica."

He tugged briefly on Phoebe's hand, and then he

zipped off toward their house. The Phoebe in the past kept swinging, stubborn as ever.

Liam felt an awe like he never had before, his heart pounding, his eyes wide. He'd tried to imagine another planet, that there really could be other places in the universe, livable places, and here was one, right here. Vehicles hummed by on a distant street. They were wider and flatter than ground transports had been on Mars, more like the "cars" back on Earth. An airship shaped like an H slid by overhead. "It's amazing," said Liam.

Phoebe watched a little longer, as her past self finally leaped off the swing and hurried inside. Liam saw Paolo and Ariana as their normal Telphon selves, busying themselves around a wide, open room with fantastic gadgets and appliances that Liam wanted to examine for hours.

"I can't take any more right now," said Phoebe, sniffing at tears. She twisted the dial and sped up. Things blurred, making Liam's head hurt again, and then there was a series of flashes and wild motions—fire, people screaming—and something massive and orange and glowing that Liam caught only a glimpse of—

Phoebe slowed time again, and they were looking out a large window from space. Below, past the spectacular rings of metal and crystal, Telos was awash in some kind of firestorm. Phoebe seemed to be viewing it from a spaceship, along with a small crowd of weeping Telphons.

"What happened?" Liam asked.

Phoebe turned to him, her eyes brimming with tears. "You did."

11

"Our people called it the Tears of Ana," said Phoebe, "because it looked like a rain of fire, but it wasn't from our star. It was Phase One."

"Phase One?" A pit formed in Liam's stomach. "Telos . . . is Aaru-5?"

"Yes."

"But . . . I thought Phase One was just a bunch of satellites and stuff?"

"*To prepare the planet for our arrival,*" said Phoebe. "What do you do when you prepare to have guests? You clean up. Make the place nice and neat."

"Oh no."

"It was a fleet of tiny, specialized bombs designed to erase every speck of life. That way, when humans arrived, they wouldn't be killed by some toxic plant or bacteria or dinosaur or, you know, a civilization of sentient beings who already had their own planet."

Liam struggled to find words. "Maybe they didn't even know you were there. Aaru was so far away. They would have scanned for radio waves—"

"We didn't use radio waves."

"Or whatever. My parents worked on Phase One . . . they would never do anything like this."

Phoebe shook her head. "Wouldn't they? If there's anything I learned in all those history lessons I had to sit through on Mars, it's that your species doesn't have the best track record when somebody else is living on the land that you want."

"Phoebe, I don't . . ." Liam could barely wrap his mind around it. "We're murderers. All of us."

"The only reason any of us survived was because we had access to the Styrlax technology. I should have been killed, along with my brother and everyone else."

"So you're trying to stop us. From invading your home world."

"You already invaded." She pointed to the flames below. "We're trying to stop you from colonizing. And then we'd use the terraforming data to see if we could fix Telos ourselves."

"And part of your plan is to destroy the entire human race?"

"Would our planet be safe if we left any of you alive?"

"I guess not," said Liam. He couldn't look at her. "I didn't know."

"Of course *you* didn't," Phoebe snapped. "But the people working on Phase One *could* have. I'm sure there was a way to escape the supernova and then find out more about Telos before you bombed it."

"We were facing extinction."

"And now so are we."

The smoldering planet went dark. Phoebe of the past was sleeping.

Liam felt a great pit inside. All his life he'd thought of the mission to Aaru as a great accomplishment, even an adventure. He'd been told by everyone that it was such an amazing feat: all of humanity coming together under one flag, finally putting aside thousands of years of conflict, working together and setting off on a great journey across the universe for survival. Everyone was so proud. He was supposed to be proud. There had been a movie; two actors played his parents in the background of a scene. Even when everyone had been making him feel like his emotions about leaving Mars, his only home, had been silly, he could remind himself that they were all part of this noble endeavor.

But they'd been wrong. It wasn't noble. Liam had always just assumed—everybody had—that Aaru was *theirs*, that all they had to do was get there. But it had been someone else's all along. They weren't pioneers; they were conquerers.

"I wish you'd told me sooner," said Liam.

"I wanted to, but . . . if I told you, even that morning before we left, you would have told your parents, and my parents and I would have been captured and maybe killed ourselves."

Liam didn't answer. Would he have told them? Probably. "But how could you stand living with us? Pretending you were human, when you knew what we did?"

"Sometimes I wanted to blow up the school," said Phoebe. "I nearly jumped up in class and punched kids a couple times. They would say such arrogant things. I knew they didn't know, but still. . . . Back here, on this ship right after the Tears happened, I wanted to kill you all."

Liam nodded. "I get it."

"No, I'm serious, I really did."

"But you don't want to kill us now, do you?"

"Not as much. Not *you*. I don't know. I did spend

three years being a human. You have some good points: grav-ball." She shot Liam the briefest smile. "On the one hand, I don't think you're murderous invaders. And it's like, if the situations were reversed, I'm not sure that my people would have done it differently." She shook her head. "But it doesn't change the fact that you actually did it. When I'm hanging out with just you, or Shawn, our parents, I can almost forget, but even then, a part of me always knows that you murdered us all, and . . . I don't know if you'd even care if you knew."

"I care."

"Liam, duh! Each of you, individually, would probably care. But I'm not sure humanity would, and I still don't think you'd leave Telos alone."

Liam wondered if she had a point: Aaru-5 had been humanity's target. There had been other possible planets, but they were so much farther, and every kilometer added to the uncertainty. He really wasn't sure that some alien race would have changed their plans.

"Maybe we could live there together," he said. "I mean, like you said, we have the terraforming data."

Phoebe laughed. "What, like we're just going to get along? You'll give us, like, our own little island or something? There's only two hundred and thirty-eight of us left. Thirty-seven now, after that body at Delphi.

And that's the best case. That's it. You can't even imagine what it feels like. Plus, we're not the same. When you terraform Telos for what a human needs, that's not necessarily going to work for a Telphon."

"So—I don't get it," said Liam. "Do you still believe in the plan to kill us all or not?"

"Liam!" Phoebe balled her fists. "I just saved your life. Multiple times! Do you know how it felt to fire on Barro's ship? Or to make those course changes, knowing it would mean I wouldn't see my people? Do you know how lonely it was doing all that by myself?" Her eyes welled up.

"I'm sorry."

"I know. It's just, I've been wearing this mask and shaving my own bristles off for a quarter of my life. Did I mention we had tails? We had to cut them off. And then . . ." Phoebe pulled down the collar of her shirt. The putty gave way to her natural purple skin. Liam saw the top of a large black scar that began just below her collarbone. "Because of the different atmosphere and gravity on Mars, they gave me a backup pump attached below my heart to compensate. We only have three chambers. You know that Martian cough I had? It was because of my pump, trying to keep up."

"So it's like a second heart?" said Liam.

Phoebe nodded. "Sometimes when I'm lying in

the dark I can hear it sort of wheezing inside me. And sometimes it gets out of rhythm with my real heart and there's this vibration that feels like my chest is going to break. And that's kind of how the whole thing has been. It was our planet, our only home. We're never going to get that back, even if we kill every human in the galaxy. And that would mean losing my best friend. I've wanted to tell you for so long. Part of me kept hoping I wouldn't have to, and another part of me kept looking for a way. If things hadn't gone sideways on Mars, I don't know if I ever would have gotten the chance. But they did. And here we are."

"So what do we do?"

Phoebe shrugged and wiped away tears. "I have no idea. This is as far as I ever imagined. I mean, I'm not even sure my people are wrong, but I—I just don't want any more of them, or you, to die."

Liam felt a surge of frustration. He couldn't quite put his finger on why. "Back on Mars, when we found the chronologist's lab and learned about the Drove, you said it changed everything. And at Saturn you told Barro that the Drove were the real enemy. But it sounds like you still sort of think we're the enemy."

"I thought that finding out about the Drove might convince my people to call off the attack, at least for a little while. I mean, anybody going around blowing up stars is pretty dangerous, and for a minute, I could imagine taking our vengeance out on them instead."

"You mean like humans and Telphons, side by side?"

"It sounded nice, but then . . . there are trillions of stars. We might never run into the Drove again. And even if we did, and even managed to stop them, what then? We'd turn to face each other, and you'd still be the ones who slaughtered us. Barro was right: it wouldn't really change what happened."

"See? It sounds like you still agree with them."

Phoebe threw up her hands. "What else do I have to do to show you that I'm on your side?"

"But that doesn't mean humanity's side."

"No. I'm not sure that it does. . . . And I don't know how you could expect it to."

Liam shrugged. "So what do we do next?"

"All I can think to do is catch the *Scorpius*, and get our parents treated and woken up. Hopefully, our cover hasn't been blown yet. Then we can get our parents together and talk to them. They might listen to us. For mine, it would be a first, but they might."

"There has to be a way to convince them to call, like, a cease-fire or something," said Liam. "And to convince humans that we need to think about this some more. Like, maybe we can share the terraforming data and everyone can go their separate ways. If your ship can make wormholes, you guys could go start over anywhere." Phoebe's eyes narrowed at him. "Right, or we could find another spot and you could have Telos back, I don't know."

"It's a solid plan," said Phoebe. "Except we'd never see each other again."

"Yeah. . . ." He wanted to refute that, except he couldn't think of any way it would work.

Outside of the timestream, the red dwarf star, Ana, was rising over the ashen rim of Telos.

"We should go back," said Phoebe.

"Thanks for showing me," said Liam. "It was beautiful. Telos, I mean. Your home."

"Thanks." Phoebe sniffled.

"I'm sorry. I don't know how I can ever make it better."

She squeezed his hand. "You've made it better."

Phoebe turned the dial two clicks forward. Time sped up in a blur, becoming little more than flashes of color, and the feeling of a wind blowing through Liam grew—

Suddenly something crackled and buzzed, like when heat lightning would strike the colony dome. There was a blinding flash of white light, and all at once Liam felt like he'd been crushed, and also turned upside down, then like he was falling, but then it all stopped.

Bright spots dotted his vision. He winced and looked around and saw that he and Phoebe were still in the timestream. Outside, he saw her view of their Mars classroom, with Ms. Avi and all the kids, and there was Liam himself, sitting a few seats over, only this moment was frozen, as if Phoebe was holding down the watch symbol. But she wasn't.

"What happened?" Phoebe rubbed her head.

Liam looked down at himself and realized that there was no more sense of his physical form, the one that was hugging Phoebe on the cruiser. There was only this timestream version of himself, and he felt dizzy and nauseated, as if he'd finished a time trip and was actually back in the present. "I don't know. We stopped. What does the watch say?"

Phoebe held up her wrist. The symbols in both hemispheres were blinking, back and forth and out of sync with each other. And the dial was blinking red again.

"That's not good," said Liam.

"What does it mean?"

"I don't know." Had the chronologist come back? Or was this the Drove? They had been moving forward.

He spun around, looking up and down the strange cloudy hall of the timestream—and froze.

"Behind you," he said to Phoebe. She turned and her eyes grew wide.

A doorway.

Here, somehow in the timestream, a trapezoid of black metal, narrow but quite tall. It was solid, heavy-looking, threaded with circuitry that glowed liquid silver, and it led into an inky darkness.

"What is it?" Phoebe whispered.

"I have no idea," said Liam. How could this be here? A door in the quiet of paused time—no, not quiet, exactly. There was a grinding sound, like power cycling in deep, humming rotations. It was coming from through that doorway.

"Try the watch," said Liam.

"I'm turning the dial but nothing's happening," Phoebe hissed. "The buttons don't do anything either. Are we stuck here?"

Liam shrugged, and yet his first thought was *yes*.

Phoebe stepped toward the doorway. "Well, where does this go?"

"Wait—" Liam followed her.

They crept up to it and stood just outside it.

That humming sound had grown, rumbling Liam's gut and vibrating his teeth. It seemed to be coming up from Liam's feet, but when he looked down, he still saw himself standing in a sort of undefined fog.

Phoebe leaned into the shadow of the doorway.

"Do you hear that?"

Liam held his breath and listened.

Voices. Faint, echoing, like you might hear at the far end of a hallway with no one else around.

Phoebe stepped into the doorway.

"Hold on," said Liam.

She held up the malfunctioning watch and raised her eyebrows at him. "Maybe it's a way out of here."

"We can't be sure about that," said Liam. "This might have to do with the chronologist. She did say she would see us later. Maybe we should wait and see if she shows up."

"I'm going to take a look."

"It's a door in a timestream. We don't even know what that means."

Phoebe stepped farther into the shadow. "It's cold." The space seemed to ripple, almost like liquid. It coalesced around her, and just like that, she vanished into it.

"Phoebe?" No answer. "Phoebe!" Liam held his breath and stepped into the doorway. He noticed that same rippling happening in the corner of his vision, but he didn't feel it. There was a sense of cold, though, deep, dark cold.

"Phoebe!" He took another step, and felt a sort of rushing movement. All at once it was pulling him, or pushing him, or both, Liam couldn't quite tell, but he couldn't fight it, and then he was rushing forward and the dark closed around him and it was dotted with stars, as if he was adrift in space itself—

The wind grew inside him, louder than ever before, and he started to fall.

INTERLUDE

SALVAGE FREIGHTER CARRION
0.3 LIGHT-YEARS FROM ACCESS PORTAL FOUR

Just under nine and a half trillion kilometers from Delphi, inside a sleek black ship with a mirrored surface that made it seem like merely a ripple among the stars, a light began to blink. The light was on a console in the ship's cabin, and it caught the attention of a young woman. She wore a gray jumpsuit uniform, and her hair had been shaved except for two thin bands that began just above her temples and arced over her scalp, meeting at the back of her neck. The remaining hair was long and dyed blue, such that it appeared as if she had two small waterfalls, one on either side of her head. This woman, Kyla, didn't love the style, but it had been a trend that had swept through the crew and such things were good for morale. In fact, she was often kind of chilly, though she did enjoy rubbing the shaved areas and feeling the stubbly promise of the rest of her hair returning. The sound and feel against her fingertips also soothed her during this stressful operation, and that was what she'd been doing when the light began blinking. The sight of it caused a nervous skip in her heart.

"Jordy!" she called over her shoulder. "I think we got one!"

"You sure?" Jordy was back adjusting the shield phasing. It had been a string of thuds followed by curses ever since he'd left the cockpit, as the ship kept rocking back and forth in the radiation storm, and the spaces in here were incredibly tight.

Slim people, the prior owners of this ship, Kyla thought. Very slim. The straps that held her in the pilot's chair were extended to their maximum length and they were still cutting into her shoulders and waist. *You're no spring chicken*, her dad had said once—or a few times too often—when she was a teen, something that she'd been pretty sure he meant not just as a nod to time passing but also as a critique, and yet thinking of it made a lump form in her throat. He was probably long gone by now.

She pressed a lever on the side of the chair and it swiveled to face the front console. She tapped the blinking light and a liquid spherical map appeared. It was helmet-sized and aqua blue, floating in a concave depression. Lights flashed within it, all of them white except for one, which was red. Kyla slipped her hand into the sphere and pinched the green one. This caused a target shape to blink on the windshield, and a route map to zigzag through the debris.

Kyla locked in on the coordinates and fired the thrusters, the force pushing her into her seat.

"Ow! Careful!" Jordy yelled from the back.

"You be careful!" Kyla squinted, peering out into the radiation storm that blossomed in space all around them, a riot of maroon and yellow feathering in iridescent clouds tipped with nucleic fire. Nothing visible through that target finder yet.

There was, however, something much larger and closer, a growing silhouette against the background inferno, heading in their direction.

"You got those shields realigned?" Kyla called.

"Mostly!"

She rolled her eyes. Nothing was ever a simple yes or no with Jordy. "Well, hurry up!" She reached back into the spherical map and tapped an enormous white signal. Its details scrolled on the windshield. "I think we're about to have a close encounter with Charon!"

She made a course correction and burned the engine. The ship darted but was immediately shoved by a heavy wave of charged energy, which threw them back the way they'd come. The silhouette racing toward them had grown to take up nearly half the cockpit view. A great hulking half-moon of rock, streaming a fog of melting ice behind it. Her readings flashed again. Definitely Charon, the sister satellite to good old Pluto, or what was left of it.

"Okay, they're set—ow!" The craft rocked again, and Jordy slammed into the ceiling as he floated back to the cockpit.

"Buckle up already," Kyla barked.

Jordy dragged himself into his chair and strapped in. "Why are we flying toward that?"

"I'm working on it!" Kyla hurried to plot a new vector.

They bucked and rolled in another energy wave, tossing them closer. The great chunk of destroyed subplanet filled their view, heading straight for them, impossibly large—

Kyla held her breath and burned the lateral thrusters. One . . . two . . . three . . .

They slid just out of Charon's way.

"Have a nice trip," said Jordy, looking over his shoulder.

Kyla tapped the red blinking light and corrected course toward it.

"Man," said Jordy, his face lit by the fury of magenta

and yellow ahead of them. "The old girl really had some energy in her."

Kyla opened her mouth to agree, but her voice hitched up and she clenched herself against a tremor of sadness. No more tears, she told herself. Especially not in front of Jordy, of all people. *And especially not for something that can't be helped.* That was her mom talking. Keep that steely exterior! That had always been Mom's way, and Kyla had never been able to live up to it. Besides, it was okay to be sad about the death of your home star, no matter whether you could do anything about it or not. And yet it seemed like there must have been a way to stop it, but how? These choices had been made before they'd even known any better.

And it was far too late now.

"Looks like a small cruiser," said Jordy, analyzing the data from the red dot. "About five thousand klicks out. I'm not getting any engine readings."

Kyla shook her head. "No way that thing has power. They'll be lucky if they even have a hull, being out in this storm."

"What's the point of this assignment, anyway?" said Jordy. "Nothing can survive a supernova."

"Captain said it's our duty to be sure. We owe it to humanity. No soldier left behind, right? If anyone was stupid enough to stick around here and somehow survived, it's our duty to bring them home safe. And besides, if we do find survivors, you know we need the help."

"Can't argue with that. Maybe we can finally start getting actual downtime and have some fun."

"Fun?" said Kyla. She tensed up. That feeling again . . .

"Okay, there it is," said Jordy, pointing. "I have visual."

Kyla saw it now, too: a small metallic flashing, reflections of the roiling storm. They were closing fast. Kyla reversed the thrusters and burned, slowing them down. "Anything?" she said.

"I'm running scans now. It's hot enough, but so far no life-forms."

The shape grew, and Kyla could make out the curves and jagged edges. A military transport, she thought, or what was left of one. The front half was intact but it was blown apart at its middle, trailing a tangled mess of electrical innards and chunks of its fuselage. "Doesn't look promising."

"Nope. Life signs officially negative. Oh well."

Kyla watched the wreck drift by. No signs of fires or light inside. She turned away, biting her lip. "Maybe it was left behind."

"Maybe," Jordy said quietly.

"Attention, Gamma Fleet, all ships reporting top-off

and our safe window is closing. Break off your current course and return to the portal, over."

Kyla keyed the mic. "Roger." She reversed course and burned the engine. "Guess that's that."

Jordy exhaled. He gazed out the side of the cockpit as a V-shaped formation of five ships soared past them, their wide, oval-shaped wings glowing iridescent green. "Looks like success. Man, I bet those things are fun to fly."

"Yeah." Kyla lingered on the supernova storm, its undulating waves making the stars behind it wobble and shimmer. *I'm sorry*, she thought, and had to clench her gut again. It didn't seem fair to anyone, least of all to her and Jordy and the rest of the crew. A hopelessness gathered inside and shuddered from her stomach to her shoulders. What kind of universe let this sort of thing happen?

An alarm flashed on the dashboard.

"Aw, man," said Kyla. She bent and fished into the leather bag she'd attached to her seat belt.

"Really?" said Jordy. "Another cascading event?"

"Looks like it."

"Why can't they get these things under control?"

"Have you ever looked at those portal systems? It's a wonder we don't end up with two heads using all this crazy technology."

Kyla produced a copper-colored metal cube.

Through a clear window she saw the current date and time on a digital watch face held inside. "All right, we should be okay, just hang on."

The alarm went from beeping to buzzing, and all at once the space around them and within them seemed to light up in sizzling white.

Kyla's head split with pain, and she felt a flash of burning, followed by a sensation as if her arms and legs were gone, as if she was floating, nothing. Except also everywhere. Sound was gone. Just white. She opened her eyes—or maybe they had been open and her brain simply needed a minute to believe what it was seeing—and saw many versions of herself, as if she were standing in a square of mirrors reflecting infinitely back on one another. Except this wasn't quite that, because in one direction she saw herself younger, and a teen, a child, and yet somehow many, many versions of each, fanning out, and in the other direction she got older, her hair graying, skin sagging, her body eventually suspended in some sort of gold-plated geriatric suit. And even further in the first direction she was an infant and then there was a red darkness and then something like starlight and back in the other direction there was something like a brain in a clear box of turquoise liquid and then also red darkness and more starlight.

All of this was very large. And getting larger by the

moment, except it seemed that there was no moment, just more versions of her expanding and expanding outward from her present self—

And just as suddenly all of it was gone and Kyla was back in the cockpit, singular, buckled in her seat, blinking and looking out the cockpit window at the yellow fire of the supernova.

"Aaaooow." Jordy winced, rubbing his palm against his temple. "That always hurts!"

"No kidding," Kyla croaked. "What does the computer say?"

"Hold on." Jordy fished an injector out of his thigh pocket and stabbed himself in the side of the neck with it. He spasmed, briefly, and held it out to her. "Want some?"

"No, thanks." She was still seeing double and her head felt like she imagined a piece of synthetic steak felt as it was being freeze-dried, but the pain blockers Jordy preferred dulled her reflexes too much for flying.

Jordy checked the comms. "The ship thinks it's the year 8047."

"Okay." Kyla opened a panel in the bottom of the copper box, whose internal clock hadn't changed. She uncoiled a small magnet cup and affixed it to the console. "Resetting actual time."

The box hummed. All the lights on the console

flashed and the readouts spun and realigned themselves with normal old present time.

"Everyone all right out there?" the captain asked.

"No!" Jordy moaned.

"We're fine, Cap," said Kyla, "just rebooting the clock. That one seemed more severe to us, sir."

"They are getting worse."

"Did we lose anybody?"

"Negative. No reports of paradox psychosis. But the sooner we wrap up this mission, the better."

"Copy that—we're on our way." Kyla burned the thruster again, increasing their speed. She closed her eyes and breathed deep, trying to move away from that strange sensation, the vision of herself in so many forms. All of them had seemed like ghosts. And yet more. And it made her feel like she herself, here and now, was somehow less real.

"Whoa, heads up," said Jordy.

"What?" Kyla turned her head too fast and it lit up with pain.

Another red light had started blinking in the navigation map.

"Looks like we've got one more out here."

"It's probably just another ghost ship. We're on beam for the portal." She looked back at the nova storm again. "You heard the captain—sooner we wrap, the better."

"Mmmm . . ." Jordy tapped the controls. "I don't know, scans are showing a more organized heat map from this one."

"Like what?"

"Signatures consistent with life-forms."

"How many?"

"More than one. Fewer than five."

"Jeez, be a little less specific."

"Scanners are on the fritz with this storm, not to mention that time freak-out back there. We'll have to get closer to find out."

"Captain won't like it."

"Captain doesn't like anything."

Kyla flexed her fingers and sighed.

"Okay, wait—" Jordy adjusted the scanner. "There, two life-forms. Confirmed."

"What kind of ship are they in? If it's military—"

"I can't tell. Not getting a reading from the ship anymore. I— Come on!"

"What?"

"They're gone."

"How can they be gone?"

"Well, I don't *know*. All this interference. Might just be an error. Or they might have just died while we were watching."

"Can you lock on their last known coordinate?"

"Already done. It's close to the portal, actually.

We'd barely have to slow down."

"You had to say that."

"It is *technically* our mission."

Kyla sighed, still heavy inside. *Do what needs to be done,* Mom scolded.

"Miss you," Kyla said to herself. Suddenly she was back at the launch on Mars, hugging them both, crying and secretly hoping they might cry too, but of course they didn't.

"Huh?" said Jordy.

"Nothing." Kyla shook her head. "All right, I'm initiating intercept. Captain," she hailed. "We've got a possible live one out here. Won't hold us up too long, over."

There was a long pause.

"I told you," Kyla muttered to Jordy.

"Affirmative," the captain finally replied. "Make it quick."

"All right, let's go save some lives," said Jordy.

"Right." As Kyla burned on an intercept route, her heart leaped. A little bit of good they could do. It would be nice, considering what was already done.

12

Liam's next thought was that he had just been without thought, without anything, like a wave was receding, but instead of water there had been nothing—a hollow, cold absence. For a moment, he couldn't remember where he'd just been, and a new fear spiked through him, as if he couldn't actually recall *anything* about himself—

But then he remembered that doorway in the timestream, their classroom on Mars frozen around them, and then that rippling black and the feeling of falling. In the dark, it had seemed for a moment as if he had seen something huge and geometric, like a cityscape, or a ship, black and smooth and hulking . . .

but it had been only a glimpse.

Before that, they'd been on Phoebe's home world. Telos, which was Aaru-5. Before that, on the cruiser, escaping Delphi.

Shouldn't he still have been able to see his body back there? Except Liam felt a cold sensation on his cheek. He picked up his head and saw that he was lying on a floor made of carpeted panels and gazing at a wall with a closed door. It was very quiet, just a sort of breezy sound, a distant whirring like fans. Cold, too. But the light was red. Flashing.

He turned his head and saw that he was on a walkway. There was a railing beside him. Beyond the railing, hundreds of meters away across a vast space, he saw a long swath of green grass crisscrossed by white paths. And even though he was looking sideways at it, it was somehow also beneath him.

He lurched up to his knees and took in the huge cylindrical space around him lined with walkways that each passed hundreds of doors. A starliner core—the *Scorpius*! Unbelievable! Somehow they had traveled across space. Could that be possible?

Red lights flashed silently on every deck. Everyone must be in stasis, part of the emergency protocol.

Phoebe groaned. She was lying on her back a few meters down the walkway, rubbing her face. Liam saw that the watch was blinking blue on her wrist, and while that at least meant it was working normally again, it also meant they were in danger.

"Phoebe." Liam crawled over to her and shook her shoulder. "Look where we are!"

"Everything hurts," said Phoebe. She blinked, and as she saw what was around them, her eyes went wide. She bolted up. "The *Scorpius*? How did we get here?"

"I don't know. That door. It's like we teleported or something."

Phoebe slowly got to her feet and looked down at herself. "I can't see my body back in the cruiser anymore." She tapped her arm. "Feels solid. Are we really here?"

Liam hopped up. "I think so." He glanced around, half expecting to find that trapezoidal doorway still nearby somewhere, except he didn't see it.

The staterooms were all closed, with red lights beside their entry panels, indicating that the doors were locked, the pods inside in stasis. Liam leaned on the railing. The park, the glass domes of its restaurants and common halls, all still. No movement on any of the other walkways either. Just the whirling of the red emergency lights. He pulled out his beacon and pressed the glass top. It didn't blink back.

A low rumble shook the ship and pressed on Liam's ears.

"That didn't sound good," said Phoebe. She looked out over the railing. "This core seems different than it did in our orientation, doesn't it?"

"I guess. I don't know. Let's find a VirtCom port and figure out where we are." Liam started down the walkway. As he walked, he realized that Phoebe was right; there was definitely something different about this core from the one he'd seen in the orientation guide. He couldn't quite put his finger on it. But his head still ached, his thoughts were still foggy. How in the world had they gotten here?

He reached a gap between staterooms, expecting to find a panel where he could access the VirtCom and other passenger systems, but the wall was blank. He noticed, too, that the door to his right had a green light instead of a red one. He pressed the access panel and it slid open. Empty inside. No stasis pods. No personal effects. Not even any furniture other than the modular desk and table that were built into the wall. He was surprised that there could be any spare rooms, especially with one of the cores damaged. And the stasis pods clearly hadn't been ejected, because then the back wall of this stateroom would be open to the vacuum of space.

The ship shook again, the rumble interrupted by a distant crashing sound.

Liam turned around and studied the expanse of

the core. "There aren't any of those cable transports," he noticed now, "the ones you use to get from one deck to another. They were everywhere in the orientation."

"Maybe this core doesn't have them?" said Phoebe.

"No climbing domes, either, the ones that could simulate gravity on different planets. And . . ." He noted other doors here and there on other decks with green lights. "I don't get how there could be so many empty rooms."

"Maybe they didn't have time to finish all the cores?" said Phoebe. "I mean, the departure date kept getting moved up."

"Yeah, but that doesn't explain the empty rooms. Unless . . ."

"What?"

"Maybe they belong to people who were lost in the attack, like who were on the bridge at the time. Except that one I looked in had no pods or personal effects."

"Maybe they were trying to reduce weight since they lost those engines."

Liam shuddered with a surge of adrenaline. It was partially due to their travel through that doorway, but worries about Mina and Shawn were also fresh in his mind. "We should get to the bridge." Liam tapped his pockets. "We can give the data to command and see if there's a way to find the cruiser." His heart faltered for a moment as he wondered just how far away their parents and JEFF were and how they would even contact the cruiser with no comms.

"Which way is the front?" asked Phoebe.

Liam pointed. "The stateroom numbers get smaller as you head forward."

They hurried down the long walkway, through the quiet and flashing red light. Liam kept looking around, and his nervous feeling grew. It took them ten minutes to reach the end of the core segment. The ship rumbled again, this time so hard that Liam lost his balance and—

Suddenly he was back in the skim drone. The great red sun was before him, spinning its flares, and Liam was watching it, terrified, certain it would destroy him. But he wasn't alone this time; Phoebe was slumped over against him in the cockpit. Her face was Telphon blue, all of her makeup gone. Her eyes were closed, and there seemed to be something shiny on her lips. *Ice*, Liam knew, and she was so cold, but at least she was breathing. And yet he also knew that there was so little time—

"Liam?"

A hand on his arm. Things sliding around loosely, no direction or balance. Liam thudded into something hard and found himself leaning against the walkway railing.

"You okay?"

He blinked at spots in his eyes. Phoebe stood beside him, still in her human makeup, and they were on the starliner. "Yeah. I'm fine." He pushed himself upright and fought off a wave of dizziness.

"You didn't seem fine."

"It's just from going through that door," he said, but as he continued down the walkway, he worried it was more than that.

They reached the far end of the core segment. Elevators led like spokes from all the decks to a central platform where the airlocks were located. Liam pressed the button to call one. No response.

"Are they shut down?" Phoebe asked.

"Looks like it. Maybe to save power. Let's take the stairs."

They switched back and forth down flight after flight of metal stairs, gravity shifting as they did, so that they were always upright. When they reached the airlock platform, the walkway they'd come from was nearly above them.

They stood before six sets of wide, clear airlock doors that led into the next segment. Liam worried for a moment that these doors wouldn't work either, but their panels were lit, and when Liam pressed the button, the first of the double sets slid open.

The next segment was as quiet as the last one had been, and as spartan: no cable transports, no climbing domes, and while many of the staterooms had red lights as if they were occupied, again there were others that were empty. The emergency lights still twirled on each deck, lighting the space in red.

It took them twenty minutes to cross this segment, and Liam's fear gripped him tighter.

"There should be more people," he said quietly.

"Or at least bots," Phoebe agreed.

"It's like a ghost ship."

They reached the next set of airlocks, and Liam saw a much smaller space beyond.

"This must be the front section," said Liam.

They passed through the doors and found themselves in a wide, dimly lit hallway with many branching corridors. A shrill alarm sounded steadily. There was no one around.

"There." Phoebe pointed to a pedestal up ahead in the center of the hallway with a diagram of the ship. They approached the glowing map, and the tremors of worry in Liam's gut became a full-blown earthquake.

The diagram showed a starliner with a single core, not six. It had only two egg-shaped fusion engines, a shorter bridge section, and a smaller X-shaped array beyond that. Liam leaned against the pedestal and his breath caught in his throat as he read the name of the ship, in glowing white letters across the top of the map:

ARTEMIS.

"That's impossible," Liam said after a moment.

"I don't understand," said Phoebe.

Liam's mouth had gone dry. "The *Artemis* was the prototype starliner."

"So we're somewhere else in the fleet?"

Liam shook his head. "The *Artemis* was never part of the fleet. It left our solar system on its own, but it was lost . . . almost thirty years ago."

Phoebe kept staring at the screen.

"It was eight years into its mission when it disappeared," Liam continued. "Nobody knows what happened to it. It stopped transmitting and vanished."

"So we just found it?" said Phoebe, gazing around. "When no one else has?"

"I guess so." Liam tapped his link and pulled up his location settings, but a message flashed: *ERROR: UNABLE TO DETERMINE COORDINATES*.

"If we're really on some lost ship that's been floating through space for thirty years," said Phoebe, "who knows how far we are from the cruiser and our parents. Let's go back into the timestream together. We have to find that door again."

"We should talk to the captain first," said Liam. "We can send help to find this ship once we're back with colonial."

"But how are we going to explain how we got here?"

"I don't know. Tell the truth, I guess. How we used the watch. They need to know about the Drove and the chronologists and everything, too."

"Are you going to tell him about me?"

"No. They need to know about the war with the Telphons, though."

"I guess. But how do we know we can trust them? What if they want to take the watch—"

"They may not be your people, but they're mine," Liam said. "I have to tell them."

"I didn't mean it like that," said Phoebe.

"It's okay." Liam pointed ahead. "The bridge should be at the end of the hall."

The ship rumbled again, causing them to stumble as they hurried toward a wide, open doorway. Beyond it, they started up a short flight of stairs—

Hands instantly grabbed them both by the shoulders.

"What are you two doing up here?" The soldier lifted Liam momentarily off the ground, then dropped him back to his feet and pinned his arm tightly and painfully behind his back.

"We need to talk to the captain," said Phoebe, who had been similarly pinned by another soldier.

"No one's supposed to be out of stasis," said the

272

soldier holding Liam. "You're violating direct orders."

"We're not part of the crew!" said Liam. "We're from another ship: the *Scorpius*."

"The what?" The soldier gripped Liam tighter.

"It's another starliner, the last one in the fleet. We might be able to help you."

"What are you talking about?"

"We know you've been out here for thirty years—"

"What's going on, Corporal?" A tall woman had turned from where she was overseeing a few officers sitting at terminals.

"Caught these two sneaking around, Lieutenant," said the soldier. They pushed Liam and Phoebe the rest of the way up the stairs, to the top of a wide room with levels stepping downward, all curved like an amphitheater and facing an enormous window. The levels were lined with workstations, though only a few of them were occupied, by soldiers wearing gray uniforms. Red lights flashed throughout this room, too.

Another wicked vibration shook the ship, but Liam barely noticed, because of what he saw out the giant window.

There, in space before them, floated a great black doorway, illuminated by the massive lights on the *Artemis*'s front array. It was exactly the same trapezoidal shape as the doorway Liam and Phoebe had found in the timestream, except that this one was far larger. Liam guessed that it was over a kilometer tall and nearly as wide, like one of the skyscrapers he'd seen in pictures of old Earth. There was a small ship hovering closer to it: a military cruiser, its lights probing the inky black within the doorway.

Liam shared a wide-eyed glance with Phoebe as the guards pushed them over to the lieutenant. She wore a black uniform, and her gold-streaked brown hair flowed over her shoulders.

"Sorry, Lieutenant Lyris," said the soldier holding Liam. "We were just about to take these two back to their quarters."

"It's all right, Corporal." Lyris peered at them. "What were you saying about being from another ship?"

"We—" Liam began, but he was cut off by a flash from outside and a rumble throughout the ship. Everyone staggered, metal creaking beneath their feet.

A wild, jagged scar of light seared across the dark, like a burst of lightning. It crossed diagonally in front of the doorway but also seemed to pass through it. As it did, the structure lit up with a complex threading of silver circuitry. Sparks flew. The *Artemis* shuddered and lurched forward.

"Lieutenant!" shouted another officer. "Gravity emissions are increasing."

"Burn the retrorockets at ten percent!" Lyris said.

"Electromagnetic scans are off the charts," said another officer.

"Are the rockets holding?"

"Barely, sir; we're not going to be able to maintain this position much longer."

"Any word from the captain?" said Lyris.

"No, sir!"

"Hail him again! And again after that." She turned back to Liam and Phoebe. "Is there another ship around here? As you can see, we're caught up in whatever that thing is, and we could sure use some assistance."

"We're from a cruiser that's part of the fleet," said Liam, "but we're supposed to be on the *Starliner Scorpius*. Though I don't think either of them are nearby, or anyone else."

Lyris peered at him. "Starliner? The fleet? As in the colonial fleet?"

"Yeah. The *Scorpius* is the last ship. We've been trying to catch it. We just left Delphi."

"Hold on. Delphi? Where is that?"

"It's the first waypoint," said Liam. "I guess you probably wouldn't know about it, as you never got there."

Lyris winced. "Let me try to understand this. Are you saying that you are from a ship that has left Mars, and that has already departed the first waypoint en route to Aaru-5?"

"Yeah. We left Mars ten years ago. Right before the sun went nova."

Two different officers turned in their seats as Liam said this.

Lyris turned to the soldiers who'd grabbed Liam and Phoebe. "Did you scan them?"

"No, sorry, sir." Liam's soldier pulled a small wand-like device from his belt and pressed it against Liam's neck. It buzzed with electric current.

"Ow."

The soldier studied the readings on the device.

"Anything?" asked Lyris.

"DNA scan's negative. He's not indexed."

Lyris tapped one of the officers sitting at a nearby workstation on the shoulder. "Bring up our latest images from Kazu-4." The officer flashed through screens. Lyris pointed to one. "Is this what you mean by Delphi?"

Liam saw the dim blue-and-white orb. "Yeah, that's it."

"What year is it?" said Lyris.

"What do you mean?"

"What year is it, right now, for you? What Earth year?"

"It's 2223," said Liam.

One of the officers gave a sharp intake of breath. Lyris bit her lip. She pointed once more at the image of Delphi. "This planet is called Kazu-4. A rogue planet that we are scouting to be the first waypoint. It's part of our mission, here, now, in 2194."

Liam repeated the number to himself and glanced at Phoebe. Her eyes were wide. Nearly everyone on the bridge was staring at them now.

"And you're telling me that you're from a starliner thirty years in the future. You realize you're standing on the prototype, right? That no other starliners exist yet."

Liam swallowed. "Yeah."

"And how exactly did you get aboard this ship?"

Liam pointed to the window. "We came through that. Well, a smaller version of that."

"Lieutenant!" an officer a few rows below called. "We're getting a signal from the captain!"

"Put him on."

A large screen appeared, overlying the window. It showed a static-filled image that was hard to make out; maybe some kind of structure, illuminated by floating lights. The image clipped and sputtered.

"—you copy, over?"

"Captain Barrie!" Lyris called. "We read you! What is your status?"

The captain breathed hard over his microphone.

"It's incredible," he said.

"Where is he?" said Liam, looking from the video feed to the view of the doorway.

"He went into that thing, or through it," said Lyris. "He's on a tether, from that military ship. I told him it was a completely crazy thing to do, but he's the captain."

The video feed clarified—it seemed to be coming from a camera on the captain's helmet—and now a great geometric structure became visible, like a cityscape folded on top of itself, all made of glistening black metal. There were giant towers, long twisting arms, stretching far beyond what the camera could capture.

"What kind of readings are you getting from this?" asked the captain.

Lyris bent over one of the officer's shoulders. "Metallic molecular composition, but whatever it's made of is definitely not on our periodic table. It's giving off a strong radioactive signal as well as gravity emissions like nothing we've ever seen."

"Unbelievable," said the captain.

"Sir, we need to pull back," said Lyris. "We're having a hard time holding this position."

"Did you put all nonessential crew in stasis lockdown? Reroute core power to the engines?"

"Yes, sir, but I'm not sure that's going to be enough. We need to get away from this thing before it breaks us in half."

"Any word from colonial command?"

"Communications are all messed up," said Lyris. "Our transmissions might be making it through the interference, but there's no way to be sure."

"It's massive," said the captain, awestruck.

Liam peered at the great structure, and it reminded him of ancient Earth cities—the pyramids, the Roman temples—but also of the strange black buildings on Phoebe's world. And he was fairly certain he'd glimpsed it before—when they had traveled through the smaller doorway.

"And this is only one arm of it," said the captain. "I . . ."

"Captain, you should come back through. We can study this gateway, and whatever that complex is, further once we get to a safe distance."

"They're connected," said the captain. "And there are more of them. More doorways, I think. . . ."

"We also have new evidence here, sir, that you really need to see."

"What new evidence?"

"Well," said Lyris, eyeing Liam and Phoebe, "two kids have shown up here who claim they traveled through a doorway like this one, and they're from the future—our future, thirty years from now after the sun is gone."

There was a long silence.

"Captain?"

"I'm here. Future humans . . ."

"Here comes another gravity spike," an officer reported.

The lightning flashed again, the doorway's circuitry igniting, and the *Artemis* bucked and lurched closer. A new siren wailed.

"There's a partial meltdown in energy cell two!" an officer shouted. "We're losing power."

"Retrorockets to full!" Lyris called. "Captain, sir, Peter . . . please come back through."

"I need a closer look. If this is what I think it is—"

"Captain! We're not going to survive a closer look!"

"Nobody survives," the captain said, almost dreamily, "if you tell the story long enough."

A huge rumble shook the *Artemis* to its core.

"Gravity is off the charts!" an officer called. "We're losing our position!"

"Get him out of there!" Lyris shouted. "Extraction team, go!"

The military cruiser edged toward the great doorway. Suddenly the ship upended into a spin and tumbled through, vanishing from sight.

"Report!" Lyris shouted. "Captain!"

The *Artemis* lurched again, throwing everyone across the room. There was a huge whumping sound from somewhere behind them.

"We've lost the stabilizers completely!"

"Reroute all power to the retrorockets!" Lyris yelled.

"They're gone too, sir!"

The *Artemis* began to career toward the doorway in space. Officers tumbled and ran to their workstations. Sirens blared. There was shouting everywhere.

Liam stumbled and watched the giant structure growing to fill their view, with its empty blackness inside. He grabbed Phoebe's hand. "What are we going to do?"

"We're going through it again," said Phoebe quietly. "Don't you get it? This is how the *Artemis* was lost."

"I do not think that is the best course of action," said a voice from behind them. A hand fell on each of their shoulders. A hand with more than five fingers.

Liam spun to find the towering, spindly chronologist standing right behind them, blinking her filmy white eyes. Phoebe suppressed a shocked scream.

"I have been looking everywhere for you," said the chronologist.

"What is it saying?" Phoebe asked.

"I'd suggest you come with me before you pass through that portal. If you're confused about space and time now, trust me: you do not want to go through that thing again." She produced her orange crystal and pressed her fingers against the top and the bottom. It split open at its equator, bursting with bright light.

Liam glanced back and saw Lyris looking up from a workstation, eyes wide. "Can we help them?" he asked.

"Not right now," said the chronologist.

The light ballooned around them and the view of the *Artemis* began to fade. The doorway crisscrossed with lightning, the ship rocking back and forth as it barreled toward it.

"Where is she taking us?" Phoebe asked.

"To my office."

Then they were gone, in a blinding flash followed by total darkness.

Liam felt a cold nothingness seeping into him and had a sense of traveling farther, this time, than ever before.

13

"Well," said the chronologist, closing her version of the orange crystal. "That is a relief."

"What is?" asked Liam, getting to his feet. He was covered in cold sweat, his head splitting with pain. He stumbled as he stood, and Phoebe caught him by the shoulder.

"I wasn't entirely sure that I'd be able to transport you." The chronologist studied the orange sphere as if she was reading it. "But it appears my theory was correct; your interaction with my chronometer has continued to alter your subatomic fingerprint since we last spoke. It's affecting you, too," she said, nodding to Phoebe. "Oh, sorry." She pointed to Liam. "Can you give her your version of my crystal for a moment?"

Liam fished it out of his pocket and handed it to Phoebe. The two versions of the crystal started flashing in unison.

"Can you understand me now?"

Phoebe's eyes widened. "Yeah."

"Good. As I was saying, there was still some danger that trying to bring you here would tear you apart, but you seem to have developed a tolerance for it."

"What does that mean?"

"It means that exposure to the timestream is making your subatomic particles behave, in very subtle ways, more like waves."

"That doesn't help," said Liam.

The chronologist sighed. "You are starting to experience time differently. Have you been feeling all right?"

Liam shook his head. "Not really." He turned to Phoebe, who looked nauseous. "You okay?"

"I think so." She winced and handed him the crystal back, along with the watch, which had stopped blinking. "Where are we?"

"You are in my office," said the chronologist.

Liam looked around and nearly screamed: they seemed to be standing on nothing, suspended in the center of a giant space shaped like an oval tipped up on its end. In all directions he could see out into the depths of space, except straight ahead, where a massive nebula shaped like an eye wafted and shimmered in purples and greens and blues. After a second, he was able to discern a sheen beneath their feet, a sort of crystal floor, or perhaps an energy field. This same slight reflection of light also indicated walls.

Around Liam, Phoebe, and the chronologist floated an uncountable number of luminous sparks all dancing in a slow spiral. The swarm of lights extended above and below as if, for them, the floor was not there.

And this was not the only room. To his left and right, this oval-shaped space was connected by narrow archways to more rooms of the same shape, curving out of sight, and each of them was filled with fields of glowing embers. In the nearest one, Liam saw another being similar to the chronologist—this one had a few more arms and was waving them around, which caused the points of light to move in great currents and folds.

"What is this place?" Phoebe asked, awestruck.

"The regional managers' offices," said the chronologist. "I know they appear connected, but they are actually each separated by hundreds of thousands of light-years. I am in charge of the sector that includes your home galaxy as well as approximately a half billion others."

"What do you mean you're *in charge* of it?"

"I help to compile the long count," said the chronologist. "A complete record of what happens in this universe. We are its official observers and keepers."

"Like, from the very beginning?"

"Yes, and from the end."

"The end . . . ," said Phoebe. "You know the future?"

"Well, future and past are a bit of a three-dimensional way of looking at things, but, to keep it in terms you would understand, that would be accurate."

"And you also go around fixing problems like tears in the fabric of the universe and stuff," said Liam.

"We mostly just watch and chronicle. Generally speaking, it is not our policy to intervene in the mechanics of the universe, except in cases when events may prove fatal to its entire existence."

"What does that mean?"

"It means that if this universe collapses, we'll all be out of a job. And also dead."

"Aren't you already dead? Back on Mars?" asked Phoebe.

"Ah, not yet." The chronologist checked her version of the watch. "But I will be, very soon. In fact, I'm heading there right after this lunch break. Figured now was as good a time as any to get that data of yours, since apparently I will not be returning."

"Time's different for her," said Liam. "What happened to us, back there? How did we end up on the *Artemis*?" He pictured the locked staterooms, all the people inside who had no idea of their fate, and those officers on the bridge, struggling to control the ship. Had they really been pulled through that doorway? "And how did you find us?"

"All excellent questions. I have some data here to analyze." She waved her hand and the drifting lights swarmed out of the way. A map appeared around them, or something like a map. It hovered from just above the floor to just over their heads, three-dimensional, and yet Liam sensed that there was more to it; they'd seen a similar map in the chronologist's observatory on Mars. *Time*, he thought now. The map also showed time. He could almost see it—but not quite.

The chronologist made a second waving motion, and a clear pedestal slid up from the transparent floor. A small black crystal reader sat atop it, as if it were floating in air. It looked just like the one Liam had found on Mars. The chronologist placed her version of the orange crystal into the curved depression and spun it. Streaks of light emanated from the crystal, and columns of scrolling data bloomed here and there in the map around them.

"Tell me what you remember before you ended up on that ship," she said.

Liam explained about using the watch to see Phoebe's timeline—this made the chronologist frown, but she didn't interrupt—and then about the malfunction and the appearance of the doorway.

"Did the watch blink red?" the chronologist asked.

"Yeah."

"And this door you went through was similar to the one that spaceship encountered."

"A lot smaller, though."

"And you say you traveled together? How did you accomplish this?"

"We kinda hugged," said Phoebe.

The chronologist cocked her head.

"We tricked the watch into making a time field around both of us," Liam added.

"The watch cannot be tricked. What is a hug?"

"It's when you put your arms around each other, you know, like this?" Phoebe made a fake hug, her arms circling the air around Liam.

"Curious," said the chronologist. She studied her crystal, and it glowed brighter, as if she was interacting with it in some way that Liam couldn't perceive. Then she raised her arms and began to move them among the flittering embers. The sparks dipped and darted and whirled, creating a small space, and then a new light burned itself into existence between the chronologist's thumb and the tiny finger protruding off it.

"What are you doing?" Liam asked, watching the light grow.

"I am adding an entry to the long count for 'hug.'"

"You didn't have that in there?" said Liam. "It's a pretty important human thing."

"Forgive me for saying this, but I am also currently creating an entry for 'human.' I will certainly add to it when I visit your system."

"Do you have an entry for Telphon?" Phoebe asked.

"I did recently add one, yes."

"Thanks a lot."

"If it's any consolation," said the chronologist, "the entry on you two is quite long."

"There's an entry on us?" said Liam.

"Very much so," said the chronologist. "Now, you say you employed this hug operation to use the watch—"

"It's not an operation," said Phoebe. "It's just a hug."

"I see." She squeezed the little light again. "Participant in hug describes act as *not an operation, just itself.* You were saying?"

"Then we walked through the doorway," said Liam. "We thought our bodies would still be on the cruiser, but the door seemed to transport us completely. Do you know what that was about?"

The chronologist finished blooming the ember of light and then, with a wave of her hand, ushered it off into the swarm overhead. "Remember how I told you that there was a weak spot in the fabric of space-time, near where we last met?"

"The one that made my two realities overlap?"

"*You* made your two realities overlap—the weak spot just provided the necessary conditions. Anyway, yes, that tear extends forward and backward through space-time. And this doorway you encountered is its cause. Well, technically it's less of a doorway, more of a mathematical anomaly, a paradox held in multiple states that makes travel between universes possible. That ship you ended up on, the *Artemis*, ran into that very same door, many years before you did. And then you ran into it on your way back through time."

"How could those two doorways be the same? Theirs was huge."

"Remember, I told you it's not exactly a door. I should have noticed it when we first met, but at the time I hadn't even considered its possibility."

"So does that mean the *Artemis* is now in a parallel universe somewhere?"

"If their ship was not destroyed by the transit, that is likely."

"So why didn't we end up in another universe, then, when *we* went through the door?" asked Phoebe.

"I believe you may have, briefly."

"It did get really dark and cold," said Liam. "And I thought I saw something, maybe like what the captain of the *Artemis* was looking at. A big ship, or a city." The thought of it chilled him. "It seemed dead, though."

"Indeed. I believe you initially transited the doorway; however, the interaction between it and the time field that my watch creates resulted in a malfunction that, in essence, spit you back out. When this happened, the watch found the *Artemis* as the safest place to put you. Again, the watch has many advanced features for protecting itself."

"It thought it was safe to put us thirty years in the past?" said Phoebe.

"That is extremely close by, all things considered."

"Last time we met," said Liam, "you said that weak spots in the universe could cause realities to start collapsing."

"Yes, and in the millennia since, I have—"

"Wait, hold on," said Liam. "We met, like, yesterday."

"For you, yes, but I've been extremely busy with our Inquiry. We have since confirmed the presence of these anomalous supernovas, like the one you described. At first we did not know what connected them, but we have recently discovered the bigger problem, which is the appearance of these doorways."

"How many are there?"

"We have found evidence of six around the universe, including the one you encountered. There have so far been eight infected stars, all of which have been located in close proximity to these doorways, most of them near the one in my sector."

"Does that mean the Drove are the ones who made the doors? And they're using them to come to this universe and blow up stars?"

"That seems the most probable answer. The problem is, every time a door is activated, the tear in space-time around it gets worse."

"So there might be one of those paradox cascades you were talking about?"

"Yes, the probability of this universe collapsing on itself and the others around it is increasing rapidly."

"Does every star they pick put a group of people in danger?" asked Phoebe. "Like the sun did?"

"One other species was wiped out, that we know of," said the chronologist, "but if you're asking whether the Drove are targeting living beings, there is no evidence of that."

"Then why are they blowing up these stars?"

"That is the next question in our inquiry."

"Why don't you just go through that doorway and find out?"

"It's curious," said the chronologist. "Our four-dimensionality makes us so fully bound to this universe that we cannot in fact leave it. You two have traveled farther than I have, in that regard. Higher levels of sentience do have their limitations."

"But you—you're trying to stop this from happening, right?" said Liam. "This isn't, like, how the universe is supposed to end?"

"Correct. Up until recently, the most probable end of this universe was many trillions of years from now."

"Have you been there?" asked Phoebe. "To the end?"

"Of course."

"What is it like?"

"It *was* very dark, and very quiet."

"And what about after that?"

"After what?"

"After the end. Of the universe."

"Well, surely we don't know."

"But you know everything about the universe."

"We know a lot, but as I said we are still part of this universe; therefore while we can travel through time, we cannot travel outside it, nor before or after it."

"Didn't you say words like *before* and *after* are three-dimensional words?" asked Liam.

The chronologist made a long sound, like a lonely breeze. "I am trying to speak your language. Time and space are intertwined. If there is no more universe, there is no more time. This, anyway, is our theory. No being can know everything, or they would cease to *be*.

"That said, we experience time the same as you experience the three dimensions of height, width, and depth. You can move in them, measure them, manipulate them. You can see the length of something. I can also see the *time* of it. And this perception has allowed us to craft technology for moving in time, just as you've built ships for moving through space."

"We sort of move through time," said Phoebe. "Seconds and days and years are passing."

"Yes, but you only experience it through its effect on the other three dimensions. I experience time as a dimension itself. I am aware of my entire life at any moment, including my death."

"That must suck," said Liam.

"It has always been known, therefore it has never troubled me."

"You're okay with that?" said Phoebe. "With dying?"

"Well, these things happen," said the chronologist. "Have happened and will be happening, at every moment of this universe. Every birth and death is a part of its intricate fabric, vital to the flow of energy and the long count. To take away a death is to deprive the universe of its function."

"Which is?"

"To be what it is."

"And that is?"

"This." The chronologist motioned to the orbiting sparks, which fluttered in response. "This universe. All of it. Does it need to be any more than that?"

"I guess not," said Phoebe.

"One of the unfortunate things about a life lived in only three dimensions is that you do not know how or when you are going to die. You'd be surprised how much easier things are, knowing how long you have and what part you play."

"But if you know about your death," said Liam, "why didn't you know about the Drove all along? They're the ones that kill you."

"My experience isn't fully formed until I actually get there. No doubt you noticed that when you are traveling with the watch, you do not have the full experience of being in the future or past. Sounds, textures, the detail and intensity of things, it is all at a distance."

"I did notice that."

"That's because those are three-dimensional details. You have to be *in* a moment in all four dimensions to fully know it. So while I may be able to perceive my future, I have yet to experience it. I am still a being made of matter and bound to this universe. I cannot change those fundamental laws."

"So you're solid, like a *thing*, like we are," said Phoebe. "You were born and stuff."

"I was. Nearly thirteen billion years ago, along with the first wave of stars in this universe."

"You're thirteen billion years old?" said Phoebe.

"More like a billion and a half."

"I don't— You know what? Never mind."

"But why not go there and take a look?" said Liam.

"Go where?"

"To when you die. You could see what happens, or even prevent it."

"That is possible, but it is not advisable."

"Why not? Because it will it cause a paradox or something?"

"It's more of a wellness thing," said the chronologist. "Some of my colleagues have tried what you are describing: go see how you die, then change things to stop it, but then you just have a new death to go prevent, and on and on. It's not a great way to live. Better to be a part of your moment. And in my case, why would I change it? You have, after all, brought me the very data I am going to get, as well as information about the Drove. If I don't go and die, you can't find my crystal. None of this happens, and I'd say this sequence of events is turning out pretty promising just as it is."

"But there might still be a way to—"

The chronologist made a sharp hissing sound. "I understand that this concept scares you, but you must accept that this is how we see it. When we say, *These things happen,* we are expressing our wonder and appreciation for the universe as it unfolds, the causes and effects, no matter how large or small. Our ability to experience time only makes this more profound. And so, as a state of being, we prefer what happens to what could have happened."

"Sorry," said Liam.

"It's perfectly fine. Now, could you please place your version of my crystal in the reader?"

Liam waited for the chronologist to remove her version, and then he placed his crystal in the grooved depression. It hovered and spun, and emitted its own series of light beams that synced with the map floating around them. The map zoomed in on five lights: four red and one yellow, blinking in a tight cluster. Again, Liam felt like he couldn't quite see all there was to see.

The chronologist touched the yellow dot. The Milky Way galaxy came into view, zooming all the way into their old solar system. Seeing even just this little graphic of their former home caused Liam's eyes to prickle.

Data scrolled around them, and that voice Liam and Phoebe had heard in the observatory on Mars spoke again: *Infected star five exhibits the same abnormal growth pattern. . . .*

"You said you've met one of the Drove?" asked the chronologist.

Liam nodded. "He said they were from somewhere called Dark Star. I wonder if that's the city or ship we saw on the other side of the doorway."

"And what kind of being was he?"

"Oh, um . . . I guess I don't know. He was wearing a suit, and I couldn't see his face. Two legs and two arms, though."

"How was he communicating with you?"

"I'm not sure. I mean, I could understand him, so maybe he spoke my language? It happened in the timestream."

"I see." The chronologist kept studying the data. "Ah, okay, here it is, in the elemental analysis: they're seeding the stars by injecting them with protomatter. Sort of like spraying a fire with a fire extinguisher, except from the inside out. This causes rapid fuel loss in the star, which leads to the supernova."

"Not that rapid," said Phoebe. "It took like forty years."

"Forty years is fairly quick in the ten-billion-year

life cycle of a star." She checked her watch. "Well, this data will be invaluable as my colleagues attempt to determine what the Drove are trying to accomplish. However, I need to get going. My break is over."

The chronologist zoomed the map back out, but stopped as a new green light began to flash on it. "Ah, good. My successor has located the next activation of that doorway." Another light popped up, this one yellow. "And there is the correlating infected star and supernova. Interesting. . . ."

"What?"

"The Drove have advanced their methods since injecting your star. In this more recent attempt, they now seem to be able to cause star collapse in just under ninety-six hours."

"They went from forty years to four days?" said Phoebe.

"Yes. That's really not that out of the ordinary; technology tends to advance at an exponential rate."

Liam peered at the map. This new light wasn't that far from the one indicating their sun. "Which star is it?"

The chronologist spun her map around. "They only target main sequence yellow dwarf stars, like your sun. This new one is in a binary system."

Liam's chest tightened. "What's it called?"

The chronologist checked her crystal. "You refer to it as Alpha Centauri A."

"Our entire fleet is heading for Centauri B."

"That is close enough that the supernova will have devastating effects."

"When is it going to happen?" asked Phoebe. "Like right now?"

"No, the supernova will occur approximately thirty-three years from when you left your ship."

Liam and Phoebe locked eyes. "That can't be a coincidence," said Phoebe. "The Drove must be trying to wipe us all out at once!"

"I have to admit," said the chronologist, "that timing is more than a bit suspicious. That said, it is still possible that the Drove are merely targeting the most convenient star. Asuming they are coming and going from another universe, they might not even realize you exist, let alone that you are headed for that location."

Liam's heart raced. He thought of how the metal-suited man had offered to take him to Dark Star. That didn't seem like something you'd say if you were planning to exterminate the human race. "But it won't work," he said. "Even at only ninety-six hours, the fleet will still have time to detect the supernova and change course. The Drove must know that."

"But the *Scorpius* and the cruiser are flying blind," said Phoebe.

"The fleet will send someone to intercept," said Liam.

"Unless they're too busy fighting my people," said Phoebe.

"Can you get us back there?" said Liam.

The chronologist checked her watch again. "I believe I can." She removed Liam's version of the orange crystal from the reader, and the map blinked out. "I will make it the final function of this device. It will be fitting. Where should I deliver you?"

"The *Scorpius*?" said Liam.

"Our parents," said Phoebe.

"Okay, but when? If we go back to where we left, we'll just have to go into stasis for decades and hope we even got there in time."

"Let me see." The chronologist spread her arms and blew into the lights drifting above them. They swirled, scattering and darting. She pulled one close and pinched it. The light bloomed around her.

"What are you doing?" Liam asked.

"Reading your future," said the chronologist.

"You're— What does it say?" asked Phoebe.

The chronologist made a sound like a laugh. "I of course cannot tell you. Very curious. . . . All right." She blew the light closed and then spun the map around them and pulled on a new area. "If I send you ahead in time, your bot will have piloted your ship and caught up to the *Scorpius* just prior to reaching Centauri B. I could place you on your ship at that point."

Liam checked with Phoebe.

She nodded. "Then we can save the whole *how did we magically appear on the* Scorpius *bridge* part and just focus on the *there's an alien race tearing apart the universe* part."

"Okay," said Liam. "Let's do that."

"Sounds good." The chronologist tapped her many fingers over the orange crystal.

"I, um, have one more question," said Liam. Something had occurred to him, something that was tightening his insides in a knot.

"I have one more answer." The chronologist almost seemed to smile.

Liam couldn't quite return it. "Would it be possible," he asked quietly, "that because of the, um, subatomic change you saw in me, with the waves and particles or whatever—"

"Multiprobabilistic quantum behavior."

"Sure, that. Could that make me, maybe, see part of *my* future?"

"You mean with the watch?"

"No, more like visions."

"Are you talking about dreams?" Phoebe asked.

Liam's throat was dry. "They don't feel like

dreams. And they happen while I'm awake."

The chronologist peered at Liam. "That would be unprecedented, but possible."

"Great."

"What are you seeing?" Phoebe asked.

The image flashed through his head—the growing sun about to go nova, Phoebe, her face cold beside him in the skim drone. Except maybe that wasn't actually the sun.

"I'll tell you later."

"Just remember," said the chronologist, "what you see of the future is a function of probability until you actually get there. That said, this moment that you are seeing is likely a key probability node, perhaps even a keystone event for many timelines in the universe."

"What does that mean?"

"It means you are remembering it because it is important."

"Remembering? But it's—" Liam shook his head. "Okay. But how probable is it?"

She gave him what seemed to be a pitying look.

"What am I going to do?"

"You asked me this before, and what did I tell you?"

"You mean about trust?"

Her thin hand patted him on the shoulder. "Indeed. Okay, time to go." She held out the crystal.

"It's ready. Just press the top and bottom."

Liam held up his wrist. "Do you want your watch back?"

The chronologist held up her own. "I already have it. As I believe you say: *finders keepers.*"

"Okay, um, thank you," Liam said. "And good-bye."

"I'm sorry," said Phoebe.

"Please don't be," said the chronologist.

Phoebe took Liam's hand. "Do we need to hug for this to work, too?"

"No," said the chronologist, "I programmed it to take you both without using the hug function."

Liam pressed the crystal between his fingers. Its top and bottom hemispheres spun in opposite directions, and a bright light washed out from its equator.

"Until next time," said the chronologist.

"Wait, what next time?" Liam shouted over the rising wind.

But the chronologist, the crystal room, the field of drifting lights, and the eye-shaped nebula were all lost in white light.

14

Liam felt a wide space, like he was in a giant room, only the giant room was inside him. Completely dark, and cold—

"Liam?" he heard Phoebe call from somewhere impossibly far.

He blinked, and now there was a light in the darkness, growing rapidly, ballooning to fill the space. A great orange light. Lines sketched in around him. The geometry of a cockpit windshield, blinking controls. The skim drone. The growing star writhed with solar flares, would go nova at any moment— His heart began to race. Beside him was Phoebe, slumped over, her chest barely rising and falling, her alien skin now an even paler blue, like the ice of Delphi. He noticed too, that she was wearing the chronologist's watch, which also sparkled with frost.

"Liam?"

He blinked and the orange faded. Dim light around him.

"Hey!"

It was Phoebe. For a second, he couldn't feel his feet or hands or anything, like he had no body. Then all at once electric bolts seemed to jolt through him. He gasped and rolled in zero gravity, bumping against the wall. They were back in the main cabin of the Cosmic Cruiser. He was no longer holding the orange crystal, and it was nowhere to be found.

Sound was confusing, and at first he couldn't hear anything, but he saw that Phoebe was mouthing something to him.

"What?" he shouted at her.

"We're back!" it looked like she was saying.

Now he started to decipher what was wrong with his ears; there was tremendous noise all around him. The wailing of guitars and the pounding of synth drums and the electric knives of key filters.

Also his sister's voice:

When I don't know what's up or down,
And you're nowhere to be found

The Gravity Minus, Mina's band, blaring through the ship. Meanwhile Liam had rotated and he was upside down, his head bumping the floor, which was shaking with the bass.

His insides spun, and suddenly he was going to vomit. He kicked for the bathroom, and barely made it to the toilet and hit the vacuum flush before barfing.

His vision prickled with spots. He breathed in deep, fighting back not only the nausea and its accompanying headache but also a frigid pool of fear inside him. The supernova he'd been seeing. Could it really be his future? Not the sun, but Centauri A. In the skim drone with Phoebe, too close to escape . . .

All along it had felt like more than a dream, more than some kind of miswiring from stasis. Because it was real. Or at least probable. And it was coming. Soon.

"Hey," Phoebe shouted, leaning through the door. "You okay?"

"Yeah," Liam shouted back. "What's with the music?"

Phoebe's face was flushed like she wasn't feeling so well either, but she grabbed his arm. "Come on, you've got to see."

She pushed across the cabin, and Liam followed her to the cockpit. They stopped just at the entrance, peering in. The music was a little more bearable here. Liam's eye was drawn out the windshield, where three stars gleamed like jewels before them: the Alpha Centauri system. The closest was Centauri B, pale and whitish blue, the size of a fingertip. Centauri A was slightly farther away, swollen and blood orange. And then much farther beyond that was a small deep red dot: Proxima.

JEFF was sitting at the controls, talking to himself, except it didn't sound like JEFF.

"Rear thruster has shorted out again," he said.

Then his voice shifted to a different pitch. *"Is that a problem?"* It shifted again to an even, purely analytical tone: *"Spoken by Liam, age thirteen, son of Gerald and Lana, sibling of Mina.*

"It would be if we needed to take off again," JEFF said in his normal voice, *"but hopefully this is the last trip this vehicle has to make.*

"What's that flashing? Spoken by Phoebe, age thirteen, daughter of Paolo and Ariana."

"Checking diagnostics. . . ."

Liam glanced at Phoebe, eyebrows raised. JEFF had recorded their conversations? Except the voices for Liam and Phoebe weren't theirs. These were more like transcripts that he was playing back, like reading a script.

"We're trashing this poor ship, aren't we?"

"HA HA HA."

"JEFF!" Liam called over the blaring music.

"That's only—" The conversation halted. For a moment, JEFF didn't move, his eyes flickering; then he spun around. "Hello there!" He stood and magnetized his wheels to the floor.

"Hey, JEFF!" Liam shouted. "Turn it down!"

"Acknowledged!" JEFF tapped a button on the console and the music ceased. "Welcome back—" His voice shifted again, to that cold, analytical tone. "Facial recognition negative, gather secondary identity confirmation."

"Why does he sound like that?" said Phoebe.

"Forgive me," JEFF said in his normal voice again. "In order to better serve you, I must verify your identity. Please provide me with your colonial i-i-identification." He held out his palm. "Your fingerprint will be adequate."

Liam pressed his index finger against a subtle depression in the center of JEFF's palm. "It's me, JEFF. Liam. You were just listening to us talk. You've been our bot for, like, my whole life."

JEFF's eyes flickered. And flickered. . . . "Identity confirmed" he said. "Hello, Liam. Please confirm user settings. Would you like to continue using the assistant setting JEFF? Other options include JENNY, or MORGAN."

"JEFF will be fine."

"Acknowledged. Loading. . . ." His eyes flickered for another long moment. Then his whole panda body seemed to jolt. "My friends! I am quite pleased to see you again!"

"Thanks. Are you all right?"

"I am suitably op-p-perational."

Liam considered the trio of stars out the window. "How long have we been gone?"

"It has been thirty-two years, three hundred and nineteen days, twenty-one hours, and forty-two minutes since active human links v-v-vanished from the local network. Mission logs indicate that *you* were those passengers who departed."

His voice altered again. "Scan of ship and surrounding space negative. Primary function altered: seek medical treatment for injured adult passengers. Correction to course: none."

"Yeah, that was us," said Liam.

"My friends!" he said again. "I did not know what had happened to you!"

"JEFF," said Liam, rubbing his plastic shoulder. "We had no idea we'd be gone for so long. We're sorry."

"Is that why you were playing back our conversations?" Phoebe asked.

JEFF's eyes flickered. "Diagnostic records indicate that over the journey, my core storage circuits have developed a faulty code, affecting my memory. As more packets have become corrupted, I have been replaying our conversations daily, as a way of reminding myself who you are. That way, I can refresh the code before it is permanently lost. However, other systems are beginning to s-s-suffer."

"And you've been doing that for thirty-three years?"

"I initiated this subroutine twenty-four years, one hundred and eight days ago."

"Is that why you're listening to the Gravity Minus?"

"Oh, no. I just really like that band. The singer is very accomplished at pitch, and her lyrics convey a high degree of emotional depth."

"That's Mina singing," said Liam. "My sister."

JEFF's eyes flickered again. "I . . . did not remember that! But now I have reconnected those pathways. Very good. Mina! Sibling of Liam. And who are the adults I am carrying to the location"—he turned and checked the navigation screen—"Destina? In the Alpha Centauri system?"

"Those are our parents," said Liam.

"Excellent! That satisfies many correlative processors."

"How are they?" Phoebe asked. "It was going to be risky, leaving them in stasis for so long."

"They are alive and their vital signs and brain

activity are stable. The concern will be their cognitive state and awareness when we actually wake them up."

"Do you think it's going to be bad?"

"I calculate that they will have a slow acclimation to consciousness and movement, but that in time they will regain normal function."

Liam exhaled hard. "That is good news."

"JEFF," said Phoebe. "What else do you remember about me?"

More flickering. "You are Liam's friend, and he b-b-believes, despite evidence to the contrary, that you are not a traitor to the human race nor a war criminal."

Phoebe frowned. "Okay, so you didn't forget everything."

"Where have you been?" asked JEFF.

Liam explained their journey through space and time as best he could.

"I find certain elements of your story difficult to reconcile with the information in my l-l-logic libraries."

"Yeah, well, so do we. How close are we to Destina?"

"We are four hours from arrival," said JEFF. "I have determined that Destina is the second planet orbiting Centauri B. It is currently on the far side of the star. But I have a visual on the *Scorpius*, here."

He tapped the navigation screen, highlighting a small blinking light. "We are traveling at maximum velocity, and must begin to decelerate m-m-momentarily so that we can safely dock, but we should be within local link range very soon."

"Good," said Liam. Relief flooded through him, and he pulled out the beacon and pressed it, his fingers jittering—but at the same time, his eyes drifted to that roiling orange star, slowly growing as they got closer, and the supernova and skim drone flashed in his mind again. The beacon didn't blink back, but it didn't need to; they would be there soon. And yet Liam peered out one side of the cockpit, then the other, looking for any sign of enemy ships.

"Do you think your people are out here, somewhere?" he asked.

"I don't know," said Phoebe. "I don't have a clue what they're up to now."

Liam also wondered if the Drove might be lurking out here already. He remembered that oily teardrop ship he'd seen at Saturn.

"I am picking up highly unusual readings from Centauri A," said JEFF. "It appears to be collapsing in the same way that our sun did, only at a much faster rate."

"Can you tell how long it's been doing that?" Phoebe asked.

"I calculate a minimum of ninety hours, possibly more."

She turned to Liam. "The chronologist said ninety-six hours, right?"

When Liam blinked, the vision of the supernova flashed behind his eyes. *I don't want to die here.* "Why are they still heading toward it?" Liam wondered. "You don't need comms to figure out that that star is about to blow."

"It would seem logical that the fleet would relocate," said JEFF. "However, there are two other starliners in the vicnity." He pointed to the navigation holoscreen. "The *Saga* and the *Rhea*."

"There they are." Phoebe pointed past the *Scorpius*, two long strands of blinking lights.

"Something doesn't feel right about this," said Liam. "You know?"

"Yeah. How soon until we can hail them?"

"Fifteen minutes," said JEFF.

"Okay. I'm starving," said Phoebe. "It's been thirty-three years since we had anything to eat."

"I do not believe that is possible—"

"It's a joke, JEFF," said Phoebe.

"Oh, yes! Humor! I remember! And my appropriate response should be ha, ha, ha."

Liam surrendered the briefest smile, as did Phoebe.

"Let's eat something," she said, floating out of the cabin.

"JEFF," Liam said, "are you going to be all right?"

"Of course, Liam."

"I mean, like, with your memories."

"All packets are stable and functioning normally at this time."

"Okay." He patted JEFF's shoulder. "We'll get you all patched up on the *Scorpius*."

Liam pushed out of the cockpit. Phoebe wasn't in the galley. He floated to the back of the ship and found her between her parents' pods.

"Checking up on me?"

"No," said Liam. But maybe he had been, a little. "How do they look?"

"My parents need a serious makeup job, but otherwise all right. Alive."

"Do you need to do that now?"

"I'll wait until we dock. It's a lot easier with gravity."

Liam floated over his parents, a lump forming in his throat. Their faces were virtually unchanged. It was nearly impossible to comprehend that thirty-three years had passed. "Almost there, guys."

They started back to the cockpit. As they crossed the galley, the oven beeped.

"Here." Phoebe handed him a round, covered bowl of freeze-dried mac and cheese. "Is JEFF going to be all right?"

"He's forty years overdue for servicing," said Liam. "Hopefully he's got a little more time in him." He barely got the words out when the supernova flashed in his mind again.

"Are *you* okay?" Phoebe asked.

"Fine." He scooped up a bite with a covered spoon and pulled it out of the hole in the side of the bowl. The food was a tangy mush, not all that different from slow fuel. Liam had never even had real cheese, so he had no idea if this approximated the taste or not, but his stomach growled hungrily and he shoveled it in anyway.

Roiling ball of fire. Phoebe's pale face—

"Hey." Phoebe had put her hand on his. "Stop lying to me."

"I'm not—"

"Liam, I think I know what lying looks like."

Liam breathed hard, his insides flipping around worse than ever. He didn't want to tell her, didn't want to worry her, but she had trusted him. . . . "I've been having this sort of vision."

"What you mentioned to the chronologist?"

"Yeah." He described the scene in the skim drone, with the exploding star. "I thought it was just a bad dream about our sun, but not anymore."

"You think it's our future?"

"Maybe, yeah." Just saying that lifted a huge weight off his shoulders; he hadn't even realized how much it had felt like he'd been lying to her simply by not telling her. But still . . . "I'm sorry. It doesn't seem fair to give you something else to worry about."

Phoebe smiled. "We can worry about it together. And it's just probability, right? We can change it. Whatever happens, we won't end up in the skim drone near a supernova." She slapped his shoulder. "No problem!"

Liam tried to laugh.

"We have local link connection," JEFF called.

They shoved in a few last bites while floating to the cockpit. The *Scorpius* had grown into a small geometry of blinking lights up ahead. Liam tensed as he and Phoebe buckled into their seats. Once again, they were close enough to see the ship they'd been chasing for so long. . . .

"It's not the usual signal for the *Scorpius*," said JEFF. "They seem to have set up a backup link system. Their original network must have been damaged in the attack, with the rest of their comms. I am hailing them now."

Liam blinked and saw the fiery star about to explode. There were spots in his eyes as he looked at the *Scorpius* again—but now a strange new feeling overtook him, a cold and dizzy sensation, as if he had floated upside down. His vision swam, and his sense of the world seemed to shimmer. Liam clutched the sides of the seat, wincing as the stars blurred.

So strange. . . .

Tell him you want to hail the Scorpius, Liam thought. Except it felt more like an actual voice had just spoken inside his head, *his* voice. Maybe it was the dizziness, disorientation from their travels—

Hurry! Before he talks!

Liam shook his head. He looked down and saw that the watch had begun blinking blue.

"Starliner Scor—"

"Hold on, JEFF," Liam blurted out. "Can I hail them instead?"

"O-o-of course," said JEFF. "You are the captain."

"Thanks." Liam wiped fresh sweat off his brow. He blinked hard; the world seemed to be right side up again, as much as it could be in zero gravity.

"What's up?" said Phoebe.

"I don't know. Just . . ." He didn't finish. That feeling had been so odd. He barely knew why he'd asked to speak, but he leaned over and tapped the console's link screen. *"Starliner Scorpius*, this is Cosmic Cruiser Delta Four Five, inbound from Delphi, come in."

They all watched the screen. Waiting.

He repeated the message.

Out the windshield, the starliner had grown. Liam could see its four remaining engines and the five cores in their parallel arrangement, with a gaping space where Core Three had been.

The link lit up. "Cosmic Cruiser Delta Four Five," said a woman's voice, "this is Captain Freeman. You are a sight for sore eyes."

"Yes!" Liam pumped his fist. He and Phoebe shared a grin.

"Thanks, *Scorpius*," said Liam. "Requesting permission to dock. We have six on board, four adults with serious injuries. They need—"

"Understood, Delta Four Five," said the captain. "As you can see out your port side, we have a bit of a situation here. Red Line for the Centauri A supernova is in two hours and thirty-one minutes, so let's get you on board as quickly as possible. Please proceed to the docking bay at the forward core junction immediately. Copy?"

"Copy that. Is everyone on board all right?"

"Affirmative. At the moment all passengers except for essential crew are in stasis lockdown so we can conserve power."

"Okay, but we saw the wreckage at Delphi and are wondering about the status of our family and friends from Core Three."

"Roger that, Delta Four Five. Good news: Ninety-eight percent of the pods were rescued and are accounted for. They're stacked a bit unceremoniously in the various hangars and cores right now, but we have them. You can check the logs for your family and friends once you're on board."

"Has there been any sign of the attackers from Delphi?" Liam asked.

"Negative."

"Where's the rest of the fleet?" Phoebe asked.

"Apparently they broke off and retreated to a safe distance as soon as the first readings came in from Centauri A. As you can tell, our long-range comms are down, so the *Rhea* and *Saga* maintained course and intercepted us, as we're nearly out of fuel. See you soon. Command out."

"I have locked course on the forward docking bay and am beginning d-d-deceleration," said JEFF. Retrorockets fired and they strained against their seat belts.

Liam breathed deep, and yet his head still spun. *Ninety-eight percent.* That still meant tens of thousands were lost. . . . It was too awful to imagine, and yet, after everything they'd seen, he'd take those odds. "This is going to work." He eyed the distant boiling star and thought, *Maybe you don't get to have me.*

Phoebe nodded but her face was tight, her fingers

gripping the armrests of her chair.

"It's going to be all right," said Liam. "They won't know who you are."

The *Scorpius* grew before them, and a few minutes later, they were flying past its four remaining engines, which glowed a mellow blue now as retrorockets fired intermittently from points along the great ship's side, making bursts of white steam, and steadily slowing the ship down to prepare for the rendezvous with the other starliners.

They passed diagonally over Core Four, which rotated slowly along with One, Five, and Six and seemed to be undamaged, across the gap where Core Three had been, and then past Core Two, which had stopped rotating and was striped with burn marks. Halfway down its length, a great gaping hole had been punched completely through its side, perfectly round with melted sides, as they'd seen on Delphi. Liam spied the outlines of decks inside, as well as floating pieces of debris.

They reached the front of the cores and JEFF slowed the cruiser further. Long structures connected each core to the front section, which always seemed small from a distance but from here was a massive tubular structure, with myriad branches extending off it, some just machinery and antennae, some larger corridors with windows looking in on workspaces.

Whole sections were missing here and there, with dark burn marks and twisted metal on the remaining areas. Shards of golden material hung off what remained of the great, X-shaped framework on the very front of the ship.

Liam was tingling all over. He wanted to believe they were almost safe, but he couldn't stop thinking about the star behind them, a ticking bomb. The watch kept blinking, as if in agreement.

JEFF brought the ship on approach to the large airlock doors. As they neared, a button flashed on the console, indicating that the cruiser had paired with the docking system. JEFF pressed it, and the enormous double doors slowly slid open. JEFF guided the cruiser between them. The ship shuddered and lurched as they entered the starliner's gravity field, and JEFF fired the stabilizers. Liam felt himself suck down to the seat, his body seeming to stick tighter together. They hovered, facing the inner set of doors as the outer set shut behind them. There was a rush of air and a whoosh of sound as the airlock pressurized, and then the inner doors rumbled open.

They flew into the massive hangar, a C-shaped platform around a wide opening that led to multiple decks both above and below. Catwalks extended from the platform to a bank of elevators on the far wall. There were ships of all kinds parked around them:

boxy military vessels, sleeker private craft, a couple Cosmic Cruisers like their own, a tall rack holding hundreds of skim drones.

As the giant doors closed behind them, Phoebe rubbed his arm. "We finally made it."

Liam nodded. He spied stacks of stasis pods along the side of the hangar. There were hundreds: could Mina be in one of those? More likely that she was among the tens of thousands scattered throughout the ship.

A ring of lights flashed on the metal floor ahead of them, signaling their landing spot.

"I am surprised that there is not a landing crew," said JEFF.

"The captain said everyone except essential crew was in stasis," said Liam.

"Yes, but I would consider a basic landing crew essential."

"They probably weren't expecting us to show up," said Liam.

JEFF tapped the navigation screen. "VirtCom appears to be down." He unbuckled and stood. "I was unable to completely repair the landing gear after we departed Delphi, and will need to lower one of the stabilizers manually. I will be right back." He rolled out of the cockpit.

The cruiser hovered over its landing spot. Liam

and Phoebe sat silently. Liam heard JEFF talking to himself back there. He'd be better soon: fully updated and serviced. Their parents would be treated and awake. And he'd get to see Mina and Shawn.

And yet why didn't he feel more relieved? Because too much was still uncertain. When he knew his sister and friend were safe, when their parents were in the medical center, when they were away from that supernova . . . *But I don't get away.* The thought chilled him, the star flashing in his vision. And the watch kept blinking.

The cruiser's legs clanged down on the deck and the ship settled at an angle. As its thrusters powered down, Liam turned to Phoebe. Her face was stony, staring out the window. He realized that, for her, this was, if not enemy territory, a place where she would be considered an enemy. "We won't say anything until we can tell my parents. They'll understand. They'll have to, especially after we tell them about Phase One. And then with the Drove—"

"Liam."

Phoebe was still staring out the windshield. She almost looked sad. Liam followed her gaze. On the far side of the hangar was a strange ship: large, oblong, made of brilliant silver metal, and it seemed to be hovering just off the deck floor. Liam didn't remember it from when he and Shawn used to look at ships in the

VirtCom, but maybe it was a classified military vessel, or something that had been designed during these last few decades in flight. Hadn't he read that there was a division of the ISA that planned to keep working on faster spaceships during the journey; that way if for some reason Aaru-5—Telos; he should call it by its real name—didn't work out, they would be able to scout for new planets more quickly—

And yet despite all of those thoughts, he knew there was another possibility. So did the watch, blinking faster, almost as if it was synced to his heart.

Elevator doors slid open on the far side of the deck, and a team of colonial personnel emerged, coming toward them.

Phoebe turned to him, her eyes wide. "I'm sorry."

"What?" But Liam knew, before he could even put the thought into words.

The party coming toward the ship: ten officers wearing the maroon colonial uniforms—but their skin was lavender and spotted, their eyes black and gold.

15

"No!" Liam jumped up.

"Listen—" Phoebe began.

"Did you know?"

"I didn't!" said Phoebe. "I swear!"

"We have to get out of here!" He bolted into the main cabin—

And ran straight into JEFF.

"It's the Telphons! They're here! We—"

JEFF grabbed his arm. "This what you requested." He poked Liam sharply in the shoulder with an electric syringe.

"Ow! What are you doing?"

But JEFF was already holding out something else in

326

front of Liam. It was the dampener Phoebe had used to knock him out. "I have modified this, per your instructions." He started rolling toward the cockpit. "I must hurry and set the timing system before they enter."

"What are you talking about?" Liam rubbed his aching shoulder. "Your memories are messed up again. I didn't tell you any of that! What did you do to my arm?"

JEFF's eyes flickered. "I suppose it makes sense that you do not know what I'm talking about, given the circumstances."

"JEFF—"

"I must also tell you," said JEFF as Phoebe appeared beside him. "When you are both taken into custody, please mention that I had a processor malfunction that resulted in terminal system f-f-failure, and that you haven't been able to reboot me."

"Why would we say that?" asked Phoebe, her voice quavering with worry.

"Liam knows," said JEFF. And he turned and rolled into the cockpit.

"No," said Liam, "I have no idea what you're talking about!"

Someone banged against the outer airlock door.

Liam turned to Phoebe. "What do we do?"

She shook her head. "There's nothing I can do except try to reason with them. If I make them understand that the Drove are trying to wipe out all of us, and that we need to work together—"

More banging.

"They're not going to listen."

"They will," said Phoebe. "They have to."

Liam tried to nod, but his nerves were wound so tight he could barely move.

Phoebe threw her arms around him, squeezed him tight, and pulled quickly away. "I'll be right back."

She ducked into the bathroom.

The banging ceased. A moment later the walls rumbled and Liam heard the shrieking whine of a magnet drill.

"JEFF?" he called out of sheer panic. "Can we take off?" He leaned back toward the cockpit and saw that JEFF was now slumped over, his eyes dark. "Why would you—"

The magnet drill rattled through the floor, through his bones. He was breathing too fast and his heart was hammering and he felt like walls were pressing in on him. He sprinted back to his parents' pods. "What do I do?" he said uselessly to their peaceful faces. Maybe the skim drone? Could he take off? Could he attach his parents' pods to it somehow? But he'd never get past the soldiers outside.

"Hey."

Phoebe stood in the doorway. Her mask and hair

were gone. And she must have seen the fresh fear in his eyes, because she added, "It's still me. I swear."

Liam moved around behind his parents' pods. "Was this all a setup?" All his thoughts and feelings were a blur.

"No! I had no idea they would be here." Phoebe stepped toward him.

"Stay away from me. I shouldn't have trusted you. You're all murderers, you—"

"We're the murderers?"

"I don't know!"

A sharp bang rumbled through the ship as the outer airlock door sprang open. A pause: the drill began to rattle the inner door.

"What are they going to do?" said Liam. Tears welled in his eyes. He looked down at his parents. "Will they kill us?"

"Liam"—Phoebe held out her hand—"I won't let them hurt you."

Liam could barely breathe. Maybe Phoebe was his only chance right now. He looked at the chronologist's watch: still blinking rapidly.

There was a sound like tearing metal, and the inner airlock door crashed open.

"Hello?" It was Barro.

Phoebe turned toward the main cabin.

Give her the watch. The thought pushed through

his head in that dizzying way again, almost like an actual voice speaking in his head. Liam turned—

And saw himself standing there, just beside him. Except not. Sort of flickering and watery, a version of him similar to the one in the other future that he'd seen beneath the Delphi station.

Give her the watch, this other version of himself said. *Tell her to hide it*. He smiled.

Liam looked at himself looking back at him and winced against a sensation of empty spinning—was this real or a memory? Now, before, or even his future somehow? He had that stretchy feeling like he was moving in time. Could this version of himself be from another timeline? But they weren't near a weak point in space-time out here, and he wasn't even using the watch. Maybe this wasn't real at all. Maybe his brain had finally started to break—

Liam stumbled against the pods, his vision swimming.

"Come on," said Phoebe, turning back to him. Her blue, black, and gold eyes were rimmed with tears. "We have to."

Liam glanced to his side—his alternate self was gone. He pushed himself upright. *Trust is a powerful adaptation*, the chronologist had said. He slipped off the watch and held it out to Phoebe. "Take this. Hide it. Keep it safe."

"Okay. Why?"

"They won't search you."

Phoebe slid it onto her wrist. Liam had thought it might stop blinking, but it didn't. She pushed it beneath the sleeve of her thermal wear.

"There you two are." Barro appeared in the doorway. His human mask was gone, too. "Well, this has been fun. I'm glad to see you looking like your true self, Xela. Now, no more games. Outside."

Phoebe gave Liam one last wide-eyed look. *Trust me*, Liam hoped it meant. She turned, and Liam moved around the pods toward Barro and the doorway. He tried to make his face expressionless. He wouldn't show his fear.

"Don't look so glum," said Barro, shoving Liam into the main cabin. "I know you thought you'd left us far behind, but our people came back for us. We have a very fast ship."

"What did you do here?" Phoebe asked.

"Well, obviously we commandeered the ship," said Barro. "A regular old hijacking. The team learned at Delphi that taking out a starliner is a tall task from the outside."

"How were you able to board?" said Phoebe. "It doesn't look like you blasted your way in."

"Didn't have to," said Barro. "We had a backup plan. All we had to do was wait until it was Captain

Freeman's turn at the helm. She's one of us. That was a few months after Delphi. Once we had control of the ship, we realized that with some patience, we could score a much bigger victory by biding our time until the fleet arrived here. We made a few trips to bring some of these stasis pods to our people. Since then, we've been asleep ourselves. Very comfy."

"But what about those other starliners? When they find out that you're here—"

"Already taken care of," said Barro. "We were just going to fire on them, but unfortunately we damaged the ship's weapons guidance systems at Delphi. Whoops. But it turned out fine: Freeman put the other captains at ease, and then we posed as teams coming over for technical supplies to begin repairs. We boarded, took out their command crews, shot down their military escorts, and shut down their bots. The passengers were all still in stasis, just like here, and that's how they'll stay until that star goes . . ." He made an exploding motion with his hands.

"But you can't," said Liam. "That's three hundred million people. It's—"

"Efficient," said Barro. "Three ships down, just like that. Of course that's not nearly as efficient as what your species did. Now let's go." Barro motioned Phoebe through the airlock.

Liam followed her, his heart pounding. She

trudged down the steps, but Liam paused at the threshold. The squad of Telphons waited for them on the deck, all holding rifles. He could barely breathe— Barro shoved him and he stumbled down the steps, landing on his knees.

Liam gathered himself and stood up straight, feeling as alone and terrified as he ever had. Tarra was at the front of the group. She put her arm around Phoebe, who gazed at him sadly, and yet Liam couldn't help thinking that she looked like one of them. Aliens. She belonged with her people, not him. It seemed so obvious now. *No*, he told himself. *You can trust her.*

Tarra motioned to a Telphon soldier beside her. The man grabbed Liam by the arm, ripped off his link, and reached into his pocket for the data key.

"Stop it!" Liam squirmed, but the man struck Liam across the face. Bright pain, stinging and pounding all at once.

"Don't!" Phoebe shouted.

Liam stopped resisting, stunned.

The man hurled Liam's link off the deck and handed the data key to Tarra. She smiled at Liam, pocketed the key, and patted Phoebe's shoulder. "Mission accomplished." Phoebe tried to pull free but Tarra held her tightly to her side. "Don't worry, Xela—when your parents awaken, we will tell them that you served the cause ably while they slept." She motioned to Liam. "There's no reason to bother them with all of this confusion you've been having."

"He saved my life," said Phoebe. "So many times."

"Humans are funny that way," said Tarra. "What about the bot?" she said to Barro, who was still in the cruiser doorway.

"It's dead. Won't reboot."

"He had a system failure," said Phoebe. "During stasis. He'd been messed up ever since I used the dampener on him."

Tarra motioned to three other Telphons beside her, then to Barro. "Get the pods." She looked at Liam. "I guess I should say thank you for taking care of our girl." She patted Phoebe's shoulder. "This must be quite the shock, finding out who she really is."

"I showed him back on Delphi," said Phoebe.

This seemed to take Tarra by surprise.

"Please just let us go," said Liam.

"I'm afraid we can't do that," said Tarra, as Barro and the other soldiers appeared, carrying the pods with Phoebe's parents. They climbed down the steps and moved toward the sleek ship that hovered nearby. "We have a mission to finish here, and time is growing short."

"But it's not their fault!" Phoebe wrenched herself away from Tarra and darted over to Liam. She stood beside him and faced her people. "They were desperate!"

"Xela," said Tarra, "we are not going to go over this again. You're young and you've spent a long time with these humans. It's understandable—"

"Tarra! Listen! I know they did what they did, and we can't ever forgive them for that, but we have bigger problems."

"Bigger problems than an alien race heading for our home world?"

"Kind of, yes! You don't know about the Drove!" shouted Phoebe.

"The who?"

"They're another race of beings. Maybe from another universe. They're blowing up stars on purpose. That's what happened to the humans, and it's happening to Centauri right now. But it's even more dangerous than that. We have to work together if we're going to stop them."

Tarra peered at her like she was speaking another language. "And how do you know about this?"

"We saw it. There are these other aliens. Chronologists. We found a dead one on Mars and she showed us the proof."

Tarra cocked her head. "Do you hear yourself? None of this makes sense."

"It's true! Don't just discount what I'm saying. Please let us show you."

Tarra seemed to think about this for a moment. "Even if it is true, we can worry about it once the existential threat to our people has been eliminated." She turned to another Telphon soldier. "Take her to the ship."

"This IS the existential threat!" Phoebe shouted. "You have to listen! What they're doing is endangering the whole universe!"

"That's enough."

The soldiers grabbed Phoebe by either arm. She struggled against them but they were too strong. "The humans didn't mean to do it! They—" Phoebe made an inhuman sound, like a high-pitched whistling, her face contorted, and the effort made her double over, coughing.

"Stop!" Tarra shouted.

The soldiers paused, holding Phoebe between them.

"Phoebe . . ." Tarra pointed at Liam. "They *knew*. Tell her."

"What?" said Liam.

"I don't know what lies you've been feeding her on this journey," said Tarra, "about your poor, innocent humans, but it sounds like you conveniently left out one thing: you knew. We hacked the archives of the Phase One project. There was a faction of scientists on the team who were convinced that your data showed a reasonable chance of evolved life on Telos. But the rest of them didn't listen. They chose to destroy our world anyway."

"They wouldn't," said Liam. "There's no way if my parents knew that they'd—"

Tarra's eyes narrowed. "Your parents were part of the group that overruled that faction. Your father gave the launch order."

A surge of cold raced through Liam. He locked eyes with Phoebe. "That can't be true."

"Put her on board," Tarra said, waving Phoebe and the two soldiers away.

"Phoebe, it's not true! I swear!" And yet Liam didn't feel sure of that at all.

"Don't hurt him!" Phoebe called. "Tarra, please, don't."

Tarra hesitated, then motioned to Liam. "Put him in a stasis pod." She turned to two other soldiers. "Double-check our setup on the bridge." She strode toward her ship. "Then we depart."

Liam tried to run—he barely made it a step before two guards had him. "What about my parents?"

Tarra spun around, her voice razor thin. "Thank

you again for taking care of Xela."

"Liam!" Phoebe shouted from the stairs to the alien ship.

Liam fought against his captors, but they dragged him across the hangar, his arms burning in their grip, his feet skidding on the floor. He twisted and writhed, but it was no use. They took him to the edge of the platform, the dizzying view of decks above and below, and for a moment he thought they might just throw him off the edge, but instead they forced him down switchbacking flights of metal stairs, two decks below, then over to another haphazard pile of stasis pods.

Many were full, but there was a line of about ten that were open, their insides empty, the fluid lines and stimulators hanging unceremoniously over the edge. As the soldiers pushed Liam toward one, he saw a smear of blood on the pillow.

"Don't do this," he said.

The Telphon soldier spoke in strange chirping, whistling sounds. The other replied, and they shoved him in and slammed the top down.

"No!" Liam pounded his hands against the flex-glass top. One of the Telphons held it down with both hands while the other activated the pod. The locks engaged. The lights lit up around the inside edge. The two Telphons stepped away.

"No, please! Don't!" Liam screamed and kicked,

sobbing now, slamming his hands, and they hurt, everything hurt. They couldn't do this—

The gas jets began to hiss.

"NO!" Liam fell back, his body limp in shock and terror. He lay there, blinking, breathing out of control, chest heaving.

There was a hum and a rumble that shook the pod. Liam saw a shadow above: the Telphon ship moving out over the edge of the hangar decks and rotating.

Phoebe . . .

The ship slipped out of sight, heading toward the airlock.

He was going to die. They were all going to die.

His fingers and toes started to tingle. His head swam in that familiar way as the stasis gas took hold. He blinked against tears and saw the supernova, saw himself facing it—

Blinked: to the balcony on Mars, Mina frowning at him as he made a move on the game board—

Blinked: to the basement levels of Delphi, saw the explosion that killed him—killed the other him—

He felt like he was in all those places at once, felt that rush of wind inside him, that sense of being unstuck, adrift, like he had just turned the watch dial, like he was traveling in time, except Phoebe had the watch.

Liam saw himself outside the pod, saw himself

back on the cruiser as Barro rattled the door, standing there between his parents, saw the Telphons
approaching the starliner.

His head spun like he was in zero gravity, but it
was more than that. It was as if forward and backward
were places he could see, could reach, if he pushed
toward them, like he didn't even need the watch.

And yet what did it matter? There was no way out
of this pod, no one to help him. In moments, he'd
be in stasis, as good as dead. Maybe he could call
JEFF—but no, JEFF was shut down, and he didn't
even have his link. . . .

I have modified this, per your instructions, JEFF had
said before deactivating himself. But Liam hadn't
given him instructions.

Or had he?

He thought of that voice in the cockpit that had
sounded like his own, and then that vision of himself
by his parents' pods.

Maybe he hadn't given JEFF those instructions . . . yet.

Liam closed his eyes and focused, through the
wind and fog in his mind, and he could almost see it,
the cruiser, himself standing by his parents' pod, in
his past, the memory of it—

But this was more than that. Like Liam really

was seeing it, even like he could *be* there if he concentrated, if he pushed.

Stasis gas filled his lungs. Liam's hands and feet felt distant. His skin far away. He was going under— but also maybe somewhere else entirely.

You are starting to experience time differently, the chronologist had said. Could he? He pushed harder, felt that breeze in him, like his very molecules were seeds on the wind.

Pushed . . .

The gas completed its cycle inside the stasis pod.

But Liam was no longer there.

16

Liam pushed through the wind, a cold liquid feeling. He saw the stasis pod, the confrontation with Tarra, the cruiser leaving the *Scorpius,* all passing by in reverse, and now he saw himself standing between his parents' pods—remembered it, too, a strange sensation of seeing something new that was also a memory, of being both inside and out.

There was Phoebe, a few feet away, her human face just removed. The rattling of the magnet drill on the cruiser doors. He could hear it, feel it in his feet. This was different from when he'd traveled with the watch. It didn't feel like he was merely observing. He seemed to actually *be* here, in his past. Liam remembered this moment, how there had been two of him here. Now he was that second version of himself.

Inside his head, though, something else was happening. Liam had a sensation as if his entire life were somehow all around him, each moment like one of those glass bubbles in the baths on Delphi. His past: the chronologist's office, landing at Delphi, kissing Phoebe, leaving Mars, the balcony with his family, and so many more. And in the other direction his future, though these moments were less defined, perhaps because he hadn't lived them yet. He saw a dark area lined with stasis pods, flashes and explosions in the blur of space, and then the vision he'd had so often: stuck in the skim drone with Phoebe, facing the coming supernova. What happened after that? Liam tried to see farther, but everything beyond there seemed to be blurry, almost as if he'd reached the limits of what his human brain could handle.

We experience time the same as you experience the three dimensions of height, width, and depth, the chronologist had said. Was that what was happening to him? Was Liam experiencing his life four-dimensionally? Whatever this was, he wanted to stay and visit all these moments—

Yet this ability didn't change the fact that he was still, at some point in his timeline, stuck in that stasis pod, with Phoebe gone and hundreds of millions of lives, including his family's, in grave danger. It was astonishing that he could experience time like this, but right now he needed to *use* time.

And he already had. He'd moved himself backward from the pod to this moment in the cruiser. Somehow he had done this without the watch. *The watch changed me,* he thought, and the idea turned some of his wonder to fear, but he would have to worry about that later.

Right now, or then, the watch was what he needed to worry about. The past version of himself was still wearing it. Liam already knew from being in this moment the first time that this was what he was here to do. But why give the watch to Phoebe? Because they'd take it from him, that seemed certain. Maybe he could think of a place on the cruiser to hide it, but Barro was already inside.

And he also remembered his future, in the skim drone: he'd seen the watch on Phoebe's wrist.

Liam leaned toward his earlier self: "Give her the watch."

The Liam in the past turned and looked right at him, and he remembered how odd that had been.

"Give her the watch. Tell her to hide it." Liam smiled at his earlier self, as if to say, *It's all right, I know what I'm doing.* And yet, did he? He wasn't entirely sure.

Phoebe started to turn back around, and Liam pushed away, out of the moment, through the time-stream as if on a breeze. Okay, what was next? He still needed to come up with a way to get out of that stasis pod. Could he just go to the future and open it himself? But he wasn't sure if he could move past that moment when his physical body was trapped. Wasn't that still technically his "present"? Also, even though he was doing this without the watch, wasn't there still some danger that traveling into the future would alert the Drove, same as when he'd tried it before?

That moment just before they'd landed still seemed like the best place to start. JEFF had behaved strangely. Maybe Liam could be the cause.

He pressed himself back into the world again, saw his earlier self and the others in the cockpit as the cruiser entered the *Scorpius's* docking bay.

JEFF got up to lower the landing gear. Liam ducked into the galley as the bot rolled by.

He wondered if he could just tell himself to leave, to fly off right now, or go back further to tell himself to get out of the Centauri system before they even hailed the *Scorpius*, but that wouldn't solve anything—he was the only hope that Mina, Shawn, and the rest of the humans on the starliners had.

So then, should he warn himself about the Telphons? But he wasn't sure what good that would do, either. Maybe his best chance was to let the Telphons think they had taken care of him, and leave the *Scorpius* unguarded.

JEFF had opened a panel in the floor and was manually cranking down the landing gear. When he stood, Liam stepped out.

"JEFF."

"Yes L—"

Liam threw a hand over JEFF's mouth. "Don't say anything. It's me, but not the me who's in the cockpit now. I'm from another time."

JEFF leaned and looked into the cockpit. Then back. Liam slowly took his hand away from JEFF's mouth. "I can calculate no other possible explanation for your appearance," JEFF said quietly, "unless you are the result of a malfunction in my perception pathways."

"It's really me. I'm here, but I can only stay for a second. Listen, we're going to be in trouble soon. Is there a way for you to shut yourself down for a while, so that you seem to be out of commission, but then turn back on?"

"Let me calculate." JEFF's eyes flickered. "Yes. I could put myself into a lockdown state that would appear to be a total system failure. I could use Phoebe's dampener to initiate it."

"Okay, good. And when you wake up, I'm going to

346

need you to come find me fast. I'll be in a stasis pod."

"Where?"

"A couple decks down."

"Which stasis pod? My sense was that there are many stored on each deck."

"I'm not really sure. It was a blur."

"Then I will just home in on your link."

"I won't have my link."

JEFF checked the cockpit again. "All of this is extremely complicated."

"Yeah, I know, but can you do it?"

"If you will not have your link, perhaps I could find you via a subcutaneous tracking beacon."

"Yes. That will be perfect."

"Okay, I will need to inject that in your upper arm. Just wait right there."

"No, JEFF, it's not for me. It's for . . ." Liam pointed to the cockpit. "That me." Then he pointed to himself. "I'm going to leave now. Oh, and don't tell *that* me about *this* me. I mean, you won't, but maybe that's because I'm telling you not to now."

"I am not following."

"Just do all this, okay? You'll need to be shut down for like fifteen minutes. Then come find me."

JEFF's eyes flickered for a long moment. Liam worried that he'd shorted out JEFF's systems, but finally, he said, "Acknowledged."

"Thanks. And JEFF. Don't forget, or we'll all die. Make a backup of this conversation log or something."

"Will do, Captain."

Liam breathed deep and turned in on himself and moved again. He remembered that he had one more stop to make, just a bit further back in his timeline. He pushed along, like swimming in one of those circulating lazy rivers they'd had back at the athletic complex on Mars, the world blurring around him as it ran in reverse. He felt a quiver in his stomach but realized that he felt far less nauseated and achey than he had in his prior trips through the timestream. And yet maybe he should be worried about that, too; what was happening to him?

He watched himself in the cockpit, the starliners shrinking out of sight, the stars of the Centauri system retreating. He stopped and slipped forward, to the moment when JEFF was just beginning to hail the *Scorpius*. He understood this now: JEFF and past Liam and Phoebe had no idea yet that the Telphons had hijacked the ship, so if the Telphons and their sleeper agent captain heard JEFF over the link, then they wouldn't believe the story later about JEFF being broken.

He pushed into the moment, standing just behind his past self, and leaned down behind his own ear.

"Tell him you want to hail the *Scorpius*," he whispered.

His past self twitched, and Liam remembered hearing this very voice, his own voice, and felt a strange sort of spiraling inside himself. Past Liam sat there frozen—he'd been confused by this—while JEFF began the hail. "Hurry!" Liam told himself. "Before he talks!"

Liam watched his past self lean forward, remembered leaning forward and cutting JEFF off, asking to hail the *Scorpius* himself.

Okay, everything was in place. Liam let go of the moment, drifting back into the timestream, and as he did so, his insides fluttered with fear. Now he had to return to himself, to stasis, and hope it all worked. But again he wondered: Did he *have* to just return to his present? Should he at least try going forward just a little, to be sure JEFF showed up?

Maybe he should even try visiting that moment in the skim drone. Why were things blurry beyond it? Was it because he died there? How? If he knew, maybe he could figure out a way to avoid it.

And yet, the chronologist had said that was not advisable. And even if it was possible, the Drove might just find him on his way there.

Liam felt himself winding tighter, his emotions

knotting in a ball. Maybe it was simpler than all that.

Maybe he just didn't want to know.

He was nearing his present now, and he felt the terror again, of being locked in that stasis pod, his body going cold. Returning also meant losing control and hoping JEFF would come through and wake him up.

One unknown at a time, his mother had said.

Okay. He pressed into himself, like sinking into a frigid gray fog, and the world dissolved around him.

A gasp, and he was suddenly back. On his hands and knees, the freezing metal floor wavering into focus. His eyes stung, his hands were clammy, body was shaking.

"Welcome back, Liam."

He struggled to raise his head, gulping air. JEFF lifted him gently to his feet.

"How long was I under?"

"Approximately twelve minutes. I apologize—my reboot took slightly longer than expected. I had to briefly replay recent conversations to recover my damaged memory."

"It's okay, JEFF. How long until the supernova?"

"I calculate just under two hours." JEFF's head swiveled around. "Do you know the status of this ship? I detect no awake personnel, and without the VirtCom it is impossible to access its systems."

"Everyone's in stasis," said Liam, glancing back at the pod they'd put him in. "Or worse. And Phoebe—they all left. We need to get to the bridge." Liam tried to turn and stumbled into JEFF.

"Acknowledged, but first you need a stasis booster. You were put into that chamber unprepared, and even that short period in hibernation has compromised your systems."

"JEFF, I'm not a computer, we can worry about how I feel later—" Liam tried to brush him off, but bright spots bloomed in his vision. JEFF didn't know the half of it, with the effects of stasis compounded by his time traveling. It made him want to sink back again, try to get outside himself, this weak body that was trapped in the present.

"I'm afraid this time, Captain, my safety protocols compel me to overrule you."

"Fine," said Liam, still breathing hard. "Let's hurry."

"Allow me." JEFF twisted and scooped Liam off the ground in his arms.

"Whoa, JEFF—"

"Remain calm, Liam. I have you." He began to wheel across the deck, a sound like crackling electronics coming from somewhere inside his body. "That's nothing to worry about."

"Whatever you say."

JEFF rolled to the elevators, and they zipped up to the level where the cruiser was parked. As they crossed the deck, there was a rumble and whine through the walls of the ship.

"That star is becoming very unstable," said JEFF. "Just hurry."

They reached the cruiser and the bot clomped up the stairs and set Liam on the couch. He rolled to the cabinets and returned with two orange pills in one hand and a syringe in the other. "Take these." He gave the pills to Liam. "And—"

"Ow!" Liam flinched as JEFF jabbed the needle into his shoulder, the opposite one from where he'd inserted the tracker, and depressed the syringe. "Now both shoulders are killing me."

"You will feel notably better in a minute. Please take those pills." JEFF rolled into the cockpit.

Liam swallowed the pills dry, then made his way into the galley and filled a cup with water.

"I am no longer getting a link signal from the bridge," said JEFF. "Nor can I establish communication with the other starliners."

"They killed the active command crews and shut down the bots," said Liam, joining him in the cockpit. Liam looked at the dots on the navigation holoscreen—the giant starliners just sitting there. "All the passengers are asleep. Is there any way to wake them?"

"We will need to check the condition of the *Scorpius* bridge," said JEFF. "We may be able to reestablish the local link channel to send an activation command to the bots on the other starliners, who in turn can wake up another command crew."

"Can you do that in time?" asked Liam.

"I will not be able to say for sure until I reach the bridge."

"Okay, let's go, then."

JEFF put his hand on Liam's shoulder. "I would advise that you stay with your parents until I determine the extent of the situation. In the event that I cannot for certain get the *Scorpius* to safety, you must have the cruiser ready to depart."

"But you'd come with us, wouldn't you?"

"My programming instructs me to pursue the safety of the most lives possible. If there is any chance I can save the millions aboard this ship, then I must do that, even if it means being here past Red Line." He patted Liam's shoulder. "You may have to leave without me."

"JEFF, I can't pilot the ship alone, find fuel, all of that."

"Let me assess the situation." JEFF rolled out of the cockpit.

Liam felt as if he was freezing up inside. "Wait!" He darted out into the living area. JEFF paused on the stairs outside the airlock. "What about Mina? And Shawn? I'm not leaving without them."

JEFF's eyes flickered. "I calculate that you will not accept the reasoning that it is too risky to try to find them in the limited time that we have."

Liam clenched his jaw. "Correct."

"Acknowledged. In that case, I will access the logs once I am on the bridge and let you know where she is."

"Shawn too."

"But Liam, what about Shawn's father? And Shawn's grandfather? They are on board. Shawn won't want to be rescued without them. And Wesley's cousin—"

"Okay, I get it. We can't get them all. But Mina . . ."

"The sooner I go, the sooner I can tell you." JEFF lowered himself down the steps.

Liam's throat tightened. "JEFF, be careful."

JEFF reached the deck and looked back. "Thank you, Captain Liam. I will follow all safety protocols." He raised his arm and saluted, his panda face fixed in its permanent grin, then rolled toward the elevators.

As soon as the doors slid closed behind him, Liam slammed his forearm against the wall. He hated being stuck here, waiting helplessly.

He checked his parents' pods—they were still functioning normally—and returned to the galley, where he found a nutri-bar and wolfed it down. Then he sat in the cockpit, his head still aching.

He wondered where Phoebe was. Were they even still in this part of the galaxy? Or had they left, perhaps searching out the next starliner to attack? Had they awakened Phoebe's parents yet, and did they know what she had done? Had she tried to convince them to stop fighting? He doubted they'd listen to her.

He missed her—she was the only person on his side, perhaps in the universe, unless being with her own people had changed her mind again. He doubted that, too. There was no one as stubborn as Phoebe.

His fingers drifted to his wrist, wishing he could go back to Mars and find her somewhere before everything had changed, but then he remembered he'd given her the watch. Of course he didn't even really need it now. . . .

The cruiser's link blinked to life: *Scorpius Command*.

"Liam, this is JEFF, come in."

"How's it look?"

"It is more serious than we realized; it . . ." JEFF paused as if he was searching for what to say. "Sorry, Liam, most of my processors are being rerouted. The Telphons wrecked the bridge. All of the comms and guidance systems are down, and they slaved the ship's central operating systems to some sort of dampening program that is . . . keeping the bots from activating on their usual cycles. Therefore I am using my own processors to m-m-mirror the *Scorpius* systems while I repair them. . . ."

"Are you sure you can handle that?"

"I am uncertain, but I cannot calculate another option."

"What about Mina?"

"Yes, I . . . The logs indicate that she was recovered. So, for that matter, were Shawn. . . ."

Liam slid down in his chair and pumped his fist.

"And Wesley. Mina's stasis pod is stored in Core Two, S-S-Segment Three, but the log does not indicate a more specific location than that. It must have been compiled in haste."

"Core Two—wasn't that the core with the big hole in it?" Liam asked.

"Yes, Segment Three is in fact the one that was damaged. The hull breach shorted out its systems and gravity, but this actually made it easier to float the stasis pods into position. Each pod has a magnetic lock, which they used to attach them to the walkways."

"The segments are huge," Liam said, remembering how long it took him and Phoebe to get from one end to the other when they had been on the *Artemis*. "Isn't there a way to scan for her?"

"All scanning functions in Core Two are offline. . . ."

I may be able to spare . . . some processing space to repair them. . . ."

"No, that's okay, I get it. You have to focus on fixing the ship." Liam sat back, clenching his jaw, breathing hard. He checked the time: one hour and forty minutes until red line. Less than a blink of an eye in this universe. He felt like he was melting down inside, his hands balled into fists. He imagined Mina in her stasis tube, in the dark of that core—

Liam looked down at his shirt. He pulled out the beacon and pressed its green top. It didn't respond, of course, but Mina's beacon would still be lighting up.

He stabbed the link. "JEFF, I know how to find Mina. You can reach me in the skim drone, got it?"

"Acknowledged . . . but Liam, remember the time—"

"Don't worry," said Liam. "I got this."

17

Liam hurried into the cabin. Core Two was depressurized; he should use a space-grade suit to be safe. He pulled one from the closet and slid it on. He grabbed the helmet and a jet pack and had turned to go when he spied his Dust Devils jersey balled up in the corner. He grabbed it and stuffed it in his helmet, then ran for the hatch.

He climbed into the skim drone, buckled in, and hit the main power. Lights began to flash around the console. Liam flexed his fingers on the controls and his mind slipped—there was the giant star, the supernova imminent, Phoebe beside him. He shut his eyes and took a long, deep breath, fighting the adrenaline coursing through him. Just because he was getting into the skim drone near the supernova didn't mean that future was destined to happen. Phoebe wasn't even here. Had to keep his mind on what was happening right now, in the present.

All systems came online. Liam checked the battery level: 97 percent, even though it had been charging for decades, but the level was holding steady. JEFF's patch seemed to be working. He detached from the cruiser and moved out from beneath it using short bursts of the lateral thrusters, then flew to the edge of the landing platform.

Liam surveyed the decks above and below him. Which way would lead to Core Two? But he couldn't be sure the skim drone would even fit through all the corridors and airlocks. It would be faster to fly outside and through that hole in the side. He rotated the drone and darted over to the airlock, where he sent a departure request. Yellow lights flashed around the perimeter, and the giant inner doors slid open.

He flew into the airlock. Once the set of doors behind him had locked shut, red lights flashed and all the air and sound sucked away. The outer doors slid silently open in the vacuum of space. As soon as the gap was wide enough, Liam shot out into the dark. His fingers danced over the thrusters, arcing the skim drone along the front section of the starliner.

It seemed so much bigger when you were in a ship this small, like it might roll over and crush you at any moment.

He flew out from beneath the front section and angled toward Core Two. White light from Centauri B shone down from directly above him, and to his port side, the fiery orange light from Centauri A. Liam frowned. The star looked even bigger than it had when they'd arrived.

He zipped along the great curving hull of the core. Thousands of little windows beside him, all dark.

Ahead was the blast hole in Segment Three, like some interstellar shark had taken a bite out of the ship. Liam centered himself outside the gaping darkness and, holding his breath, flew in. Mangled metal beams and tangled, twisted wiring reflected in the skim drone's lights, reaching out at him from all sides. He zigged and zagged through the wreckage, at one point catching a glimpse into a stateroom that seemed almost perfectly intact, except that its wall had been ripped off, the bathroom bitten in half, all its pods gone.

Then he was through and into the cavernous core. He pivoted and flew beside the nearest walkway, lined with stateroom doors. The park was below him, its grass brown and frozen. Ice coated every surface: the walkway railings, the walls and doors, and the thousands of stasis pods that had been salvaged from Core Three and were now lined up end to end on each walkway. Around him at the edges of the skim drone's lights, the cables of the transport system—some of them snapped—gleamed like webs, as if this core were the lair of some giant spider.

Liam tugged the beacon from his suit and pressed the top, peering out the cockpit for a glimpse of the tiny green light. But the drone's lights were too bright, causing a million glittering refractions of ice, and it was too dark beyond their reach. Liam slowed to a stop and turned off the lights. He pressed the beacon again. No sign of its twin. He turned the drone lights back on, shot forward a few hundred meters, stopped, and tried again. Only darkness.

He repeated this sequence over, and over, until he'd reached the end of the core segment. He flew along the inner curve of the wall and reversed direction, a new set of balconies in view beside him. He started back up the core, flying short distances, extinguishing his lights, and pressing the beacon.

As he went, he checked the battery: 88 percent. Was that lower than it should have been at this point? Maybe. But there was still plenty of juice left.

He'd reached the end of his third sweep when the drone's link activated.

"Liam, this is JEFF. What is your status?"

"I'm still looking for Mina." He checked the time. One hour and fourteen minutes until Red Line. He'd scanned barely a quarter of the segment so far, at best. "What's going on there?"

"I have analyzed their d-d-dampening program, and I have calculated a way to disrupt it. I am testing it here on the *Scorpius*. If it works, I will have to wake a bot on each of the other starliners to do the same thing. But I will need to access fleet logs to get the identification codes for exact bots to contact directly, as the ship-wide link systems are down."

"That sounds like a lot to do in just over an hour."

"Yes . . . I would advise that you begin returning to the cruiser soon, to prepare for departure."

"I'm not going without Mina."

"You may have to, in order to save yourself and your parents."

"Just tell me when your test is done."

Liam slammed the controls and screamed in the cockpit. He needed to go faster! There were too many decks, and not enough time, and he only had two eyes—

Wait. He opened the options for the navigation screen. Of course! He could change the display to view all four directional cameras at once. He turned off the lights and pressed the beacon. Nothing, but he could see many more pods this way. He moved along, trying over and over. Reached the end. Moved and started back again.

He'd checked nearly half the segment now, but fifteen more minutes had passed. Under an hour to Red Line.

"How's that test going, JEFF?"

No response.

Liam darted farther up the core before doing his next test. But if he went too far, he might miss some. *I have to risk it. I'm running out of time.* Still nothing. He flew again. Pressed the beacon.

Wait. Was that a flash of light on the port camera? He tapped the beacon again.

There she was! A weak green glint, on the far side of the segment. Liam held his breath, tapping the spot and setting navigation. He rotated the ship and shot toward her, dipping and darting to avoid the glittering transport cables. As he flew, he doused his lights and hit the beacon, and the green light glimmered brighter, and a moment later he was there, hovering in front of a walkway, where a single stasis pod among all the others had a tiny green light flashing through its icy top. Liam tilted the skim drone and pressed the beacon and the light bloomed inside, illuminating a faint outline of Mina's shoulders and chin through the frost.

"Hi," Liam said quietly. He laughed to himself,

and tears leaked from his eyes, and he kept pressing the beacon and looking at the faint impression of his sister, right there, finally, after so long.

"Liam," said JEFF. "Are you headed back to the cruiser?"

"I found her, JEFF!" Liam couldn't help shouting. "How's it going there?"

"I have successfully disabled the Telphons' programming. I am rebooting ship systems, and will attempt to contact bots on the other starliners in a few minutes. However, you still need to be prepared to take action if this does not work. Time is running out."

"I know. It's okay now," he said. "I'll be back there in a second."

Liam figured the skim drone was strong enough to override the pod's magnet. He rotated so that the bottom claw was facing Mina's pod, tapped the thrusters to line up, and then extended the claw, watching on the underside camera. He closed its bulky metal fingers around the sides of the pod, breathing with as much relief as he could ever remember feeling. He fired the thruster gently—

The skim drone shuddered but didn't budge. Liam tried again, to the same result, then stopped. He couldn't risk damaging the pod or skim drone.

"JEFF," Liam said into the link. "How do you detach the magnet lock on the pod?"

"Just a moment. . . ."

Liam bit his lip. He checked the time. Forty-nine minutes. Cold sweat dripped beneath his arms.

"JEFF, I need to—

"Apologies, my processors are nearly maxed out. The lock mechanism is on the right side of the main control panel of the pod. Look for a small blue lever."

"Okay."

"Liam, you really need to—"

"I know! Hold on."

Liam put on his helmet and activated his suit. He opened the canopy, and sound and air sucked away, his suit humming against the frigid cold of space. He unbuckled and floated out of the drone, guiding himself down the front of the ship using the gold towing rings. He moved quickly but carefully to the underside of the ship and then pulled himself along the claw until he was beside Mina's pod. He rubbed his glove over the top, scattering a cloud of ice crystals, and there was Mina, her face serene and asleep. "Hey, sis."

The controls on the side of the pod were frosted over. Liam located the little blue handle, pulled the lever, and felt the pod shift beneath him, floating free. He pushed off the balcony railing back up to the side of the drone, and climbed inside. As soon as the cabin repressurized, he yanked off his helmet and fired the thruster. The skim drone lurched and lifted away from the balcony. On the camera, Liam could see his sister safely in the grip of the claw beneath him.

"JEFF, I have Mina. I'm headed back to the cruiser."

He nearly burned the thruster at full power, but Mina's pod immediately buffeted off one of the transport cables, and Liam reminded himself that the ship had a bigger profile now with her pod, and snagging on one of those cables could send them spinning to a crash.

He checked the time: forty-one minutes until Red Line. But he had Mina now. It would be enough.

Liam threaded his way back to the gaping hole and then shot out through the jaws of debris. He emerged into space and found himself face-to-face with the boiling orange star. *Sorry to disappoint you*, he thought, *but I'm not dying here.*

He flew along the side of the core and then back under the front section of the starliner to the docking bay airlock. He sent the landing request, and moments later, he was back inside the hangar.

"All right, JEFF, I'm back. Is it working?"

"Good news. I have successfully contacted a bot on each ship. The *Saga* has rebooted and awakened a command team, and they have also confirmed that they can fly the starliner at least enough to execute a burn out of the system. I expect the *Rhea* will be in the same condition. However, I have also confirmed that one thing the Telphon commander told us is true: The *Scorpius* is too low on fuel to depart on its own. It will need to be towed by the other starliners using their magnet tethers. This will require a more gradual engine burn, but I believe we can reach a safe enough distance to then compensate by using the solar sails to harness the energy wave of the supernova."

"And there's time for that?"

"We will find out shortly."

"JEFF, translate! Does that mean we're going to make it or not?"

"My calculations indicate that your odds for survival will be better staying with the *Scorpius* at this point."

"Okay, well, I'll wake up Mina. Keep me posted."

He gently lowered Mina's pod to the floor beside the Cosmic Cruiser. As he retracted the skim drone's claw, he gazed at her through the underside camera. He could still see her sleeping face through the hole he had rubbed in the frost. He tapped the thrusters to dock beneath the cruiser—

A great rumble shuddered through the *Scorpius*, rattling the entire hangar. Mina's pod skidded on the floor. There was a wicked crack, and a section of paneling crashed down beside the cruiser.

"JEFF, what was that?"

"We appear to be under attack from the Telphon craft."

"They're back?"

"One of our engines has been hit with their particle incinerator weapon. I am scrambling our defensive fleet of drone fighters to engage, as is the *Saga*. The *Rhea* is nearly online."

"But you can't destroy it! Phoebe's on that ship!"

"We must protect the hundreds of millions of lives on board," said JEFF. "That said, the Telphon ship has some sort of cloaking device and is difficult to target. It just fired on the *Saga*, taking out its primary shielding. I am running analysis to develop a counterstrategy, as we cannot defend ourselves for long against their weaponry—"

A muted sound distracted Liam. Like a voice. Liam checked the skim drone's link, but only JEFF was transmitting on it. He glanced around the hangar; had someone called to him from the deck? But there was no one around.

Are you there? it sounded like the voice had said. It seemed to be coming from inside the craft—Liam pushed aside his helmet. A light flashed within the folds of his Dust Devils jersey.

"Of course you're not. But I didn't know what else to do."

Phoebe!

Liam grabbed the jersey. There was something tucked in its front pocket: Phoebe's link. That strange symbol she'd shown him was flashing on its screen.

"We'll never see each other again," Phoebe said. "I guess I just want the universe to know that I'm sorry, and I was wrong. I—"

Liam tapped the symbol. "Phoebe! Phoebe, it's me! I'm here!"

"Liam! You're okay!"

"Where are you?"

"I'm on our ship! They don't know I'm contacting you. Where are you?"

"In the skim drone."

"Still on the *Scorpius*?"

"Yeah. What's happening? I thought you left."

"Liam, I couldn't talk them out of it. We'd moved to a safe distance, to see what we could learn about the Drove after the nova. But then we detected your ships coming back online. It's my fault they knew about the Drove—otherwise we would have just left. Even when I'm right, I'm wrong. You have to get out of there."

"Where am I going to go?" said Liam. "We're trying to get the starliners to safety. JEFF is on the bridge. I'm alone with my parents and sister."

"You found her? She's alive?"

"Yeah. Shawn is too."

Phoebe made a sniffling sound. "Liam, I'm sorry,

my parents won't listen. Neither will Barro or Tarra, or anyone else. They don't care about what I'm trying to tell them. About the Drove, the chronologist, that everything is so much more complicated than we know. They just want you all dead. I don't know what we're going to do, I—" There was a loud screeching sound.

"Phoebe?"

"Your fighters are firing on us. But they won't be able to stop us. This ship is too fast."

"I know." Liam looked at Mina's pod. He could load her onto the cruiser and run for it. Get his family to safety. But then what?

"Hello, Liam," said JEFF over the link. "Are you all right?"

"Hold on a sec," Liam said to Phoebe. "Yes, JEFF, um . . ." He probably shouldn't tell JEFF he was talking to Phoebe.

"Liam, you should dock the drone and buckle in on board. Things are about to get bumpy."

The entire ship lurched sharply around Liam.

"That was the magnet tether from the *Saga*," said JEFF. "The *Rhea* is moving into position."

"All three of us attached makes us sitting ducks, doesn't it?" said Liam.

"Momentarily, but do not worry. It is also a part of our counterstrategy against the hostile craft."

"Counterstrategy?" Liam eyed Phoebe's link. With a shaking finger, he pressed the icon so that she would hear their conversation. "What strategy is that?"

"I am now synced up with the other two commands. The enemy ship is too fast to pinpoint with our standard warheads. However, the *Rhea* was able to run scans, and we have determined that while the ship's engine possesses technology beyond our understanding, it still operates according to standard electromagnetic theory. Therefore, we are deploying the drone fighters in such a way as to draw the ship to a target location, at which point we are going to fire an array of warheads with timed detonation from all three starliners, encasing the ship in an electromagnetic blast that should render it inoperable."

"Inoperable, and then what? We just leave it there?"

"Then we will be able to target the ship directly."

"But JEFF—" Liam's insides squeezed tight. "Phoebe's on that ship."

"Acknowledged, but you must understand: she is part of a hostile alien force that is responsible for many thousands of lives lost already, and is currently attempting to kill many more."

"We're responsible for— Never mind."

Liam switched off the drone's link. "Did you hear that?" he said to Phoebe. "It's a trap."

"I heard it."

"You should tell your people our plan," said Liam, his heart racing.

"But then we might kill you!" Phoebe sniffled. "I told you I can't stop them. I'm powerless here. Just a stupid kid to them."

"I know the feeling."

A silence passed between them. Outside the drone, the *Scorpius* rumbled.

"I guess this is good-bye," said Phoebe.

As Liam listened, a great hole opened up inside him, like all of his emotions were spiraling down it. He closed his eyes and slid along, letting the breeze blow. Once again, he saw himself at different moments in time, all floating like bubbles. He saw the future, close now, the boiling star about to explode, Phoebe's icy face . . . but his thoughts slipped backward too, to sitting on the couch with her before Delphi, to being trapped on that ledge on Mars with her, to catching her eye and laughing when Shawn made a joke in class, and all the moments compressed into a ball inside him, heavier than anything he'd known.

He even remembered her makeup melting away and her true face becoming visible underneath it, the truth she'd dared to share with him. In her own way, she had probably seen that moment, that future, coming for a long time, but she had been brave.

He would be brave.

"Phoebe," he said calmly. "It's going to be all right."

"How?"

"Just a sec." Liam tapped the drone's link. "JEFF, how long until we fire those warheads?"

"Approximately ten minutes."

"Okay, thanks." Liam flexed his fingers on the controls. There was no point fighting it anymore. "JEFF, I need you to do something for me. Make sure my family is safe, okay?"

"Liam, I do not understand the circumstances of this order."

He breathed deep, then fired the thrusters and spun toward the airlock.

"Liam, where are you going?"

The inner doors slid open.

"Liam, please: I cannot calculate any scenario in which leaving this ship leads to a favorable outcome."

"Neither can I." He slid into the airlock, and when the outer doors opened, he fired the skim drone's thruster at full power. "Phoebe, can you turn on the location beacon on that link you're using?"

"Yeah, but why?"

"I'm coming to get you."

18

"Coming to get me?" said Phoebe. "How?"

"In the skim drone."

"But Liam, your vision—"

"I know—I think this is it."

Phoebe didn't reply right away. Liam maneuvered the drone out from under the starliner. The battery level was at 73 percent. Enough, maybe. And yet he wondered with a sinking feeling if he would need it.

He paired Phoebe's link with the skim drone and opened the tracking screen. A dot lit up, indicating Phoebe's position. "Okay, I've got you."

"You shouldn't do this," Phoebe finally said. "You should just get out of here."

Why?" Liam nearly shouted. "So we can watch our people slaughter each other and not be able to do anything about it? So one of us can watch the other die? All of this feels pointless if we're not together."

"But how are you even going to get to me? We're in a firefight."

"Those drone fighters should recognize me as a friendly ship," said Liam. "I think I can get close to you. If you can just get in a space suit and get outside somehow—"

"We don't have space suits that work for us. Just these weird things that the Styrlax use."

"Are there escape pods?"

"No, but . . ."

"What?"

"You said in your vision I seem cold," said Phoebe. "Do you remember what JEFF said about space? About surviving in the vacuum?"

"You mean that you can't?"

"No, you can, for about sixty seconds. And he was talking about humans. Might be a little longer for me."

"Or shorter, but—are you saying what I think you're saying?"

"You've seen it, Liam. It works."

The pit inside Liam grew deeper. "But we haven't experienced it yet. We don't know for sure."

"Then why are you flying toward me?"

Liam nodded to himself. She was right.

"The watch is blinking," said Phoebe.

"I'm sure it is."

Liam burned the main thruster. It shoved him back against the seat. Out the cockpit, he saw a series of bright flashes dead ahead. The giant red star was somewhere beneath him.

"So . . . ," said Phoebe. "I'm going to jump into the vacuum of space, and you'll catch me before I turn into an ice cube."

"That's the plan."

Another long pause. "How soon will you be here?"

Liam checked his acceleration, then the battery. Sixty-eight percent. It was draining faster than it used to. "Three minutes."

"We're getting shot at from all sides. What if I just get blown apart by enemy fire?"

"I don't think you will," said Liam.

"I guess I just have to trust you."

"That's what we do, right?" Liam watched the dot closing on his navigation screen. Out the windshield, the flashes of the firefight grew closer. And every time he blinked, he saw that vision, the boiling star through the cockpit window—

But no! He'd changed the future how many times? He could do it again. This vision was still probability, just one outcome. And it was one that included saving Phoebe.

An explosion caught his eye up ahead. He flew by a damaged drone fighter, spitting sparks. The drones were oval-shaped discs, with thrusters on all sides, each rotating around a spherical center like a giant metal marble.

He could see the Styrlax ship now, dead ahead, explosions flashing off its sleek exterior. It zigged and zagged through the swarm of drone fighters, a couple of them smashing against its hull. In a wicked burst of light, it fired a wide beam that incinerated two fighters, then continued burrowing through the dark. Liam lost sight of it, until moments later there was an explosion from one of the cores of the *Saga*.

Liam noticed that the *Rhea* had moved into parallel formation with the *Saga* to tow the *Scorpius*. Their engines were bright, as if they'd slowly begun to accelerate. The Styrlax ship was on a course that would bring it to the port side of the starliner formation.

"JEFF," Liam tried, but JEFF was no longer on his link screen. They were out of range, or maybe it was the interference from the firefight. How soon would they launch those warheads?

"Phoebe, I'm one minute out."

He heard Phoebe breathing hard. "Everyone's distracted. I'm—I'm in the airlock. Liam, I'm so scared."

Fifty seconds. "You're going to be all right. Just hold on to that link with both hands. Remember to close your eyes, and breathe out before you jump."

"It's going to hurt, isn't it?"

"I think so."

"But you're going to catch me."

"I'm going to fly right up and pull you in and you're going to make it." Liam felt determination coursing through him. They could do this.

Lights flashed all around him now, fighters swerving this way and that in flurries of quick rocket bursts. The skim drone drew closer to the alien ship, but it kept changing course, and Liam had to manually adjust his approach with the lateral thrusters. He was trailing only a couple hundred meters behind it.

"I'm here," said Liam.

"Okay, I'm going to do it," said Phoebe through rapid breaths. "Going to hit the button and jump. Wish me luck."

"Good luck. And you're holding the link tight?"

"In a death grip."

"Okay, go for it."

"You got me?"

"I got you."

"Here I go—" Liam heard her exhale, and then a metallic sound of rushing air.

He thought he saw a flash of light on the side of

the Styrlax ship, the airlock door opening. It swerved again, and the dot of Phoebe's link separated from it. Liam tapped the thrusters, counting the seconds.

Three, four, five . . .

He slowed slightly and lined up his intercept. A fighter shot by above him, was just past when it exploded in a silent flash. A chunk of it raked the skim drone's side and a warning light flashed.

Liam realigned, slowed further.

Eight, nine, ten . . .

He slapped on his helmet and locked it in place with shaking fingers.

Thirteen, fourteen, fifteen . . .

He opened the cockpit. With a great whoosh, the skim drone coughed out all of its air and silence engulfed him. Flashes of the firefight everywhere. Another drone fighter exploded nearby.

Liam double-checked his course and speed. They had to be lined up just right.

And there she was! Straight ahead, a tiny object just silhouetted in his lights. Her body an infinitesimal thing against the backdrop of the stars.

Nineteen, twenty . . .

"I'm coming," he said to himself. She was probably already unconscious, but he was close. Fifty meters.

Liam grabbed a safety line from its compartment and hooked it to his belt. He unbuckled his seatbelt and attached the hook on the end of the line to the tow handle beside the cockpit.

He started to float up. Phoebe was right in front of him now, her arms straight out in front her, hands clasped, and it was like they were both flying, seemingly in slow motion and yet at over a thousand meters per second. Her eyes were closed and her skin looked frosted in his helmet lights, her body stiff, literally freezing in the vacuum of space right at this very second. Had to hurry. He tensed, opened his arms.

Twenty-six, twenty-seven . . .

She was just above the drone, and he kicked gently against the hull to move closer—

Suddenly he was yanked hard and there was a bright flash and everything spun, the stars tumbling over and over.

A flash of shrapnel—the skim drone had been struck by a piece of fighter wreckage. Liam twisted, somersaulting away. *No!* He grabbed for the tether, the strap slipping through his gloves. Finally he gripped it and pulled himself hand over hand back toward the ship. This righted him with the skim drone but everything else was tumbling, the suns and explosions blurring by again and again. He gritted his teeth and focused only on the drone until he reached the cockpit.

The controls were dark.

Liam pulled himself inside and grabbed the booster pack from the floor.

Thirty-four, thirty-five—or maybe forty. He'd lost count.

The pack was clipped to the seat belt and he fumbled with that, too, before finally freeing it. He slid the straps over his shoulders and unclipped his safety line. He kicked off the side of the drone, and as he floated away from it, he wrestled to the get the thrust control free of its holder on the shoulder strap, and then hit the autostabilize. A series of small bursts fired on the back of the pack, stopping him from spinning. The skim drone was now above him. The firefight beneath his feet. *Keep it together!* he told himself.

How long had it been now? Fifty-five?

He rotated, peering into the dark—

There she was, so far now. . . . He straightened toward her and fired the main thruster on the pack, sailing toward her. Fired again, and again, trying to match her speed.

There was an explosion above, a silent flash, and chunks of pulverized fighter spreading in a fountain, but it had been heading away from him and the shrapnel continued in that direction.

Almost to Phoebe. A full minute now? More? She

was upside down relative to him. Liam fired again, coming at her on a sharp angle. All of a sudden too fast—

He slammed sideways into her back and wrapped his arms around her stiff, unmoving body. He nearly tumbled right over her but held on. *It's too late, too late—*

He fired the lateral thruster, turning until he spotted the skim drone, then the main thruster at full, wrenching them to a stop and sending them hurtling back toward the craft.

Had to be well over a minute by now. They neared the drone and he fired the reverse thrusters in pulses, slowing, slowing, but not slow enough—a quick burst of the lateral thruster and he was able to crash into the front of the drone with the booster pack rather than Phoebe's body. He felt it crunch through his suit. They bounced, tumbling over the cockpit and colliding with the open canopy, which caught them. For a moment he worried it would snap off and that would be the end, but the canopy held, and Liam grabbed the side of the ship with his free hand and pulled them down. He pushed Phoebe's frigid body into the seat, her legs wedging in the footwell, and then yanked down the canopy. The controls still dark, the cockpit as cold and airless as space.

He jammed his finger on the power button.

Nothing. Held it down. . . .

The craft hummed to life and began its restarting procedure, the welcome logo appearing on the main console screen. Systems flashed on in turn, and the blowers roared. A few seconds later, the air pressure and oxygen indicators blinked green. Liam tore off his helmet.

"Phoebe!" He turned her cold body toward him. He unzipped his suit, pushed it down to free his arms, and started rubbing Phoebe's shoulders. They felt so cold. "Come on, Phoebe. Come on." She wasn't breathing. Her lavender, dotted skin and black thermal wear crusted in frost, crystals beaded on the tips of her gray eyelashes.

Outside, lights strafed by and another drone fighter disintegrated a few hundred meters away. Liam wondered if the skim drone appeared on the Telphon scopes. He wondered if they knew that Phoebe was with him, or even that she was gone yet.

Liam made a two-handed fist, trying to remember the CPR lessons he'd gotten at the research station. Once every couple years he'd been forced to sit through them, assuming it was something he'd never need to know. Had it been thirty compressions? That sounded right. Then breathing, then more compressions. It was an ancient technique, but one that had proven its worth throughout the centuries.

He pressed his fist against Phoebe's chest, about to start—something vibrated there. Her artificial second heart. It was still working, or trying to. Would he damage it if he pressed? He started pumping anyway, his fists against her cold, cold sternum, watching her still face.

"Come on, Phoebe."

Thirty compressions. He held her nose, prickly to the touch, wiped away ice from between her lips, and leaned in and breathed three times. More compressions. He still felt the whirring of that pump, but nothing else.

It was taking too long.

He breathed into her mouth again. It had to have been nearly two minutes by now, if not more, and it wasn't working! More compressions. Five, ten—

She gasped and convulsed and drew in a weak, cold breath.

"Phoebe! It's okay, you're in the skim drone. I've got you."

Her lips moved slightly, like she was trying to say something, but her wheezing breaths made her wince, like they caused great pain. Shivers racked her body. Her eyes stayed closed.

Liam kept rubbing her shoulder with one hand but also reached for the drone's link and brought up available connections. *None.* He twisted around, trying to find the starliners. There they were, above and behind him. He fired the thrusters, rotating toward them. They were moving away, their engines glowing bright. Bursts of light flashed around them, and to and from a cluster of lights maybe halfway between the starliners and Liam. The swarming patterns of drone fighters, the white-hot blast of the Styrlax weapon.

He brought up navigation, found the *Scorpius* with the scanner, and selected it. He set the computer to calculate an intercept velocity. As long as they hadn't accelerated too much yet . . . A green line flashed between Liam's location and the starliner. It would take a 55 percent burn to catch them. He checked the battery level. He had 57 percent.

He glanced down at Centauri A. *See ya.* And he burned the thruster.

"Phoebe?"

The voice had come from inside the skim drone cockpit. A woman, speaking quietly.

She sniffled. "Phoebe, please respond."

Liam gently pried the link from Phoebe's wet, frigid fingers, but it was coated with melting ice, its screen dark. The voice was coming from elsewhere. Liam reached under Phoebe's legs and found her old link, the one that she'd left for him. It was blinking with the white signal.

"Phoebe . . ." Liam gazed at the link. It sounded

like her mother. He thought about turning it off.

"This is Liam," he said instead.

"Liam," said Ariana. "Where is Phoebe?"

"She's with me."

"Is she—"

"I think she'll be all right."

"We were fighting. She disappeared and she . . . jumped. What did you tell her?"

"I didn't tell her anything. You're all trying to destroy each other, but we're all in danger, and none of you would listen."

"What are you two planning?" Ariana asked. Liam could hear her choosing her words carefully.

"We're going to find another way."

"She belongs with us," said Ariana.

"That's not what she thinks."

Ariana didn't respond, but Liam sensed that she was still there.

He watched the Styrlax ship and its spiraling firefight, drawing closer to the starliners. Any second now, they would fire. Phoebe must not have told them about the human plan. . . . Liam's mouth went dry, his stomach flipping. If he just turned off the link—

"It's a trap," he said, and immediately wanted to take it back.

"What is?"

"They're drawing you into range; then they're

going to trap you with warheads, to disable your ship."

Just then, light burst from the starliners. Dozens of streaks of white, creating a spiraling ballet of glowing embers. The missiles were all in a tight cluster, heading straight for the alien ship.

"We can outmaneuver that with ease."

"That's what they want you to think," said Liam. "Until it's too late. You have to get out of there now."

Another pause: "Why would you help us?"

"Because I'm Phoebe's friend."

No reply again. Liam watched the dancing lights, the cluster speeding toward the Styrlax ship. Their weapon flashing, firing countermeasures at the warheads. All at once, the missiles broke formation and fanned out in wide arcs. It looked like a net, unfurling around the Telphons, creating a sphere—

There was a brilliant orange flash, like a disk of light, and just like that, the alien ship was gone. Not a second later, the warheads detonated, a sphere of stars all born at once, massive blinding flashes, making a giant corona of light that radiated out from the blast zone in all directions.

What had he done?

Liam watched in awe as the explosions merged, seeming to boil for a moment before dying out. All the lights of the fighter drones were gone, the blast having either destroyed them or knocked out their power, while that glowing corona expanded in all directions—

Including right toward him.

Oh no. Liam checked the navigation. Their burn wasn't complete yet. They were still accelerating to catch the starliners, gaining on them steadily, but with more to go. The battery was down to 15 percent and the wave of blast energy was hurtling toward them.

"Come on," said Liam, trying to will the drone to move faster. His speed was up to 89 percent of what he needed to catch the starliners . . . now 91. The battery down to 11 percent.

But that blast wave was closing.

The drone's link flashed.

"Liam, do you copy?"

"JEFF!" Liam shouted. He must have just crossed back into range. Burn at 94 percent. "I'm coming! I'm almost there, just hold on—"

A sizzling hiss grew around him, the ship vibrating, and Liam felt a static rush through his body. A bright flash—

The skim drone went dark.

"No, come on, no!" Liam jammed the power button and held it down. Nothing. The thruster was dead. All controls dead. The ship's link, their links, even their suits—knocked out by the electromagnetic pulse from the warheads' blast.

Liam slammed the controls with both fists and fell back against the seat, stunned. He stared uselessly at the starliners, so close . . . but he knew the math. Though the skim drone was currently hurtling toward them faster than they were departing, they were accelerating too. He hadn't reached a fast enough speed to catch them, and they couldn't turn back, not when that amount of mass was already in motion, and not with Red Line so soon.

Mina and his parents and JEFF and Shawn. . . . They were going to make it, but Liam had no idea where they were going, no way to catch them, and no way to survive out here.

He and Phoebe were marooned.

He shivered. It was already cooler, and without power, the tiny cabin of the skim drone could only keep out the icy cold of space for so long. Red Line couldn't be more than twenty minutes away. And how long after that before the supernova? Maybe an hour. But they would be frozen or out of oxygen long before the energy storm turned them to atoms.

The blast wave from the warheads had put the skim drone in a slow spin, and now the huge fiery eye of Centauri A slid into Liam's view directly in front of them, its orange light bathing his face.

Liam glanced at Phoebe, slumped on the seat beside him, breathing weakly, making tiny clouds of vapor in the rapidly cooling cabin.

This was it, then.

The future he'd seen.

He almost laughed, his eyes welling up. A dead end, literally. He'd been so stupid to think it might be anything else. They were going to freeze to death here. And then a supernova would wash them away. Their people would destroy each other, or most of each other, and one by one the stars would keep going dark until reality tore apart and collapsed on itself.

The feeling closed in on him from all sides. Liam fished the beacon out of his shirt and pressed the top. No response, of course, but he at least smiled momentarily, imagining Mina's pod lighting up, his glow around her, even if she had no idea, as she was whisked to safety, at least for the moment.

The skim drone kept spinning, as it would in the vacuum with nothing to slow it down, until it was destroyed. Liam saw the brilliant shine of Centauri B. He saw the glimmer of the trio of starliners, mere dots now. And back around into the angry glow of Centauri A. He almost wished he could stay alive long enough to see it explode. Maybe if he put on his space suit, he could conserve what little body heat he had left. But then he'd just have to watch Phoebe freeze first.

She coughed. Liam rubbed her shoulder. "I'm

sorry," he said quietly, fighting back tears. Maybe she would wake up before they succumbed to the cold. He could say good-bye. Or maybe it was cruel to hope she'd wake up only to suffer.

Liam let his head fall back against the seat. He closed his eyes and listened for that wind inside him, the sense of time blowing him around. If he finally went forward, would he see his body die? Maybe he should have checked before now. Risked the Drove, or, to be honest, risked *knowing*. Then maybe he could have done something differently, but what?

There had to be something. Liam closed his eyes and pictured his timeline. Catching Phoebe, leaving the starliner . . . what could he change? He couldn't ask JEFF to alter the plan with the starliners or their attack on the Telphons. All of that was too important for far too many lives. Lives Liam had saved by having JEFF wake him up from the stasis pod and, in a way, by getting caught in the first place. And he had to arrive on the *Scorpius* in order to make that happen. What about before that? The chronologist's office: but if they didn't go there, they couldn't deliver the data that she needed. Could she help somehow if he visited her? But she was gone to die, and everything before that all the way back to Mars seemed too important for finding that data, and for saving his parents. Liam couldn't see a way to *not* do any of it. It all mattered for the lives of so many people, even the universe. None of it could really be changed.

Well, there was one thing he could try to change. Right at the very end. Right before this.

I could go back and convince myself not to come for Phoebe. Then he could leave on the *Scorpius*. He wouldn't be here at all. Except—

Would I listen to myself? Would the Liam of twenty minutes ago really not come out here?

He was pretty sure the answer would be no.

So this was it then. There was nothing to be changed, nothing to be done. He was here, in the cold skim drone, Phoebe beside him.

For a moment, he actually smiled. *Why would I change it?* the chronologist had said. Liam thought of Mars, of Lunch Rocks and running through the tunnels. He thought of before that: his apartment and his family, school, going to grav-ball games and arguing with Phoebe about the stats, gazing up at the blinking lights of the starliner docks in the night sky. Maybe it had all had a purpose. Maybe he'd played his part. Or maybe it just *was*, and if that was the case . . .

We prefer what happens to what could have happened.

It had been good, hadn't it? He'd been lucky, he'd been loved, he'd had an adventure. . . .

But his heart still raced. This was still terrifying.

His breaths were getting thin, making clouds in

the skim drone's cramped compartment. It wouldn't be long now before he passed out.

Tears streamed down his face. Maybe he should just go backward. Back to the balcony on Mars, to sit with his family for these last few moments. Maybe stop by Lunch Rocks and see Phoebe's smile one more time. He could just be there, home, and maybe he wouldn't feel what was about to happen here—

Wait.

If he went back to Mars, there was something else along the way.

The doorway.

The last time they'd encountered it, it had transported them completely off the cruiser. He could push back there, and maybe he could find it. But he couldn't bring Phoebe with him, unless . . .

Liam fought off his shivering and pulled up Phoebe's sleeve. There was the chronologist's watch, and it was blinking blue, the only thing still working after the electromagnetic wave.

"Phoebe." Liam shook her gently. She shifted, made a soft groaning sound.

He wriggled the rest of the way out of his suit, his cold fingers fumbling to get the bulky thing down and off his legs. It was hard to even lift them, feeling gone in his toes, and barely enough room in here—he yanked it free of his feet and kicked it down into the footwell. The movement caused stars in his eyes, his head swimming. Too cold. Not enough air.

"Hey." He pulled Phoebe up to a sitting position. She coughed violently, her body shuddering. Liam spied his Dust Devils jersey half beneath her. He pulled it free and struggled to tug it on over his head. Then he took Phoebe's wrist and slipped off the watch, fumbling in his numbing fingers, and put it on his own.

"Hang on," he said, teeth chattering. "We're getting out of here. I hope." He leaned as close to her as he could and wrapped his arms around her, his cheek against hers, feeling the slight bristles of her skin, her faint warm breath. Then he reached around behind her head and turned the watch two notches to the left.

The world blurred, two cold bodies in the skim drone with time running out but also traveling now, backward through time, to the *Scorpius*, to finding Mina, back through a flash of stasis and the blur of his time trips, which made his head ache. Back out of stasis, encountering the Telphons in the hangar and then onto the cruiser, retreating into space, the Centauri system shrinking.

Things spun wildly, Liam's brain stretching, and then they were in the chronologist's office, talking to her in reverse, all the little lights floating around them. Liam checked the watch. It was still blinking blue, the symbol in its left hemisphere still flashing.

And yet his vision of it seemed to be dimming, and there was a pain clouding over him. *I'm freezing*, he thought, *and losing oxygen.* Hypothermia. Asphyxiation. *Just a little farther.*

In the timestream, the world spun again, Liam's head aching like it was being torn in two, and they were back on the *Artemis*, retreating down its halls and core segments filled with red flashing light, getting closer.

But all of it was foggy. Syrupy. Like the time was moving right along but he wasn't quite able to keep up with it. Cold, so cold, the world getting gray and heavy.

Come . . . on. . . .

White spots in his vision.

Where are you?

The wind through him slowing.

And then the watch began to flash red, the two hemispheres blinking at once. Crackling and buzzing, and Liam felt like he'd been crushed back into himself. Time seemed to halt. Formless gray around them—

There it was. The doorway.

Its black trapezoidal frame flickered with silver circuitry. He'd found it! Or it had found him, as the chronologist had said.

"Come on, Phoebe," he said into her ear. He put his arm around her—so much effort just to lift his arm—and stumbled through the strange gray fog toward the dark, beckoning doorway. "We can make it."

But the door didn't seem to get closer, or maybe it did. It swayed in his vision, fading, everything becoming a gray nothingness. He struggled to press his feet down, to push harder, dragging Phoebe along, his arms and chest aching. *Freezing.* . . . Had to make it to the doorway. Its dark, liquid sheen.

We can make it. Stumbling ahead now, holding on to Phoebe, and Liam gave one last gasp and lunged for it. The door blurred, and Liam felt cold in his bones, his vision going white. He lost track of his legs, of the world around him, but still held on to Phoebe tight, telling himself, telling her, over and over, *We can make it.* . . .

We can make it. . . .

EPILOGUE

CENTAURI SYSTEM

"Go back," said Marnia-2. "Please."

Tarra studied the navigation screen, the triangle of dots blinking there. "We should attack the starliners immediately, before they reach reinforcements."

"She is one of us!" said Marnia.

"She made her choice," said Tarra. "She chose the enemy."

"She chose her friend," said Calo-6. "She's our daughter. The only family we have left. And she's our future."

"It's too dangerous to risk going back near that supernova."

"Tarra," said Barro, "you know in this ship we can afford to risk it. There are so few of us."

Tarra pursed her lips and crossed her arms. "Fine." She turned to the two Telphon navigators standing on either side of the hovering orange crystal. It was two meters in diameter and functioned not only as the ship's power source but also as its controls—accessed by placing both hands on its surface. "Take us back."

The crystal powered up and the ship hummed. Marnia closed her eyes and gripped a railing along the wall. There was a flash, and a nauseating feeling of squeezing that made it seem like your eyes were going to pop out of your head. Then a lurch as the ship transited the space fold it had created and emerged back where they'd left. Centauri A still boiling away, the supernova imminent. The starliners out of sight now.

"Retrace our course and scan for ships," said Tarra.

A clang echoed through the hull, vibrating the floor.

"Lots of debris out here," said Barro.

"Assuming it's in one piece, the skim drone should be larger than this wreckage."

Marnia reached for Calo's hand.

"We should never have let her spend so much time with them," he said.

Marnia peered at the scanners, looking for any kind of sign. Liam's words ran through her head. *We're going to find another way.* He'd saved their lives, warning them about the warhead trap. Which changed nothing. It didn't bring back Telos. It didn't bring back Mica, their sweet, wild little boy. And yet . . .

"Scans are picking up a larger object up ahead," one of the navigators reported.

"Looks like a skim drone," said the other.

Please, Marnia said to herself.

Calo curled his fist. "If the boy is there—"

"You will leave him alone," she said.

Another chunk of fighter debris caromed off the hull.

They slowed, the nearly nova star straight ahead.

"Do you really think someone is blowing up these stars on purpose?" Barro wondered aloud. "How could that even be possible?"

We could have listened to her, Marnia thought.

"Should be dead ahead," said one of the navigators.

"There it is," said Tarra. She pointed to a small black dot silhouetted against the boiling star.

They closed, and the outline of the skim drone took shape. It looked intact, but it was dark outside and in.

"No life readings," said Barro, "but there's a lot of interference." He tapped the screen, as if to try again.

Marnia rubbed the skin in the crook of her elbow. She couldn't lose another. . . .

"Pull it into the docking bay," said Tarra quietly.

They filed back through the ship and down a spiraling staircase. The skim drone lay on a wide metal floor in the center of a circular hangar. Its exterior steamed with melting ice. Calo put his arm around Marnia as Barro approached the craft.

Marnia knotted inside. She wanted to look away but told herself no. She'd have given anything to see her youngest child one more time, even dead, as strange as that sounded. She would be here for Xela, even if only to see her into the arms of Ana.

Barro peered through the icy canopy. He tried to pull it open but it wouldn't budge. "Get me something to pry it with."

Soldiers moved around the perimeter of the hangar. The walls were hung with strange contraptions that looked like combinations of space suits and stasis tubes, cylindrical and glassy with arms and feet, which the Telphons had no idea how to use. One of the soldiers returned with two bars with flat ends. She and Barro pried at the canopy, straining. With a sharp crack, it popped open.

Please, Marnia thought again as they lifted the cockpit canopy.

Barro looked inside for a moment; then he reached in and pulled out an empty human space suit. "They're gone."

SALVAGE FREIGHTER CARRION
0.09 LIGHT-YEARS FROM ACCESS PORTAL
FOUR

"Watch out for that debris," said Jordy.

"I see it." Kyla adjusted the thrusters with one hand and scratched at the stubble on her head with the other. "Do you have eyes on our target?"

"We should be close." Jordy spun the spherical navigation ball, sticking his fingers inside and enlarging it.

"How are the life readings?"

Jordy frowned. "They come and go. It's weird. Like they're there but they're not." His fingers danced around in the light sphere and then he shrank it back down. "Course plotted."

"Roger that." Kyla adjusted thrust and ducked

the craft as a huge chunk of supernova debris sailed by. She wondered if it was another bit of Pluto and Charon, or maybe one of Neptune's moons.

A light flashed on her windshield. "Okay, there it is." She fired the retrorockets.

"Kyla," the captain called over the feed, "what's your status?"

"We're closing in on the possible survivors," she said.

"We are waiting on you to shut down. Readings are starting to deteriorate and we may be in for another cascade event."

"Just for the record," said Jordy, "I am out of meds and I'm *not* okay with seeing myself as an old man again without them."

"Relax." Kyla watched on her scanners as the last green-glowing ship winked out of sight. "Just a couple minutes more, Captain." She turned to Jordy. "You do the walk this time."

Jordy groaned. "I did the walk last time!"

"And I did the flying. We play to our strengths."

"All right, fine." Jordy unbuckled and ducked out of the cockpit.

Kyla slowed, and their lights fell on a midsized ship. It was sleek and shiny, some kind of private craft.

It was also severed nearly in two, like someone had peeled it apart down its center. The sides were torn and frayed, with circuitry, cabinets and other supplies hanging out into space. Some of the frayed wires were still sparking, now and then. "Not sure you're going to find any live ones out there," Kyla called over her shoulder, "unless maybe they're in stasis pods."

"Uh . . . ," Jordy said from what sounded like just down the hall.

"What is it?'

"Can you come back here for a second?"

"You're not getting me to do the walk—"

"It's not that. Just get back here."

Kyla sighed and unbuckled. She pushed out of the cockpit, floated through the narrow hall and into the main staging room of the ship. Jordy stood with his back to her. "Stop being a wimp about—" She stepped beside him and her words caught in her throat.

There were two kids lying on the floor. Teens. A boy on his stomach, a girl half curled on her side. Her face was strange; she seemed to have lavender-spotted skin. They were dressed in black clothing, the boy with some kind of red shirt. Both alive, their chests rising and falling, but unconscious. Their faces were flecked with ice.

"Okay, that's not what I was expecting."

"Who are they?" Jordy said quietly.

"How should I know?" Kyla kept staring at them. "Where did they come from? How did they—"

"Hey, look." Jordy knelt beside the boy and fiddled with his arm.

"Don't just touch them without a suit on or something," said Kyla.

"It's fine." Jordy stood and held out an object: a strange silver watch. "What do you think this is?"

Kyla looked from the watch back at the kids. "Something the captain's definitely going to want to see." She turned toward the cockpit. "Come on, let's get back to Dark Star."

"Yeah," said Jordy. He glanced at the kids again. "Um, yeah."

The sleek ship turned away from the rolling eddies of the sun's supernova and aimed itself directly at the great trapezoidal doorway hovering in space, its sides glowing with silver circuitry, its center inky black. Thrusters burned, and the ship disappeared into the void.

END OF BOOK TWO

DON'T MISS THESE BOOKS BY KEVIN EMERSON!

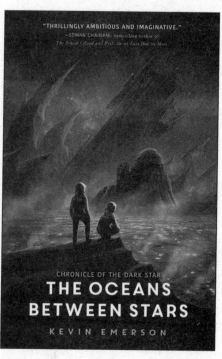

"This is perfect science fiction: a terrifying yet very cool vision of the future, lots of technological awesomeness, mind-bending alien mysteries, a mission to save the human race—and two funny, resourceful, very real kid heroes who I'd follow to the edges of the universe."

—**TUI T. SUTHERLAND**, *New York Times* bestselling author of the Wings of Fire series